Redemption

Kelly Moran

To Johnna,

Mistakes of the past
are merely lessons for
our future. Remember
them but don't let
them haunt you.

Kelly Moran XO

Cover Art Design by: Kelly Moran
Front Photo Credit: Kruse Images & Photography
Front Cover Model: Matthew Hosea
Back Photo Credit: Adobe Images

Createspace First Print Edition
ISBN-13: 978-1542652438
ISBN-10: 154265243X
Published in the United States of America

For all the men & women who serve. Thank you.
With special thanks to Drew Deaton.

Please consider donating today.
www.Honor-The-Sacrifice.org

Praise for Kelly Moran's Books:

"Breathes life into an appealing story."
Publishers Weekly

"Readers will fall in love."
Romantic Times

"Great escape reading."
Library Journal

"Touching & gratifying."
Kirkus Reviews

"Sexy, heart-tugging fun."
USA Today HEA

"Emotional & totally engaging."
Carla Neggers

"A gem of a writer."
Sharon Sala

"I read in one sitting."
Carly Phillips

"Compelling characters."
Roxanne St. Claire

"A sexy, emotional romance."
Kim Karr

Chapter One

In the private cemetery on her family's ranch, Olivia Cattenach knelt by her brother's grave and brushed grass clippings from the headstone. Six months since Justin had been killed in action. Hard to believe. The loss was still as fresh as the day two soldiers had shown up at her front door with his tags and their condolences.

Worse than losing her brother, her best friend, was the reality of a life cut short at just twenty-eight. Tragedy didn't begin to cover it. One IED, one wrong step, and he was gone. Erased as if he'd never been here at all.

Knowing Aunt Mae was standing behind her at the wrought iron gate, waiting to start the day, Olivia sighed, took a sip of coffee from a travel cup, and tried to keep her morning visit short. But, damn. The sharp stab of loneliness pierced her stomach.

She glanced past his grave and that of her parents' to the northern pasture in the distance, teeming with long golden stems as far as the eye could see. "In another month, we can harvest the winter wheat and plant the spring."

Though the crop only encompassed one-hundred of their two-thousand acres, and it wasn't near the revenue as their other income margins, it had been Justin's favorite part of the ranch. Hands deep in the soil, wide open land, and silence.

His last days hadn't had any of those elements. Instead, he'd been in a decimated structure in the arid desert, surrounded by crumbling concrete. Guns, explosions, shouting...

She shook her head and eyed their house to her left, beyond the ridge where the cemetery was located. Merely a blip from her position. Justin used to race her from the cottonwood tree edging the iron fence, down the incline, through the wildflower garden, and to the three-story log cabin they called home. As the older sister by two years, she'd let him win, of course. Until he'd hit a growth spurt as a teen and grew taller than her by six inches. All legs, her brother.

A bitter wind blew across the range, bringing the faint scent of snow from the Laramie Mountains to the south. Sun beat down on the prairie grass to her right, over the eastern and southern passes. For mid-April in eastern Wyoming, the day was proving to be warm.

Overnight temps had been in the forties, but it would probably hit the sixties by lunch. Not a half-bad start to a Monday.

Feet shuffled from behind, reminding her she couldn't sit idle talking to a ghost much longer. She eyed Justin's grave one last time and attempted a smile. "Love you. Say hi to Mom and Dad. I'll see you tomorrow."

The figure of speech made her throat burn as she rose and turned for the gate. Because she wouldn't see him tomorrow. Thanks to a commanding officer who'd made a bad call, she'd never see her brother again.

Aunt Mae waited patiently, one arm propped on the post, a to-go mug of coffee in her other hand. Sunlight hit her pure white strands, cut in a neat bob above her wide shoulders. Her craggy face had seen many rough winters, the fine lines a testament to her will, but her piercing blue eyes were as kind as her soul.

She'd grown up on the ranch and, twenty years ago, had stepped up when Olivia's mother and father had died. She hardly remembered her parents, scattered fragments of memories really, but Aunt Mae resembled Olivia's father down to her square chin and solid frame.

Olivia adjusted her fitted red flannel under her canvas jacket and stepped into Aunt Mae's brief embrace. The rustling of their clothing scratched the air as they separated, then they walked toward the house with Aunt Mae's arm slung over Olivia's shoulders.

She breathed in crisp mountain air tinged with frost and soil. "Nice morning."

"That it is." Her aunt glanced at her as their boots crunched over the gravel-strewn path. "Long walk to take every morning, though."

"You don't have to come with me." She often didn't accompany Olivia on her routine trek, and those were the days she'd found it harder to leave and get to the duties awaiting her.

"I don't mind. These old bones need the exercise." Aunt Mae dropped her arm, severing the connection, and glanced ahead. "I'll bet my bison stew recipe there's a certain foreman waiting for you outside the barn."

Olivia knew better than to accept that wager. "No doubt." Bright and early, Nakos always waited for her to round the bend from the cemetery trail. He usually put in a solid hour delegating duties before she even stepped off the front porch.

"He wouldn't make a bad husband, baby girl."

True. Olivia could do worse than Nakos Hunt. With the dark skin tone and black hair of his native Arapaho tribe, combined with solid bone structure and a handsome face, he'd definitely been conceived at the deep end of the gene pool. He was also hard-working, kind, and protective. Too protective, but she shrugged that off.

Thing was, there were no sparks. Appreciation, yes. Chemistry? No. Still, she was thirty years old, lived on the outskirts of town to which had few prospects, and if she wanted to carry on the family legacy, she needed to put serious thought into settling down with someone. She got along well with their foreman. He'd been the closest to a best friend she'd had since Justin died.

"I'll think about it." She took a sip of coffee.

"You've been thinking about it for months." Aunt Mae's eyebrows pinged. "The boy's had a thing for you since you were sixteen. How long are you going to make him wait?"

One more thing to add to the guilt pile. "It hasn't been that long."

"You're right. He's probably crushed on you since his family came to work for ours. I peg that somewhere around age nine."

Olivia laughed. "Okay, stop." She shoulder-bumped her aunt. "He hasn't exactly made a move." Not that she would've known what to do if he had. Nakos had always been placed in the what-if column in her someday mental file. Biological clock aside, she was hesitant to pull out the folder and dust it off.

"Who says the man has to do all the work? Show some initiative."

Yeah, yeah.

They walked in silence the rest of the hike, and just before she parted ways with her aunt, Nakos came out of the third barn with a clipboard in hand.

"Shocker." Aunt Mae winked. "Go get dirty, baby girl. And I mean the naked kind."

With a laugh, Olivia waved goodbye, watching her aunt take the long, winding path up to the house. She turned to find Nakos's dark eyes on her and walked closer. "Good morning."

He gave a nod, and the wind caught his short ponytail tied at his nape. "*Hebe*, Olivia."

Every morning, he greeted her with a hello in his native Arapaho tongue, and something about it settled the turmoil in her chest. Not that she minded change, but she preferred certain precious things to remain the same.

One corner of his mouth curved. "A smile looks good on you. Been awhile since I've seen it."

"Thanks. What've we got today?"

"You and I have spring shearing this week. The wool supplier's coming Friday for a pickup. I put four guys on counting and moving steer farther down the eastern pasture, two on horseback checking the southern fence-line, and another three on the northern ridge. We've had some trouble with pronghorn antelope eating crops."

That accounted for all her men. Nakos made ten. They hired additional seasonal help when needed, but until the wheat harvest, they were solid.

While Nakos consulted his clipboard, she studied him. Like her, he wore jeans and a flannel, but his coat was thick wool and he donned a black cowboy hat. At his six feet, she had to shield the sun with her hand and crane her neck to look at him. Clean-shaven, thick neck, defined shoulders, broad chest, and a narrow waist. She tried to wrap her mind around something romantic between them. All she could conclude was...maybe.

But why the hell not? She'd never know if she didn't grab an opportunity by the bootstraps. "Aunt Mae says I should get dirty."

He glanced at her. "Well, we could bypass the sheep and muck stalls. Then again, shearing's sweaty work."

Sigh. "She says the naked kind of dirty." She couldn't blame him for not catching her drift. It's not as if she'd ever flirted with him before. She wasn't even sure she knew how, at any rate. In these parts, the direct approach of buying someone a beer at the sole tavern in town was the equivalent of an offer.

He went eerily still and, as if in slow motion, his gaze slid from the clipboard to her. Hard black eyes nailed her to her spot and probed as if searching for the Holy Grail of meaning.

Unnerved and feeling more than a little stupid, she shifted her weight to her other foot. "Have you ever thought about it? Me, you, clothes on the floor?" Yikes. Couldn't get any more obvious than that. She'd kill Aunt Mae later.

A harsh inhale, and he turned his head, glaring at the mountains in the far distance. His Adam's apple bobbed with a swallow and he closed his eyes for a brief moment before looking at her once again. Interest flared in his eyes, but uncertainty was gaining ground.

Finally, he switched the clipboard to his other hand and deigned to respond. "Where is this coming from, little red?"

He only called her "little red"—a reference to her size and hair color—when pissed off or if she did something he thought was adorable. She couldn't tell which extreme he was hovering near at the moment, and his expression wasn't offering any clues.

She shrugged. "We're not getting any younger and we're both single." Lovely. She might die from over-romanticism.

"That's not exactly a reason to date someone."

Lord. She wished she'd never brought it up. Irritation made her eye twitch. "I didn't say anything about dating." When he just blinked, she sighed. "Never mind. Have the sheep been kept in all night?" They couldn't shear if the herd was wet from the elements.

He shoved the clipboard under his arm and dropped a hand on his hip. "Yes."

"And they've been fasting since yesterday?" This was to avoid excess waste to keep the wool and floor clean, plus minimized the sheep's discomfort when rolled to their backs.

Not that Nakos didn't know all of this, but a topic change was sorely needed. She was beginning to wonder if her instincts and Aunt Mae's declaration about Nakos's feelings were accurate. If that were the case, Olivia might've just made things very, very uncomfortable between her and her foreman.

"Yes." He eyed her with a cross between confusion and frustration. "The first quarter of the flock is rounded up and in the pen. This isn't my first rodeo."

"I know." Most days, she didn't have a clue what she'd do without him. He'd always been her rock—silent, strong, and unrelenting. "You do a great job, Nakos. Sorry. I'm having an off day." Or year. Whatever.

He gave her a disbelieving look littered with concern. She walked around him and headed for the barn, but he gently grabbed her arm to stop her retreat.

With his face half in shadow from his hat, he drew a steady inhale. "Are we really doing this? Are we talking about crossing that line?"

"I don't know." Despite the chilly air, her cheeks heated. "Maybe we should table the discussion and think about it."

He stared at her a long beat. "Why now? I never got the impression you were attracted to me."

"You're very attractive." That wasn't the issue. And if this wasn't the most whack conversation the two of them ever had, she'd eat her own cooking. "I'm restless, I guess. Aunt Mae started in about settling down and, well...Yada."

All he offered for the longest time was a slow nod. As if an afterthought, he let go of her arm. "Let's get going on the herd. That can't wait." Posture stiff, he pivoted toward the open barn door.

"Are you angry?"

With his back to her, he paused. "No." He glanced at her over his shoulder. "I'm processing. Out of nowhere, you proposition me and then claim it was out of boredom."

Crap. She stepped in front of him, her stomach twisting in guilt. Just what every guy wanted—his pride bitch-slapped. "I'm sorry. And I didn't say I was bored, I said restless. There's a difference. If you're not interested, we can pretend the past ten minutes never happened."

"My curiosity isn't in question and you know that or you wouldn't have brought it up in the first place. Not once have I put you in a corner, little red." He stepped closer, crowding her, and looked down his nose at her. "Know why? Because *you're* not interested."

"How do you know? We've never kissed or tried a relationship on for size." In fact, she could count on one hand the number of times he'd touched her, and she'd still have spare fingers. He always stood beside her, had her back, but they didn't have a touchy-feely kind of friendship.

"You feel it or you don't. It's as simple as that." He shook his head. "Go ahead. Table the discussion, as you claimed. Think about it. I'll be right here, where I've been the past twenty years. Now, can we get to work or would you like to throw me a second punch?"

Her shoulders sagged and she closed her eyes. This was why she'd blown off Aunt Mae every time she'd tried to bring up the idea of starting something with Nakos. One comment and a failed attempt at flirting had managed to wound his pride, insult him, and dent their friendship. At a loss, she opened her eyes, only to find his gaze pinned to something over her shoulder and a determined set to his mouth.

"I'm sorry." She'd say it a thousand times over. As if reluctant, he glanced at her. "I care about you, Nakos, and I wasn't thinking beyond right this second." Which was completely out of the norm for her.

Obviously, his feelings ran deeper than attraction. She never should've toyed with his emotions. In part, she was glad she'd said something because now she knew for certain instead of simply going off assumption. If they kissed and there was a spark, they could build upon that, perhaps, since the notion was out there. But instinct sent warning knells clanging against her temples, shifting in her gut. He hadn't been wrong, either. Desire wasn't knocking on her door. Not the consuming kind worth risking their solid unit to test the waters.

Conflicted, she rubbed her earlobe between her forefinger and thumb—a nervous tick she'd had since she was a girl.

"Consider it forgotten." He pointed to the barn. "Work now. Talk later."

They wouldn't talk about it, though. That wasn't their dynamic. He had a way of reading her, and her him, without the need for words. Not that they didn't have open communication. She'd yet to meet anyone more brutally honest or forthcoming than him. But heart-to-hearts? Hell no. Even after Justin died, Nakos had offered no platitudes. He'd just stood next to her, silently watching and letting her know he was there if she crumbled.

She followed him inside the barn and took stock. *Baa-baas* rent the air and the scent of straw mixed with soil clung to the crisp cross-breeze. He'd rounded up a third of the flock and had some penned on one side of the large space, the rest in the outer holding area just beyond the open rear doorway. Roughly a hundred sheep stalked around while her faithful black and white border collie, Bones, sat idly in the middle of the room, awaiting orders. To the right was a sturdy wooden table where they could roll the wool and a large crate already on a skid for easy transport.

Nakos had sure been busy this morning while waiting for her. Quickly, she removed her canvas jacket and hung it on a peg just inside the door. Since each sheep could produce eight to ten pounds of wool, and the process of shearing required skill, it was harder than most realized. Luckily, she and her foreman had it down to a science.

With Nakos holding the animals in position, she sheared. He rounded the flock and sent them out one-by-one as she rolled and stored in compatible silence. They moved as one like clockwork through lunch and into the late afternoon before they finished with the herd slated for today.

Once the barn was locked tight and the flock out to pasture, they headed up the winding path to the house as daylight faded to dusk. Crickets chirped while their boots crunched over gravel. Bones trotted along beside her, his tongue drooping partly out of his mouth.

She swiped the sweat from her forehead with her arm, chilly now that the temp had dropped. Her muscles cried uncle as she glanced at Nakos. "Are you staying for dinner?"

"No. I've got leftovers from Mae. I'll walk you up, though."

He had a cabin on the ranch's property near the southern ridge, a good ten minute trek. His truck would be in the driveway to get him back home, so seeing her to the house wasn't unusual. But his dismissive tone kept the erected distance firmly between them. Uneasiness coiled in her stomach as they rounded the bend, and she figured she'd give him a couple days before apologizing again. Hopefully, that would get things back to normal.

Stopping abruptly, he glared straight ahead. "Are you expecting company?"

"No." She followed his gaze to his blue pickup truck, partially blocked by the corner of the house. Behind it, parked next to the pine trees lining one side of the driveway, was a motorcycle.

She only knew a handful of people in town who owned a bike, and none would drive it up to her ranch this early in the season. As they got closer, she spotted the telltale green canvas military-issued tote strapped to the back of the seat, and her heart stopped.

"Oh no. Do you think it has something to do with Justin?" He'd been dead six months, though. Who could possibly want to visit her regarding him?

Nakos, jaw tense, glanced from the motorcycle to her, then at the three-story cedar log cabin like he was searching for signs of trouble.

The lights were on downstairs, a yellow glow emitting from the windows. Nothing seemed amiss on the wrap-around porch. The rocking chairs and pots filled with marigolds were in place, the heavy front door closed. All was quiet.

"I'll follow you inside." He jerked his chin, telling her to precede him.

She walked along the side of the house to the tack room in back, where they kicked off their boots and hung their coats. Her stomach somersaulting, she opened the kitchen door, letting Bones inside, and stepped through, Nakos on her heels to close it behind them.

Nothing was going on the six-burner gas stove. The slate countertops were free of dinner clutter, but remnants of something Italian hung in the air.

Aunt Mae rose from the scarred pine table in the center of the room, a teacup in hand, while Bones trotted off into the other room. "There you are. You have a guest."

Olivia glanced at the visitor in question as he unfolded himself from a chair and stood. The legs scraped the floor, and the sound ricocheted off the white distressed cabinets and back to her like a bullet.

Holy crap. The breath backed up in her lungs. Man wasn't the word to use to describe the person standing in her spacious kitchen. Giant, perhaps. All she could do was stare, caught between confusion about who he was and avid fascination.

Easily six feet and a handful of inches, he towered over her, even with the table and several sandstone granite tile squares between them. His head was shaved bald, but he had maybe a day's worth of light brown scruff on his jaw, indicating what color his hair would be. A sleeve of tats ran up both arms and under a fitted white tee that left nothing to the imagination for the definition that lay underneath. Bulging muscles and veins and...testosterone. Yes. A huge wall of testosterone, this guy.

He shoved his huge hands in the pockets of his worn jeans, causing his biceps to bunch. He must've bench-pressed a Buick to get guns that size. "The name's Nathan Roldan, but I go by Nate."

15

Lord, his voice. Deep, guttural, and with a resounding echo that rumbled through her nervous system. She rolled the name around because it sounded familiar, but no way would she forget him had they met before.

"Do I know you?" She pegged him at close to her age, give or take a year.

"Ah." Aunt Mae smiled, and the anxious tension in the gesture made Olivia's pulse trip. "Why don't you get washed up and we can talk? While we were waiting for you, Nate and I ate. I'll reheat it for you."

Nakos, as if sensing a problem, cozied closer to Olivia's side. He offered her a look that said, *I'm not leaving you alone with this guy.*

Confused herself, she glanced at the newcomer again. His gaze darted between the two of them before he nodded in some kind of understanding. That made one of them, at least.

"I'm not here to cause trouble." He pulled a wallet out of his back pocket and strode around the table.

His gait was like that of a graceful predator, and now that he was smack in front of her, she took in the details of his face. Fine lines, barely noticeable, wrinkled his forehead. His olive skin was more reminiscent of years in the sun than heritage. A golden tan of light bronze. The soft, slight downcast of his eyelids contradicted the harsh slash of his brows. So did his full, pouty mouth with the sharp cut of his jawbone.

Damn. He was one beautiful specimen. A little intimidating and extremely rough around the edges, but wow. She wouldn't want to be caught on his bad side—assuming he had a good side—yet the naughty bad boy vibes were like an undercurrent pulling her in.

Don't-mess-with-me meets I-dare-you-to-resist.

He held out what looked like a photo, and she got hung up in the dark brown of his eyes, framed by criminally long lashes. His lips pursed when she failed to take the item from him. "I served overseas with Justin."

At her brother's name, she sucked in a sharp breath and snapped to attention. With a shaking hand, she took the picture and glanced at it.

In camo gear and holding a rifle, Justin stood beside the man before her. A military jeep as the background, the guys posed,

16

Nate's arm around her brother's shoulders. Justin's grin and blue eyes had her throat closing and longing banding her chest. Before she got too emotional, she passed the photo back to Nate and cleared her throat.

He then extracted a driver's license, courtesy of the state of Illinois, and showed her first, then Nakos, who eyed both the card and man like he was one flinch away from going postal. Nakos crossed his arms in a clear what-do-you-want pose.

Nate tentatively glanced at Aunt Mae and back to Olivia when her aunt nodded consent. "I just want to talk, and then I'll leave if you want." His gaze darted between hers, giving her the impression he was looking through her and into some deeper part she didn't know existed. "Before he died, Justin gave me a message for you."

Chapter Two

A promise. After an honorable medical discharge, that's what had sent Nate from Chicago to Meadowlark, Wyoming. The "honorable" part of his release from the Army was a joke, but his pledge to a dying comrade was not. Redemption was asking too much, but he could hope. Something told him he'd still be seeking absolution when he took his last breath on some distant day.

It should've been him six feet under with Justin standing vigil at Nate's funeral. Not the other way around. And he'd pay for it the rest of his pathetic life. He was here, as Justin had asked of him, but there was no atonement for getting a friend killed.

He stared out the massive living room window at a dark Cattenach Ranch, waiting on Olivia to return from upstairs. Justin had talked about his family and the land often, but somehow hadn't done any of it justice. Nate had envisioned a little farmhouse in the middle of nowhere, surrounded by rolling hills and cows. Showed what he knew.

It had taken five solid minutes on his Hog to ride to the front door from the local highway. He might've missed the turnoff had the arched wrought iron sign not been so prominent. Lined with pine trees on one side and solar lamps on the other, the driveway went on for miles and he thought he'd never arrive.

The three-story log cabin damn near resembled a mansion, rural style. All cedar and glass on the outside, stone and accents on the inside. Wide beams across a twenty-foot ceiling, a flagstone floor-to-rafters fireplace, and scarred pine throughout. The furniture was navy corduroy. The kind you sank into on a snowy day and never wanted to leave. Family portraits and landscapes of the ranch dotted the paneled walls. He hadn't seen but two rooms, and he was impressed. The kitchen was huge, airy, and modern with stainless steel appliances.

For a city boy used to skyscrapers and sirens, who'd had to hoard food just to scrape by, it was a culture shock. Hell, Iraq had been less of an adjustment.

Footsteps padded on the stairs and he turned. The cold ball of dread in his gut morphed into a boulder. The biggest holy shit since arriving? Olivia Cattenach. He'd seen a couple photos of her, courtesy of her brother, but the 3D version had been a blow to the head.

She rounded the landing of the enormous polished birch staircase, wearing a loose pair of gray sweats, pink socks, and a white tank top. He'd misspoken. She wasn't a blow. She was a hydrogen bomb directly aimed at his solar plexus.

Like her brother, she was slender and had legs for miles. Waifish would describe her if not for the hourglass flair of her hips and the generous endowment of breasts. That hair, though? Fuck him. His wildest fantasies couldn't conjure a shade of auburn that heart-stopping. Silky and falling just past her shoulders, he itched to ram his fingers through the strands.

She stepped into the room and glanced around. "Sorry for the wait. We were shearing today and I was filthy. I needed a shower."

He had no idea what the hell she was talking about, but he nodded. "Not a problem." When her gaze darted elsewhere again, he made a non-threatening move of sitting in one of the many available chairs. His size could be menacing, and the last thing he wanted was to frighten her. "Your aunt said she's in her room if you need her. And the man you were with, Nick? He left." Under duress, even though the aunt assured the guy Olivia would be fine.

"Nakos," she corrected and offered a polite smile. "He's our foreman and a good friend."

Nate wondered if the guy knew he was only a friend. He'd shot nothing but threatening daggered glares Nate's way, but he'd kept his mouth shut.

After a beat, she claimed a chair across from him and tucked her legs under her. "When did you get to town?"

Small talk typically made him break out in hives, but he liked the sound of her voice. Lilting, almost. "About an hour before you came in. I rode straight from Chicago."

"Is that where you're from?" She tugged on her earlobe, her gaze on her lap. She'd yet to look him in the eye for long, and he wanted a glimpse of them again more than air.

"Yes. The south side." He skimmed his gaze over the light dusting of freckles on her shoulders. Her skin was something else. Not quite fair and not rich enough to be considered sun-kissed. At her nod, he leaned forward a tad. "Don't be scared. I'm built like a bear, but I'm harmless." Actually, he could kill a man fifty different ways with his bare hands, but that was intel she didn't need.

Finally, those eyes focused on him, and the room vacuumed of air. Cornflower and bluer than anything he'd born witness. Her brother's had been a shocking shade of navy, but hers were...potent. The fine arch of her brows and her long lashes only made them seem bigger on her pretty oval face.

"I'm sorry." She worked her lower lip between her teeth. "The last time someone from the military showed up, it was to..."

To inform her Justin had died. Nate should've thought of that.

Forcing himself not to fist his hands, he acknowledged he understood with a grunt. "I apologize for missing the funeral. I was injured and in a hospital in Germany at the time. I just got back Stateside a couple weeks ago." Long enough to grab the few things he owned from Jim and hop on his Harley.

"Oh." Her gaze swept over him as if searching for evidence. "I didn't realize anyone else was hurt. Was it...the same blast? Are you okay now?"

He'd never be okay again. "It was the same explosion, and I'm healed. I took shrapnel to my leg and hip that required a few surgeries." He wished they'd given him a lobotomy, too. The scars and residual pain in his leg weren't enough.

"So, you were with Justin when he died?"

Ten feet away. "Yes." He sensed she needed more details, even if she didn't necessarily want to hear them. "What do you know about what happened?"

Her throat worked a swallow and she glanced away. "Just what they told me, which wasn't much. He was sent into a building and an IED went off. It was implied the mission went wrong because of incorrect info from his commanding officer."

Sometimes, knowing what really happened was worse than fragmented facts. Either the Army had told her placating answers or she'd misunderstood. Either way, most of what she'd said wasn't accurate. All but one thing. Justin's commanding officer had screwed up, and Nate was that man. As a first lieutenant to Justin's second, it had been Nate's job to protect him. And he'd failed epically.

He wouldn't fail with Olivia. It was imperative she not know his role in her brother's death. For Nate to follow through on

Justin's wishes, she needed to trust him. Thus, he geared himself to relay the story while trying not to relive it.

"We were sent to this tiny village to do a sweep for refugees and weapons. Most of the buildings were in ruins and we hadn't planned to be there longer than a day. Justin and I paired up and went in one structure while the rest of our unit did the same in others."

The place had been a ghost town, so when Justin claimed to see a kid, Nate figured it had been a trick of the light. He should've known better than to send Justin first while Nate radioed an update to base. Turned out, that kid hadn't been a mirage. He'd been an eight-year-old with explosives strapped to his chest.

"We saw the bomb too late." Cold sweat broke out on his face, dampened his hands.

She drew a ragged breath, her eyes misty. "Did he...suffer?"

"No. It was quick." And sometimes, lies were a necessity. Justin had been in agony. Utter, utter agony. Fifteen minutes it had taken for him to die. It had felt like fifteen years. Justin lying on the damn ground, holes riddling his entire body, gripping Nate's hand while they'd waited for an evac team, and blood every-fucking-where. Nate would never wash away the memory. "He didn't experience any pain."

Closing her eyes, she took a second to seemingly collect herself. Relief was evident in the sag of her shoulders. "Thank you." While the acid in his stomach churned, she shifted positions and resettled. "You said Justin had a message for me?"

"Yes." He pulled the *If you're reading this* letter from his back pocket and unfolded the envelope. "We exchanged notes in case something happened." He handed it to her.

She stared at the once plain white stationery, now yellow from the elements. "Did he say anything before he died?"

"Shit, it hurts, Nate. I'm so...cold. Take care of my sister. Promise me you'll...take care of...Olivia."

"There wasn't time." Nate ground his jaw, fighting the urge to scream. To run. To bash his head repeatedly against the closest hard surface to forget. "When he wrote it, he asked that I give you the letter in person and stay while you read it."

Regardless of what happened in the next few minutes, at the very least, he'd find a motel in town for tonight. That wasn't the ideal outcome, nor the plan, but he'd figure out something more permanent after she wasn't so shell-shocked.

"I have some of his things on my bike." Nate rose. "I'll go grab them to give you a moment alone. You can meet me on the porch when you're ready."

Her gaze lifted to his and he never wanted so badly to be someone else. The kind of guy who offered comfort instead of inflicting misery. A man worthy of the gratitude in her eyes. Alas, he was an asshole of the highest order.

"Do you know what it says?" Her quiet voice wrapped around his jugular and squeezed.

"No. We didn't read each other's letters." Chest tight, he strode to the door and stepped out into the chilly air.

His shoes crunched over gravel as he made his way to his bike in the driveway. Glancing up, he found an endless supply of stars winking overhead. Too many to count and more than he'd ever seen at one time. Back in that shithole of a desert, there'd been stars aplenty, but not like this. Out here in no man's land, unbidden by city lights and smog—or explosions and smoke—the sky stretched for eons.

It was quiet, too. A rustle of dry grass here, a chirp of a cricket there. Throw in a random hoot from an owl, and that encompassed the symphony. Deafening, really, compared to what he was used to.

He grabbed the small, wooden shoebox-sized package from where he had it strapped to his Hog and dropped into a rocking chair on the porch to wait. Utter darkness swallowed the ranch, save for the sliver of moonlight. He could see why Justin had spoken so highly of the place. One could get lost in the shadows of mountains, the silhouettes of trees, or the obscurity.

After a few minutes, the skittering of fingernails on planks preceded a dog's form as it rounded the corner of the porch. It sat a few feet away and stared at him. Nate had barely registered anything else but Olivia earlier, but he seemed to recall the dog following her inside the kitchen.

"Hey, boy." Or girl?

Nate patted his leg and it trotted over to him. He gingerly petted the long black and white fur until the dog pawed at Nate's pants as if to ask for a real rub-down. With a laugh rusty from misuse, he scratched behind its ears.

"I assume you belong to Olivia. What's your name?"

"Bones." The owner in question stepped onto the porch, shutting the screen door behind her. "When he was a puppy, he'd bring me skeletal remains of whatever animals he could find. Ergo, the name." She sat in the chair next to his and laid her head against the back, her eyes suspiciously red and puffy. She'd put a sweater on to ward off the chilly night.

Figuring she'd talk when she was ready, he continued petting the dog and took in what he could of his surroundings. Another ten years, and he might get used to the silence, the fresh air.

"Looks like you made a friend already." She turned her head and offered a sad smile.

He glanced at Bones again. Great name. "I always wanted a dog." Frowning, he snapped his mouth shut, unsure why he'd told her that.

"Your parents wouldn't let you have one?"

Considering his foster families claimed eating was a privilege, and those were the decent ones, he didn't respond.

"Do you have anything waiting for you back in Illinois? A job? Family?"

He had nothing but what he could fit on the back of his Hog. "A couple friends." Just Jim, actually. And as Nate's former juvie parole officer, Jim probably shouldn't be lumped in the friend category. If not for him, though, Nate would either be dead from gang wars or doing life behind bars. "I was thinking about staying in Meadowlark awhile."

"Have you ever ridden a horse or driven a tractor?"

Hell, he almost laughed. "No. I'm city bred. Why?"

She pulled a deep breath and set her rocker in motion, gaze distant. "Well, if you're going to work here, I guess I'll have to teach you a thing or two."

He stilled, staring at her profile. And here he'd thought no one could surprise him after all he'd seen. The plan had always been to hang around town, close by, and find some kind of job and roof over his head. For the rest of her life or his, he was going to watch over her from a respectable distance.

With an endearing smile that felled him, she looked him in the eye. "That is, if you're interested?"

"I can take an engine apart and put it back together. If need be, I can handle carpentry. Fix crap. I don't know anything about ranching, Olivia."

She shrugged as if his excuses were moot. "Like I said, I can teach you. I could use a handyman." She swallowed, and a tiny wrinkle formed between her brows. "I'd really like you to stay."

Just what in the hell had Justin put in his letter to his sister? Her entire demeanor had done a one-eighty. No longer wary, she looked at Nate dead on without a hint of unease or tension. Her mannerisms and appearance were so much like Justin's, Nate's heart thumped in a strange form of déjà vu.

He glanced at the dog again, thinking. Her offer solved his job issue and working on the ranch meant he could keep a closer eye on her. But he hated the idea of taking money from her, no matter how much work he did.

"You don't know anything about me." And if she did, she'd be changing her tune. "I could be a serial rapist or jewel thief."

"Are you?" The amusement in her tone had his lips curving.

"No." A murderer by shitty circumstance, former south side gang-banger, and all around loser, but he'd never stolen anything in his life. And he'd never force himself on a woman. "Still, you just met me."

"You said you were thinking of staying in town. Meadowlark is mostly a ranching community. We only have three-hundred residents. You'd be hard-pressed finding employment elsewhere."

And the closest city was Casper, a hundred miles west, forgetting the other small blips dotting the map. He sighed and stared ahead, debating. It was one thing to stick close by and another to be right on top of her. Worse, she'd have to train him how to do the damn work.

"Justin said I could trust you, that you were a good guy."

His gaze whipped to hers. Sincerity looked back at him.

Christ, she was gorgeous. Not in a runway manner or anything found in Hollywood, but in the classical, one-hundred percent natural form not often overturned just anywhere. Beauty like hers had no place in his life.

And damn. Nate wasn't a good guy and she couldn't trust him. To protect her, to never hurt her, to give up what remained of his

25

pathetic existence to fulfill a promise? Hell yes. But he was the farthest thing from a saint as they came.

"If all that's waiting for you back home is a few friends, why not try things here?" She idly rocked the chair, her posture and tone not pushy or assertive. "It can't hurt. Honestly, it would be nice to have a friend of Justin's around. It's like having a piece of him here."

Shit. How did anyone say no to her? An hour in her presence, and he was ready to hit his knees, submit to her every whim.

"Okay." He cleared his rough throat. He'd have to figure something out regarding payment because no way was he taking money from her. He'd accrued enough in savings from the Army and had disability compensation checks coming every month. "If you're sure."

"Positive." The smile hit her baby blues this time, making his skin heat. "Welcome aboard."

"Thanks." There was a special place in hell for him. He deserved the burn. Grabbing the box at his feet, he passed it to her. "These are a few of Justin's things."

She traced her fingers over the engraving of a horseshoe on the lid. "I don't recognize this."

He didn't see how she could. It would've seemed like battery acid to a knife wound to return the last items her brother touched in a grocery bag. "I made the box. His stuff is in it."

She blinked at him. "You made this?" Her gaze dropped to her lap and she ran her hand over the lid again. "Handle carpentry," she mumbled.

"What?"

"You said you could *handle carpentry*. This is more than wielding a hammer or saw. The detail is fantastic."

Well, Jim had taught Nate to whittle as a teen. Idle hands and all that. Through the years, he'd played with various forms of wood and had gotten better, started crafting other crap. In the hospital in Germany, it was the only thing that had kept him sane.

She opened the box and sorted through a few photographs. When she pulled out a necklace, she choked on a sob. "I didn't know he had this." Tears streamed down her cheeks, reflecting in the moonlight. "I looked everywhere for it last Christmas. It was my mom's."

He glanced from the tiny heart pendant dangling on a gold chain to her and back again. Give him nuclear weapons, give him an assault rifle aimed at his head, but do not put Olivia Cattenach in tears near him. He had no experience with emotional females, and this one already had him wrapped around her pinkie.

Shame, remorse, and self-loathing ate his insides raw.

Rising, he glanced longingly at his motorcycle. "I'll, uh...give you time alone." He needed to find a place to crash tonight, anyway. "What time should I—"

The next thing he knew, the box was on her chair and she was plastered against him. With her breasts crushed to his chest and every inch of her molded to him, he froze.

Slender arms wrapped around his waist, clutched his shirt, and she buried her face in his neck. The top of her head barely reached his chin as her tears dampened his skin. The scent of her shampoo and something elemental—rain?—swirled around them and...hell. Nothing before had the ability to arouse and soothe him in the same beat.

"Thank you." Her lips feathered his throat and he ground his teeth against an involuntary shudder of interest.

Lucifer was engraving Nate's name on a cage right now.

Since she seemed to need comfort and he was at fault, he carefully cupped the back of her head and set his other hand low on her back. At the contact, she curled into him, and the urgent desire to claim her warred with a fierce need to protect her—from the world, from anything that would dare do her harm, from...him.

"Sorry." She stepped away and smiled, leaving him reeling at the loss. "Meeting someone who served with Justin and seeing his things again made me a little crazy." Her laugh was like smoke and twice as toxic. "Come on. Let's get you settled."

Settled? How? With a bottle of Jack and a mind bleach? Nothing short would do.

"Are you coming?"

He shook his head and found her holding the screen door open. "What?"

"Aunt Mae's quarters are off the kitchen. My suite's on the third floor, so you get your pick of three bedrooms on the second."

Come again? She wanted him to stay here? "I'll get a place in town."

Her grin sent the world around him in a tailspin. "Good luck with that. There's no motels."

The dog nudged Nate's hand as if to say, *Move it, asshole*.

Fine. He'd figure something out in the morning. What was one more crime in comparison to the plethora of others?

Chapter Three

Olivia sipped coffee at the kitchen table while Aunt Mae flipped strips of bacon at the stove. Sizzles and pops filled the room in a sound as comforting as it was familiar. A large stack was piled on a draining plate and two of the men had already stopped by for a bite.

"Have you seen Nate this morning?" Olivia moved scrambled eggs around her plate, hoping it looked like she'd eaten more than she had, else Aunt Mae would fuss.

"No, but he's probably comatose if he drove straight from Illinois."

No doubt. "I should've discussed him living here." It had been an impulsive offer after she'd read Justin's letter, but she couldn't bring herself to regret the decision. According to her brother, he suspected Nate had no family and wanted him to find a place to call home once he was out of the service. Justin had said other things, stuff she didn't want to dissect yet, but she'd process later. "Is it okay with you?"

Up went Aunt Mae's brows. "I don't get involved in your hiring, baby girl."

"I know. But it's different since he's staying in the house."

Her aunt transferred bacon and added more to the skillet. "Well, our boarding houses are full, so I don't know where else he'd go."

"True." They had two large farmhouses edging the northern property line that her ranch hands occupied. Part of their salary was rooming because it was easier than driving in from town at all hours.

"Justin wanted him here. Besides, he's not bad to look at."

Laughing, Olivia set her coffee aside. "He's a giant, isn't he?"

"*Pfft*. Mountain, I'd say."

With a smile and a sigh, Olivia laid her head back on the chair. She'd been enveloped by that "mountain" last night for a few brief moments, and the safety he'd invoked had carried her through the night straight into this morning. Odd, since she'd never considered herself in need of protection.

"I didn't stick around long, but it seems to me he was a little smitten by you." Aunt Mae grinned. "Didn't take his eyes off you, in fact."

Lord. "Don't tell me your *getting dirty* speech again. It didn't go over well yesterday."

Her aunt laughed. "If you weren't already thinking dirty thoughts with that hunk around, there's no hope for you."

The hunk himself strode in the back door, wearing lose sweatpants on his lean hips and a gray t-shirt soaked in sweat. His bald head and bulging arms glistened with perspiration, and Olivia nearly swallowed her tongue.

Bones trotted in behind him and sat at Aunt Mae's feet, begging for bacon.

Olivia forced her gaze to Nate's when it really wanted to wander. Man, he made her skin hot. "I didn't realize you were awake."

He pulled a set of earbuds out of his ears and glanced around. "I run a couple miles every morning." When Aunt Mae handed him a bottle of water, he stared at it in confusion. "Thanks. Am I late?"

"Nope." Olivia took her plate to the sink. "I just got up. Nakos will be doling out assignments to the guys soon. We don't have to meet him for another ninety minutes or so."

Nate nodded and drank from the bottle, looking like a pornographic version of a sportswear ad. "I'll take a quick shower and meet you back here."

"Eat first." Her aunt handed him a plate and, again, he stared at it like he'd never seen eggs before.

"You don't have to feed me."

"Room and board." Olivia smiled and reclaimed her seat. "You'll want protein. Trust me. The men come and go all day snatching food."

"Okay." He stood where he was and ate a few bites as Olivia and her aunt exchanged concerned glances. "That reminds me. Where can I pick up a few things?"

"I'm going shopping today. What do you need?"

He blinked at Aunt Mae. "Gatorade. It's an electrolyte thing since my injury. Keeps the leg from stiffening. I can get it, though, if you tell me—"

"I'll add it to the list." Her aunt waved her hand when he tried to object.

Rico, one of the ranch hands, rushed through the door, kissed Aunt Mae's cheek, and grabbed two slices of bacon. "Love you."

Her aunt tsked. "You love my bacon."

"That, too." He turned and stopped dead, wide gaze roaming over Nate. "Uh, hello."

Olivia rolled her eyes. "Rico, meet Nate. I just hired him. He's an Army buddy of Justin's."

"Gotcha." Rico held out his hand. "Thanks for your service."

Silent, Nate shook his hand, his dark eyes assessing as they ran over Rico's blond hair, jeans, and denim shirt.

"Remind me not to piss you off, yeah?" Rico kissed Aunt Mae again, high-fived Olivia, and rushed out the door.

Nate's gaze slowly traveled to Aunt Mae's back as she resumed cooking and then to Olivia. Poor guy seemed a little overwhelmed and unsure what to do next. After his first tour, Justin had been like that for a few days once he had returned home.

She got the impression Nate was forcing himself to breathe, judging by the wrought expression and tightening of his jaw. She didn't know what had him out of sorts, but she tilted her head and offered him a reassuring smile.

He shook his head as if to clear it, quickly ate the rest of his breakfast, and walked the plate to the sink. "Thanks for...feeding me."

While her aunt nodded and Nate left the room, Olivia got tripped up by his odd phrasing and the humble note to his tone. Perhaps he wasn't used to people or their ways here on the ranch yet, but she was beginning to suspect no one had ever been kind to him before. The same inkling had hit her last night on the porch when she'd complimented him on the box he'd made, offered the job, and showed him to his bedroom.

"I think you should take him with you on your walk." Aunt Mae spooned eggs into a warming plate and washed her hands. "It might give him some closure."

Olivia nodded. "I will." He'd been unable to attend Justin's funeral, but she could take Nate to see her brother's grave. She'd planned on it, anyway, if only to show him where the cemetery was located.

He came downstairs ten minutes later, wearing jeans, a black baseball cap, and a sweatshirt. She led him outside and they walked in silence up an incline, Bones trotting at Nate's side. Her dog typically didn't accompany her to the cemetery.

"I think you made a lasting impression." She jerked her chin toward the sheepdog.

He glanced at Bones. "I found him outside my bedroom door this morning. He followed me on my run."

"Really? He likes you, then. They say dogs are an excellent judge of character."

He sent her a disbelieving look. "He seems very mild-mannered. Doesn't he sleep in your room?"

"Sometimes." She shrugged. "He kind of does what he wants. You're a great companion, aren't you, boy?"

Bones barked as if he understood.

Nate's lips curved as he glanced from the dog to his surroundings. "This place is massive. How many acres do you own?"

"Two-thousand."

"Christ." He shook his head. "I can't fathom."

She laughed. "It's all I've ever known. To the north," she pointed to give him a sense of direction, "is mostly wheat crops. We keep some of the harvest for feed, but the rest goes to suppliers. There's two farmhouses the ranch hands live in beyond the field. And before you ask, they're full, so you're stuck with me."

He grunted, but otherwise kept silent.

"To the south and west are pastures. We have about a thousand head of steer and five hundred sheep. The east side is mostly the main house and barns. We have twenty-five horses, plus a large storage structure for equipment. A lot of the guys prefer ATVs to horseback."

He rubbed the back of his neck, seemingly uncertain.

"I'll teach you everything you need to know. You're a smart guy. You'll catch on quick."

His gaze whipped to hers and he studied her like she was an alien life form. "You remind me so much of your brother."

There was no higher compliment in her book. "Thank you. We were very close. More like best friends than siblings."

Frowning, he jerked his gaze ahead, leaving her to wonder what she'd said to upset him. He'd spent a lot of time in precarious and dangerous situations with Justin. Perhaps being around her was difficult or brought up painful memories.

After a few moments of silence, she chewed her lip. "How did you sleep? I'll bet you were tired after the long drive."

Appearing to mull that over, he took a deep breath. "I caught a couple hours. I didn't wake you, did I?"

"No." Her chest pinched. She wondered if he had some PTSD or if it was the change in setting that had disturbed him. "Too quiet around here for you?"

"Yeah, maybe." He adjusted his hat and stopped walking to face her. Head down, he set his hands on his hips. "I'm going to be honest with you. I don't sleep much, not for long stretches, anyway. I tend to wake suddenly and..." He closed his eyes, jaw tense.

Her stomach bottomed out. "From nightmares?"

He didn't open his eyes, but his brows pinched. "Yes." The reluctant tone belied his discomfort with the situation, and a hint of embarrassment tinged his cheeks. "This is why I prefer to stay somewhere else." With a sigh, he refocused on her, and the torment in his gaze was gutting. "You should be aware of the situation if you hear me. Or if I wander around."

Lord. He sleepwalked, too? "You must've seen some terrible things over there," she whispered.

In answer, he pivoted and continued ahead as if they'd never spoken.

She strode quietly beside him, her heart aching. Justin had never said much about his time overseas, but he hadn't had the walls in place like Nate did. He didn't know her, either, so maybe he'd talk about it in time.

At the cemetery fence, he paused. "He's buried here?"

"Yes, along with four generations of Cattenachs." She faced him, watching the hard edges of his profile. "Our parents died in a car wreck when we were eight. I didn't sleep well for a long time afterward and I refused to get in a vehicle for a year, thinking I'd die, too. I won't pretend to understand what you're going through, but what helped me was coming here, talking to them."

He turned his head and looked at her, gaze sweeping over her face like a caress. Understanding and respect shone in his eyes before he broke the connection and glanced at the cemetery again.

Bones nudged his hand and, with a blink of surprise, Nate looked at the dog.

"I think he senses what troubles you. Maybe you should let him sleep in your bed, see how it works out." She opened the gate and walked to Justin's grave.

Nate's quiet footsteps padded behind her, but he said nothing. He spoke very little, actually, but his eyes gave a lot of him away. Guilt and regret collided with turmoil and indecision. After only a day, she didn't have enough fingers and toes to count the number of times she'd seen the wide array of his emotions. None of them good.

"You have company, Justin. Look who's here." She knelt and picked a couple weeds from around the stone. Shielding the sun with her hand, she looked up at Nate. "I come here every morning to tell him stuff. I bother him as much now as I did when he was alive. It's a sister's right."

After a slow shake of his head, he stared at her with furrowed brows and a hint of amusement like he didn't know what to make of her. He opened his mouth as if to speak, but shut it again.

She glanced at her brother's grave, and for the first time since dirt had been dumped over his casket, her throat didn't close. She blathered about ranch duties and let him know she'd gotten his letter. After a few minutes, she rose and brushed off her knees, Nate watching her the whole time.

"Go ahead and try it. Talk to him." She blew Justin a kiss and headed for the gate. "I'll wait over here."

He watched her leave as if she'd smacked him upside the head, then reluctantly faced the headstone. He didn't say anything aloud, not that she could hear, anyway, but he bowed his head like he was conversing mentally, his shoulders tense. Not long after, he met her on the path.

They walked back in silence, and she breathed in the familiar scents of soil and hay the closer they got to the barn. Nakos stood outside, clipboard in hand. He looked up and did a double-take.

"*Hebe*, Olivia." His tone was flat as always, but his expression was pure what-the-hell as he glanced from her to Nate.

"Good morning. You remember Nate Roldan? I hired him for some handyman stuff. He's going to follow me around for a little while."

Nakos didn't move. Not even to blink.

"He's going to be staying up at the house with me and Aunt Mae."

Nada. Nothing. Zilch. Dark eyes glared into hers and, if not for Bones trotting into the barn, she'd have sworn time stopped.

"Nice to formally meet you." Nate nodded.

Nakos's gaze narrowed on Nate's for a blip before settling on her. "Olivia, a word." He grabbed her elbow and turned her away.

She hadn't taken a step and Nate shoved between them, using his ginormous arm to push her behind him. "Hands off." The growl of his low, menacing voice stalled the breath in her lungs.

"Back the hell up." Nakos must've pushed Nate, because he stumbled into her, not that she could see around the wall of his body.

Whoa. "Time out." She ducked under Nate's arm and stepped between them. "Nakos would never hurt me."

Nate, jaw ticking, nostrils flared, dropped his gaze to hers. In a flash, he raised his arms and took a step away. "Sorry. Gut reaction."

Interesting. More on that later.

She turned and set her palms on Nakos's chest, maneuvering him several paces backward. "Testosterone, party of one. Follow me."

With a parting glare for Nate, her foreman followed her to the other side of the barn and removed his cowboy hat. "Have you lost your mind? You don't know a damn thing about this guy."

"I know he was injured serving with Justin and he said I could trust Nate."

Up went his arms in an are-you-kidding-me move. "Says who? The stranger who showed up on your doorstep six months after the fact?"

"Says Justin in a letter Nate brought to me."

Shoulders sagging, he let out a long-winded huff. "He could snap you in half with one arm tied behind his back and without breaking a sweat."

Men. Such a headache. "Yet he stepped between us when he thought you were a danger."

"We make all hiring decisions together. And why does he need to bunk at the house?"

She scrubbed a hand over her face. "He's mostly going to be fixing stuff around the ranch. If he takes well to other things, we can discuss adding more duties. And the boarding houses are full. You want him staying at your cabin?"

His eyes narrowed.

"That's what I thought." She tilted her face heavenward. "You could be a little more welcoming."

"I could chew glass, too. Doesn't mean I will." He glanced away. "You're giving me a coronary, little red. I don't like him alone with you two."

"Noted." She crossed her arms. "Trust me like you always have before. I'm not an idiot. Can we get to work now?"

"I'm calling Rip by the end of the day to do a background check."

Rip being Meadowlark's sheriff. "Fine." Whatever calmed Nakos down was okay by her. The nearest she'd seen him angry was a low simmer. Today? He was boiling the lid off the pot.

He let out a string of muttered words in his native tongue, which she assumed were curses, and stomped back to the front of the barn. He stopped a few feet away from Nate. "You lay one finger on her and they'll never find your body."

When he disappeared into the barn, Nate looked at her, his expression unimpressed. "Nice guy."

Chapter Four

After the foreman's temper tantrum yesterday morning, Nate had spent the day ten feet from Olivia while she'd shaved wool off sheep. Many, many sheep. At least he knew what shearing meant now. It looked exhausting. A week ago, he wouldn't have said so, but since watching her and Nakos for nine solid hours, Nate would've rather done eight-hundred push-ups than partake.

And he'd tried damn hard not to think about how great her ass looked in jeans every time she'd bent over. Which had been a lot. Or the way sunlight had lit her cornflower eyes and auburn hair on their walk. Or the way she'd smiled sweetly at him as if she could chase away all his dark simply by wishing it.

Justin had been like that, too—worked his way past Nate's defenses and burrowed deep. Didn't matter how many times he'd told Justin to go away or gave off fuck-you vibes, the guy had just kept at it with charm and smiles and blah, blah, blahing Nate to death. Until he'd found himself liking the fellow soldier so much, he'd considered him a friend. A rare occurrence, since Nate had never bestowed the moniker on anyone before. Where he came from, friends were only as good as your next drug run and then stabbed you in the back for leverage.

Endearing as Justin had been, his sister was worse. The he-couldn't-breathe-correctly, what-the-hell-happened-to-rational-thought kind of worse. And damn. Around her, he had no filter. At least with Justin, Nate had been able to pull up before spouting too much. With Olivia? Diarrhea of the mouth. First with the dog comment, then admitting to having nightmares.

Her reaction had been a kick in the teeth. No platitudes or flowery nonsense. Just empathetic eyes and offers of a solution. Like there was any chance of fixing him.

Then there was the aunt. Mae was a trip herself. After his run yesterday, he'd gone upstairs to shower, only to find a mini-fridge in his room that hadn't been there before, stocked with Gatorade. And a case of protein bars on his dresser. His stupid heart had shifted in his stupid chest. Most people took something as simple as eating for granted. To him, food still gave him pause, even after all these years.

Today, with his leg cramping, he jogged the last dreg to the house and slipped in the back door. Olivia was perched at the table with coffee and Mae was transferring muffins to a teetering stack on the counter.

He swiped sweat from his brow with his forearm. "I'll go shower and—"

Mae shoved a plate with two muffins and a heap of strawberries at him.

"Eat," he mumbled.

He attempted to ignore Olivia's eyes on him while he stood by the sink and chewed as fast as he could. Knowing her routine now, he didn't have to rush because she wasn't waiting on him, but he hated the way her clever, intuitive gaze tracked his every move. It was enough to make a man self-conscious.

"You can sit, you know." Her lips curved in what he called her coax-the-beast smile.

He couldn't be tamed. Best she realize that. "I'm sweaty."

She leaned back in her seat and crossed her arms over her ample chest. Who knew flannel could be sexy? "So what? Sit, please. Enjoy your food."

Forcing a strawberry down his tight throat, he avoided her gaze. Looking at her would only suck him into her orbit and he'd say the first thing that came to mind. Like how he'd never enjoyed food. It was for sustenance only.

Once he'd showered and met up with her again, they followed the same path as yesterday, except he waited for her outside the cemetery gate while she talked to Justin. Talked, as in she had a conversation with her brother like Nate hadn't killed him. Swear to Christ, he didn't know what to make of her.

Bones trotted along beside them on the way back. The dog had been glued to Nate's side since their bonding episode on the porch. Nate didn't know what to make of that, either. He'd found Bones outside his bedroom door again this morning and he'd followed Nate on his run.

Nakos stood outside the barn when they approached, looking no more eager to see Nate than the day before. The foreman gave some sort of greeting to Olivia that sounded like *heh-beh* and ignored Nate altogether. Fine by him.

Except he didn't like the way Nakos looked at her and certainly didn't care for the way they had their own kind of unspoken communication between them. There was a solid minute of what he interpreted as: *He's still here...Yes, get over it...I'm not happy...Understood.* Nate couldn't tell if Olivia had a thing for the foreman, but he was definitely in love with her.

Nate wouldn't know love if it latched onto his face and wiggled, but he could spot it on others as easily as he could weed out a lie. Call it a gift.

They slipped into the same routine as yesterday, with Nakos holding the sheep and Olivia shearing. But instead of Nate standing around twiddling his thumbs, he took the wool from her, brushed it as he'd seen her do, then rolled it like she had.

Ten head in, she glanced over her shoulder at him. "Your turn."

Nate looked from the sheep on its back to Olivia. "What?"

"I'll walk you through it. Come over here."

With a wry sneer, Nakos deigned to speak to him. "And if you screw up, it could cause injury to the animal or decrease the wool's value."

Ignoring the self-righteous prick, Nate focused on Olivia. She had her hair pulled back in a low ponytail, was covered in dirt and tufts of white fur, had not a stitch of makeup on, and was still able to cease his heart. "Are you sure?"

In answer, she lifted her brows.

He squatted next to her, but she worked her way between his legs until she was cradled against his thighs. Her rain-like scent combined with hay and became all he could breathe in. The slim, lean press of her body in such an intimate position rendered him incapable of swallowing. In sensory overload, he tensed.

He wasn't used to touch. Plain and simple. As a kid, he'd not been in an environment that doled out hugs and, as a teen, his lifestyle with the Disciples gang hadn't exactly been cuddly. Even when he was with a woman, he preferred fast, hard fucking to fondling, typically thwarting any attempts at caressing or exploration on the female's part.

Olivia was different. Other than the brief embrace on her porch and a casual arm brush, there hadn't been contact. But those couple instances didn't instill the urge to back off or erect distance. Instead, every molecule in his body screamed for...more.

Seemingly unaware of his predicament, she picked up the clippers at their feet. "The wool on the belly is the dirtiest and not valuable, which is why we start there." She took his hand and set the clippers in it, cradling hers around his. The buzz of the device vibrated in his palm, and she took his other hand, laying the blades against his fingertips. "It won't cut you, but it needs to be held at the right angle." She turned her head and looked at him. "Do you..."

Their faces inches apart, he froze as the time-space continuum imploded on itself. He'd taken enemy fire that had been less jarring than having her this close. Her cornflower gaze held him immobile, framed by long blondish-red lashes he imagined would feel like feather kisses if fluttered against his skin. She had the tiniest scar above her upper lip—a thin white mark, unnoticeable had he not been right on top of her.

At his perusal, she let out an uneven breath that skated over his jaw. His heart detached ribs as he lowered his gaze to her mouth. They weren't full or lush, but her lips had a bow shape that was part adorable and one-hundred percent groan-worthy. Sheer temptation.

The loud rasp of Nakos clearing his throat made her flinch.

"Um..." She blinked repeatedly and glanced at their joined hands like waking from a midday nap. A blush worked its way up her neck and infused her cheeks.

"You were saying how to hold the clippers and dole correct strokes," Nakos supplied in a drone that had Nate's molars gnashing.

"Right," she breathed and cleared her throat. "Start at the breast bone on the right side and shear all the way to the flank."

She'd lost him somewhere between "your turn" and "um," but he nodded.

Gently, she lifted their joined hands and encouraged him to let her guide. Together, they stripped off a section of wool on the belly. She repeated the pattern on the left side, then a center strip before moving onto the inside of the hind legs, crotch, and tail. Nakos shifted the sheep's position, and she and Nate did the shoulders and outer legs. Two more position changes, several more strokes of the clipper on the back, and they finished.

Nate preferred the Army's calisthenics, but there was something rewarding in accomplishing a new skill. After many more runs with Olivia guiding him, he did two sheep on his own to round out the day.

Nakos stopped Olivia outside the barn door and passed her a folded piece of paper while Nate waited a few feet away.

She glanced at the page and handed it back. "I told you."

Nakos headed for the driveway. "Consider our discussion off the table, little red."

Nate had no clue what the hell had just gone down, but judging by Olivia's sagging shoulders, closed eyes, and the way she dropped her head, it wasn't good. When she covered her face with her hands and sighed, Nate's pulse thumped.

"What's wrong?" He stepped in front of her when he should've left her alone. Whatever was between her and her foreman, or anything regarding the ranch, was none of his business.

Her hands slapped her thighs. "I'm mean and I screwed up."

His first instinct was to laugh. Her version of mean and his were polar opposites. She seemed pretty upset, though, so he kept mum.

"I'm going for a ride. Would you like to come?"

"Sure." He thought she meant for a drive until she led him to the barn and stopped one of the ranch hands from unsaddling a horse. Her and the dark-haired, skinny-as-hell kid made small talk, so Nate glanced around.

The carriage doors were open on both ends of the long, narrow stables, creating a breeze and filtering late-day light. Fifteen stalls lined each side, some with horses, some empty. Stacks of hay bales were piled along a far wall and, for a barn, the place was tidy.

"Kyle, this is Nate." She smiled and faced him. "Kyle is my friend Amy's little brother."

"Yeah, I heard you were around." Kyle held out his hand. "I think I'll call you Gigantor."

Not if he wanted Nate to respond. Regardless, he shook the kid's hand. "A pleasure."

Olivia glanced at a clipboard on the wall. "Anything I need to watch for?"

Kyle eyed the ceiling as if in thought. "No, but if you head up to Devil's Cross, mind the incline. The creek's low."

"Will do. Can you pop up to the house and let Mae know we're going riding?"

"Sure thing." He gave Olivia a fist bump and jogged out of the barn.

She grabbed the reins of two horses and walked them out the opposite end and into a clearing. Long prairie grass stirred in the wind as the pink sky faded to navy. She tied the brown horse to a post by a fence and held the black one in place.

Nate eyed her, then the animals. "Never ridden one of these."

"This is Midnight. He's a three-year-old stallion and very mild-mannered. Come on over here." When he did as asked, she took his wrist and had him run his hand down the horse's nose. In turn, Midnight nudged Nate's shoulder, and Olivia laughed. "There, he likes you."

She instructed him how to mount, and he climbed onto the saddle. She did the same on hers, looking way more graceful about it, and settled her horse next to his.

"My guy here is Pirate, and he's a two-year-old gelding. Now, you know how to ride a motorcycle, so you're at an advantage." She set one hand on his stomach and the other on his forearm, and he inhaled hard. "Driving a bike requires using your core and arms. You lean into the turns, right? A horse is a bit of the opposite." And down went her hands on his thighs, and he tensed. "Your lower body and gravity will do the work. Use your legs to steer as well as the reins."

Lower body? Yeah, it was paying attention. Heart pounding, oxygen in short supply, he tried everything he could to concentrate on her words. He had a sinking suspicion she could touch him incidentally every hour on the hour for a thousand years, and he'd never get used to it.

A frown marred her forehead. "You seem nervous. Know what? We'll ride together this first time."

Nervous didn't cover it. And it had nothing to do with the horse. He'd spent his entire life unafraid of anything. Balls-to-the-wall and like the hounds of hell were chasing him. Probably because they were. Yet a slender redhead with innocent doe eyes came onto the scene and panic clawed his chest.

Before he could protest or somehow explain his response, she dismounted and walked her horse to the barn. She emerged moments later with a reassuring smile, tucked her foot into his stirrup, and climbed onto his horse.

Her back flush to his front, she grinned over her shoulder. "Better?"

No. Yes. Sweet Christ, strike him now. "Sure," he grated.

With a nod, she took each of his hands and put them on the reins, then placed hers over his so she was caged in his arms. Over her shoulder, with the scent of her shampoo driving him insanely crazy, he stared at her short blunt nails and long, delicate fingers. Except she had slight calluses on her palms that contradicted the fragile appearance.

"Okay, just follow my lead. It's kinda like steering your motorcycle."

This was nothing like his Hog, barring the rev of a different engine and the free-falling sensation of the ride.

She kicked them into a slow trot and rode them across the plains, over a few hills, and to the top of a bluff. He forgot about her closeness—mostly—and took in the view instead. Shadows played with moonlight over the horizon, shaping the mountains and surrounding wilderness as dusk descended and stars winked overhead.

Nothing. No noise, no sirens, no gunfire. Just...nothing.

He shook his head, wondering if the strange sense of calm was from her or the setting. Perhaps both. A crisp breeze tinged with pine and snow swept over him, and he filled his lungs. He could see just about all of her land from their vantage point.

Something crackled and then a voice broke the peace. "You there, boss?"

"Shoot." She twisted in the saddle, wrapped an arm around his waist, and leaned over so far, he thought she'd fall. She pulled a walkie-talkie out of a bag attached near the horse's flank and spoke into it. "I'm here, Rico. What's up?"

"Nakos wants to know where you are and Mae wants to know when you'll be back."

She issued a disgusted sound. "I'm up at Blind Ridge and I'll be back within an hour. Tell Nakos to take a chill pill. I have the satellite phone, the two-way, and a revolver." She paused. "Thanks, Rico. Go home."

His laugh reverberated through the speaker. "Ten-four. Be careful."

"Yeah, yeah," she muttered as she put the walkie-talkie back in the bag. She shifted until she sat sideways in the saddle, her hip snug against Nate's crotch, and let out a weary sigh. "This is my favorite place on the whole ranch."

He could see why. "You have a gun?"

She grinned and glanced at him out of the corner of her eye. "Yep. And yes, I can shoot it, too."

"Do you have a lot of opportunities to fire a gun?" What the hell did she need to target? Dust motes?

"It's for protection. Black bear, that kind of thing." She looked at him and laughed. "Don't worry. They don't bother people much."

"I was actually picturing you shooting a bear." He rubbed his neck, wondering why the image of her packing was so hot. "Is Nakos always that protective?"

"Sadly, yes. He's been like that since we were kids." Her contemplative gaze scanned the area. "More so since you arrived. You should know he did a background check on you."

Okay, the two of them had a very long history. Noted. And a background check wouldn't turn up anything. Nate's juvie record was sealed. "He's got it for you bad."

She closed her eyes. "I know." Flicking a strand of hair off her face, she looked at him. "Speaking of protective, what was with the pissing contest yesterday?"

"Gut response." Color him crazy, but his intuition to look after her had suddenly become more than a promise. All he could do was think *mine* whenever she was within fifty yards. He couldn't seem to get his baser instincts to realize she'd never be his, though. And shouldn't be, either. Two days, and he wanted her with a fierceness he'd never known. Lust he could deal with, but this didn't lean solely that way. "I'm not sexist and I don't think women incapable, but common sense shuts off in certain situations."

"It has to stem from somewhere."

Smart little cookie, this one. "There was a girl I knew growing up. We went through the system together, wound up at a lot of the same places." He could still see the bruises mottling Darla's body and wanted to rail. She'd been the closest he had to a sibling and, years later, when he'd encountered her again as one of the Disciples' whores, he'd been just as powerless as he'd been as a child to help her. "She was mousy and I tried my best to keep an eye on her."

Except Darla had wound up dead, anyway. In an alley with a needle in her arm.

"The system? You were a foster kid?"

Son of a bitch. What exactly was the glitch, the direct correlation between Olivia and his sudden lack of filter? "If I say yes, are you going to toss the pity card?"

"No." She swallowed and stared ahead. "If not for Aunt Mae, Justin and I would've wound up the same way. All of this," she waved her hand and shrugged, "would be gone. In the hands of some stranger." She tilted her head, brow wrinkled. "It would've broken my heart. Four generations of Cattenachs have worked this land."

The farthest he could trace his family tree was a crack addict mother who'd delivered him in an ER and split. But he understood. And so did Olivia, apparently. If he didn't watch himself, he'd let her in too far and never climb back out.

"I think that's why the rift with Nakos upsets me so much." Her gaze met his again, soft and yielding. "For the first time in our adult lives, I brought up the possibility of something more between us. If I don't have an heir, the legacy dies with me. He's a good guy, but I think he was insulted." She offered a hopelessly sad smile. "We'd have beautiful babies."

But she didn't love the guy. That much was apparent. Nate was the last person to be giving advice, yet the thought of her losing the adorable part of her personality in order to settle made his gut ache. Because that's what would happen. Mediocrity would douse her light.

Her hand settled on his bicep. The contact sent a current from the exact location, through his whole nervous system, and back again. Created unimaginable heat. Had him grasping for purchase. He tensed, wanting more, but unable and unwilling to take it.

Her pretty eyes widened and she slapped a hand over her mouth as if horrified. "Oh God. You did that in the barn today while shearing, and again on the horse. I thought you were nervous, but..." She fisted her hands under her chin. "You hate being touched, don't you? I'm so sorry. And here I was..."

She went to dismount, but he wrapped an arm around her waist to stop her, frustrated and confused. "What are you doing?"

"Getting down. I'll walk us back so you don't have to ride with me."

The hell she would. It had to be two miles to the main house.

Shit. And how to explain his body's response to her? She had the impression she'd done something wrong when he was the asshole. "I'm fine like this."

She chewed her lower lip. "Reach behind you and grab the back of the saddle. Hold on tight, though. I'm going to ride faster than when we came up to get you back quicker."

"Olivia—"

"I'm really sorry." She faced front and grabbed the reins. "Hold on."

Chapter Five

Olivia spent the next few days riddled in guilt and feeling stupid. And insensitive. And then more stupid. While they'd finished the week shearing and getting the wool loaded for the supplier, she'd done everything in her power to avoid all physical contact with Nate. She hadn't realized how often she used her hands until she'd been forced to think about every move. The best way for her to teach him was by demonstration.

In bed, she flopped from her stomach to her back and stared at the ceiling. She was going on three nights of restlessness and nothing was working. She'd tried everything but the obvious path to assuage her wrongs. Because she was a coward.

Top of the list? She needed to have a conversation with Nakos to clear the air. Which was darn impossible with Nate underfoot. Nakos had been a friend since as far back as she could remember. She may not share his romantic feelings, but he was entitled to respect from her.

Lord. And Nate? What the heck was she supposed to say, to do, after learning what she had? He'd been in foster care as a child, and she wondered for how long. What had happened to his parents? Did he have no other family? Had the experience been a bad one? There was such a fine line between his circumstances and hers.

Their conversation out at Blind Ridge kept playing through her head like a bad sitcom. The way he went rigid when she'd touched him sent a pang of sorrow through her belly. It had to be a result of his injuries overseas. Perhaps a physical connection made him think of the pain from his wounds. Worse, what if it stemmed back to childhood? She'd heard horror stories about the system, and Chicago could be a rough city.

But instead of taking the time to read his signals, make sure he was comfortable and settled in, she'd set off his triggers.

So badly, she wanted to talk to him. Ease some of his pain. Justin had sent Nate to Cattenach Ranch for a reason and it wasn't in her nature to sit idly by while someone was hurting. And Nathan Roldan was obviously dealing with a lot. From his weird food quirks to his nightmares to his strong but silent demeanor, something was eating him from the inside out. She had no direction for how to help him and he wasn't exactly a chatter box.

Plus, he didn't seem to want her help.

Bones ran into the room and nudged her arm with his cold, wet nose. He bit a corner of her blanket and pulled it off her as if telling her to get up.

She rolled onto her side. "What's up, boy?"

He barked, trotted over to the door, and came back. He nudged her arm again.

"Okay, up we go." She climbed out of bed and followed him into the hallway, then to the staircase.

There was a doggy door to the tack room, thus he didn't need to go out. He could do it himself. She was pretty sure if there was an intruder or something amiss on the property, he'd bite first and ask questions later.

He paused on the landing for her to catch up, then made his way to the second floor, stopping outside Nate's door. Bones looked up at her and scratched the floor as if trying to burrow inside.

"You really have a thing for our guest, huh?" Except her dog seemed almost frantic. He barked once and pawed incessantly, scratching the wooden frame. "Okay, hold on."

She pressed her ear to the door. Heavy breathing and sheets rustling were about all she could make out. Her face heated. Was Nate, like, um...pleasuring himself? Wait. Bones wouldn't be adamant about getting inside unless something was wrong. Maybe Nate was having another nightmare?

Knocking, she called his name, but got no response. It was a complete violation of his privacy to just open the door. What if he wasn't in distress and she walked in on something? She chewed her lip.

Bones barked again.

"I'm totally blaming you if he's naked." Quietly, she turned the knob, and Bones shot through the opening.

The room was dark, aside from the light from the adjoining bathroom. Asleep, Nate was on his back and twisted in the blankets on the queen-sized bed along the far wall. Shirtless, he bowed off the mattress and resettled, but his fingers clutched the sheets at his hips as if holding on for dear life.

48

From the doorway, she pressed a hand to her chest while her throat closed. How utterly heartbreaking to witness such a huge, capable man be at the mercy of his subconscious. Bulging muscles and wide shoulders. Tattoo sleeves with more ink on his chest she wasn't aware he had. Bald head and a permanent five o'clock shadow on his strong jaw. By his appearance, it didn't seem right or possible anything could break him.

Bones jumped on the bed, sat by his hip, and barked two quick yelps.

Nate's eyes flew open and landed on the ceiling. Wide, unblinking. His chest rose and fell with uneven, haggard pants for a few seconds before he closed his eyes and swiped a hand over his face.

Bones nudged his arm and laid next to him.

Turning his head, he frowned in confusion at the dog. "Hey, there. How'd you get in here?" Reaching over, he rubbed the dog's head.

Olivia tiptoed down the hall, descended the stairs, and made her way to the kitchen to give him privacy, figuring he'd be upset if she'd seen him vulnerable. It was one thing to have a passing conversation about nightmares and another to have someone there while experiencing one. Nate didn't strike her as the kind of man who opened up to people or leaned on others.

Still a little shaken, she stood by the sink and poured a glass of water, sipping while she looked out the bay window. A patch of Aunt Mae's soon-to-be herb garden was to the right, not yet planted for the season. Beyond that and to the left were the rolling, grassy hills that led to the cemetery. The ranch was dark, quiet, unlike the emotions swirling in her belly.

She could only imagine the things he'd witnessed in his service. Justin had always tried to keep her separate from that aspect of his life, never saying much about his time away. But her brother's slight detachment after he'd returned from a tour was nothing compared to Nate's behavior. It killed her, that haunted look in his dark eyes.

"So the dog didn't develop opposable thumbs, after all."

Gasping, she jumped. The glass fell from her fingers and shattered in the sink. She whirled toward the low, hoarse voice and blinked at Nate. He'd put on a t-shirt—a crying shame, that—and a pair of nylon shorts covered his thick, hard thighs. Several red scars riddled the area and disappeared under the hem. His feet were bare and...big.

"I didn't mean to startle you." He stepped to the other side of the island, keeping it between them.

"That's okay. I was lost in thought."

He nodded, gaze roaming her face. "You let Bones into my room."

Unsure why she was suddenly nervous, she tilted her head. He didn't appear angry, but her heart pounded and she trembled. "Maybe he let himself in."

"I shut the door when I went to bed."

Her knees knocked together. "You could've not closed it all the way."

"I'm always aware of my surroundings. I shut the door."

"How do you know it was me?" She had no clue why she was arguing with him, but her nerves morphed into an anxiety-charged storm. Probably because they were alone, in the middle of the night, with both of them barely dressed. Her tank top and boy-cut shorts showed more skin than they covered.

And geez. He was a drool-worthy, panty-drenching, yummy work of masculine art.

The slightest tic, and a corner of his lip curled in a passably amused smile. "Aside from the fact you're awake and standing in the kitchen, I smelled you in the hallway outside my room."

Her mouth opened and closed. "I...smell?"

"No, not..." He let out a frustrated sigh and skimmed his hand over his bald head. "Your shampoo or perfume. It smells like rain. It's distinctive and lingers."

"Must be my bath gel and lotion. Waterfall scent." She'd had no idea it was oppressive. Embarrassed, she bit her lip. "I'll stop using it."

"Please don't."

"But you just said—"

"I said it was distinctive, not that I didn't like it." His nostrils flared with a sharp inhale and he shook his head like he couldn't believe he'd admitted as much. "It doesn't matter what..." His attention lowered to her hand. "You're bleeding."

"What?" She followed his gaze and found blood on her left hand. A lot of it. "Oh. I must've cut it when the glass broke."

Like a switch, his eyes glazed as if he'd zoned out.

"Nate?"

He flinched, and the next thing she knew, she was facing the sink, wedged between him and the counter, and he was holding her hand under a stream of water. His warm, hard body pressed against her back and the giant guns of his biceps brushed her bare arms. While he gently rinsed away the blood, she tried to get her bearings and failed.

She was surrounded by him. Enveloped. His scent of soap. His hot breath on her nape. The unrelenting muscle on every inch of his perfect form plastered to hers. He had his head over her shoulder to watch his task, and she glanced at him out of the corner of her eye, then to his tattoos. The ones on his arms seemed to be tribal designs of some sort.

Stilling his left hand with her own, she turned it over to look at the underside of his forearm. The ink continued and shifted as he moved like a living extension of his skin. It was beautiful up close. She'd only seen glimpses before. Caught up in the pattern, she traced the black lines with her fingertips from his inner elbow to his wrist and back again.

He wove the fingers of their other hands together, still under the spray, and she diverted her attention there. Like his feet, his hands were huge. His skin tone was several shades darker than hers and he dwarfed her with his size. Strong, steady hands. Yet, he slid his fingers between hers, stroking, unerringly gentle.

While her body heated at the intimate, arousing connection, he cupped her free hand and sandwiched both between his under the water, palm to palm. The contrast was amazing. His dark, tatted tone to her pale skin. Compared to him, she seemed delicate.

As if fascinated by the position, he brushed his thumbs over hers and let out a shallow, ragged breath that fanned the shell of her ear. Goosebumps skated across her flesh, but it was him who shook.

"Are you cold?"

He dropped his forehead to her temple. "The opposite." His nose brushed her cheek as he lowered his head, and she emitted a full-body tingle. "Just the opposite," he repeated, his rough voice barely above a whisper.

Shaking his head, he shut off the faucet and reached for a paper towel. He dried her hands like she were a toddler in need of assistance, then held up her hand to examine it. Only a small half-inch knick on her outer palm, but it had created a lot of blood.

He pressed the paper towel to the cut and held it there. "It's not deep enough for stitches."

She nodded, recalling his initial response. "Does the sight of blood bother you?" Half her ranch hands passed out cold at the hint of red. It was a pretty common phobia and men could be babies.

"Not usually."

"You seemed a little rattled before."

"Justin died next to me. My mind flicked back for a second." He straightened suddenly and cursed, then muttered something that sounded like *filter*. "I'm sorry. I don't know why I said that."

She turned in his arms, finding his eyes closed and his jaw tight. In all her grief after losing her brother, she never stopped to consider Nate's feelings. She'd had to bury Justin, but Nate was the one who'd been right there when he'd been killed. That kind of thing had to leave scars.

"Don't apologize. You should feel free to talk to me."

His eyes opened and he looked at her. Shook his head. "You're not my therapist and it was insensitive."

"If we're going to be friends, you don't need to bite your tongue."

"Friends." His confused expression indicated the concept was foreign.

Lord, he needed a stiff drink and a deep-tissue massage. In that order. "You know? Friends. Staying up all night gossiping and braiding each other's hair."

He frowned, but after a beat, his lips curved. "I don't have hair."

She glanced at the top of his head. "True. You have that Hell's Angels meets Mr. Clean thing going. But you're way more badass than that cartoon cleaning wuss."

As if wanting to laugh—or groan—his lips parted. Nothing came out.

"I swear, I'll get a grin out of you yet."

"I smile." His brow wrinkled as if he was affronted.

"No, you tease with traces of a smile, but only do the actual deed when being polite." She poked his chest, but nearly broke her finger for the effort. Dang, the guy was made of concrete. "I have a feeling when you actually do grin, like from the gut, you'll make panties melt."

"Panties..." He huffed a laugh-groan combination and cleared his throat.

"Don't pretend you have no clue what I'm talking about. If you didn't want females dropping at your feet, you should've thought about that, Mr. Perfect Row of White Teeth. Too late now to bypass the hot tats, bulging biceps, and abs of steel."

"I've totally lost track of this conversation."

She offered a dramatic sigh. "We'll just have to be the kind of friends who paint one another's toenails instead."

With a dip of his chin, he eyed her like she'd gone mental. "Tempting as that sounds, I'm going to have to pass on that, too." He studied her. "I started working out in the gym to bulk up, so I'd never be considered weak again. It also helps with frustration. The...abs of steel? They were just a side effect."

She stared at him, leveled once again by the verbal bombs he kept dropping amid conversation. "Who said you were weak?" She'd claw their eyes out.

Bearing his teeth, he glared at the ceiling. "Christ, it's like my mouth is under hypnosis around you."

Her heart broke. Again. He didn't seem to have anyone else in his life and, Lord knew, he needed someone to talk to. Why not her? She'd never judge him or repeat what he said.

"Nate." She cupped his tense jaw, but he stiffened and closed his eyes. She dropped her hand immediately, fisting her fingers. "I'm sorry. I forgot."

"Olivia, listen—"

"No, it's my fault. I promised to stop. I'll be more conscious about where my hands are at all times. I know you hate it and I'd never want you to be uncomfortable here."

"I don't..." He looked away, rubbing his neck. "To set the record straight, I don't hate being touched. I'm sorry I made you think you did something wrong."

"But you—"

"I'm unaccustomed to it. Okay?"

No, *not* okay. "What does that mean?" That implied he could, at some point, get "accustomed" to contact. But what kind of person wasn't used to being touched? Then again, she wasn't sure she wanted to know.

He didn't answer, but the tension drained from him before her eyes. Like he'd resigned himself to the situation, his shoulders relaxed and the stress lines on his face disappeared. Staring somewhere over her head, he sighed.

"All right. One thing at a time." She waited for him to meet her gaze once more. "Take Bones in your bedroom with you from now on."

"He's your dog, Olivia."

"I learned to share back in kindergarten."

His expression was a mix of frustration and amusement. "I can't sleep with the door open. He won't be able to get in or out."

"My suite has a doggy door. We'll switch yours for mine in the morning. You can do that, yes? Hang a door?"

"Sure, if they're the same size. Otherwise, I might need to trim. But I don't—"

"Problem solved."

His eyes narrowed. "And how will he come and go from your room?"

"I'll leave the door open. Stop being argumentative." She grinned to diffuse his irritation. Which didn't work. "He woke you from a nightmare tonight. He seems sensitive to your moods. You might get a better night's sleep knowing he'll rouse you before it gets too bad."

He studied her for so long, she had to fight the urge to squirm. At times, he could be intense to the point of scary. Not that she was concerned he'd hurt her, but whatever thoughts and memories roamed inside his head were obviously not for the faint of heart. He must've seen something in her expression because his gaze softened, swept over her face like a tender caress, and then lowered.

Taking her hand, he removed the paper towel she'd fisted and set it on the counter behind her. His thumb stroked her palm as he examined the cut. "It quit bleeding."

Her heart hadn't. It was hemorrhaging inside her chest cavity at an alarming rate. A week, and this broken soldier was nailing her emotions to the wall. "Yeah, it's fine..."

She looked down as he brought his head up, and their cheeks brushed. Instantly, he cupped the back of her head and held her in place. She couldn't tell if it was to stop her from turning her face and bringing their lips in alignment or to keep her from pulling away.

Whatever the reason, her pulse thumped, and she became acutely aware of everything. The clock on the wall and its slow, steady tick. The rasp of his stubble against her skin. His chest rising and falling at an unhealthy pace. The way her breasts were crushed between them, making her nipples bead. His hard muscle covered by hot skin and how much of it was plastered to her. He smelled like soap and denim and—

"Don't move," he grated.

"I didn't."

"I was talking to myself." His full lips grazed her cheek when he spoke, creating an unfair erotic tease.

She trembled. "All right. Why?"

His fingers clenched in her hair. "To remind myself to ignore what my body's telling me to do."

"What's it saying, your body?" Because if it was on the same page with hers—

He groaned, and the rumble vibrated her chest. "To pin you against the counter and take your mouth in a hard, deep kiss until you can't stand on your own two feet."

Lord. She whimpered. "Why don't you?" Her panties were soaked and her breasts ached something fierce. It had been ages since she'd been this turned-on and... No. She'd never been this aroused.

"Because I'm not the right guy for you." He drew a slow inhale. "In ten seconds, I'm going to back away and head upstairs. Aside from putting a bandage on your hand, you're going to forget this entire exchange ever happened."

"Nate..." Dang, she couldn't think straight.

"Ten." In a blinding millisecond, he severed all contact and strode out.

Chapter Six

While Olivia talked with Nakos outside the barn, Nate leaned against an ATV a few feet away and crossed his arms. Several sections of pre-cut pine were lying in a trailer attached to the vehicle, and he was supposed to be heading out to the southern pasture to replace fence posts with Olivia.

Except, just like she'd been doing a lot lately, she was hedging on working with him. For the past two weeks, while he followed her around doing this and that, getting familiar with the ranch, she'd barely spoken to him, never mind looked him in the eye. If learning a new skill required a hands-on approach, she'd delegated it to her foreman to teach Nate. It was starting to piss him off, but he'd mucked this up all on his own.

Put them alone together, and she high-tailed her perfect ass from the vicinity. Accidentally bump one another? She jumped like she'd been electrocuted and created more distance than the Grand Canyon. Try to start a conversation, and he swore she bit her tongue to force one word answers.

The damnedest part of all was, her behavior didn't appear to be nervousness or her acting skittish, but rather her countering as if that was what *he* wanted. She'd somehow regressed back to before they'd sat on her porch his first evening in town and formed a tentative bond. After that night in her kitchen, when he'd nearly lost his mind and succumbed to his baser needs, it was like she thought he didn't want to be around her.

Nothing could be farther from the truth.

In reality, the only thing he had to look forward to when he climbed out of bed was her. The addicting smile. The lilt of her voice. Those eyes...

The separation was, no doubt, for the best. They'd been getting a little too...close and, Christ knew, he didn't deserve a shred of the happiness she brought him. And yet, all he wanted was more of her. More everything.

Every. Waking. Moment.

And damn, but she'd helped with his nightmares. Or, Bones had, based on her suggestion. Since switching the doors around and letting the dog sleep with him, Nate was able to slip into a deeper REM knowing Bones would wake him at the first stirrings of trouble.

"It's the last ATV, little red." Nakos adjusted his black cowboy hat. "We're short as it is since most of the men had to double up in order to keep half the horses back for shoe replacement. The vet's coming next week for a six-month check."

Nate glanced heavenward, attempting to stay out of it. Again, he was torn between wanting to make things right and needing to keep her at bay. Sun beat on his face and a cool breeze swept down from the mountain, bringing the scent of pine to override hay.

Nakos sighed. "Is everything okay?"

Out of the corner of his eye, Nate watched Olivia carefully. But her only answer was a duck of her head and a nod. Early morning light hit her auburn strands, which she had tied at her nape in a braid. Between that and her fair complexion, she looked like an angelic version of a cowgirl. A fitted green flannel shirt, tight as sin jeans, and knee-high brown boots added to the image.

That was the other thing. She showed very little skin, but thanks to their episode in the kitchen, he knew what lay underneath and how freakin' fantastic she felt up against him.

She shielded the sun from her eyes with her hand. "I'll stay back and shoe the horses. You'd be more productive fixing fence sections, anyway."

Nakos gave Nate a once-over and disbelievingly eyed her. "Are you sure?"

"Yep."

"Whatever you want." Nakos thrust his thumb in the direction of the barn. "Supplies are out. Radio me if you need anything."

Nate straightened and waited for Nakos to mount the ATV before climbing on behind him. He held the back of the seat, giving the foreman room to maneuver as Nakos drove them over the plains to the southern pasture. Which took twenty minutes. It still floored Nate how much land encompassed Cattenach Ranch.

So much...breathing room. Honestly, he couldn't remember a time in his life where he could freely breathe. It was a luxury never afforded to him.

Parking next to the first post in a very long succession of fencing, Nakos dismounted while Nate glanced around. Olivia hadn't taken him this far south yet. The Laramie Mountains were clearer, peaking over the horizon like a fortress. Yellow grass in every possible direction was turning green as several heads of steer grazed over a slight hill. A two-story log cabin dotted the landscape just west.

"Is that your place?" Nate jerked his chin toward the house.

"Yes." The foreman unloaded two pine sections from the trailer and surveyed the fence. There was roughly eight feet between posts, with two horizontal boards making up the enclosure itself. "Mae had the place built when my family came to work for the Cattenachs."

"When was that?" The way Nate figured it, he and the guy had to get along if Nate was gonna stick around. Olivia throwing them together today seemed as good an opportunity as any to get to know him better.

"We left the reservation a year after the accident that killed Olivia's parents. We were nine. My parents moved back to the reservation when Justin enlisted." Nakos went to the trailer and hauled out a toolbox, then lumbered to the fence once again. "This whole section needs replacing. We can work down the line."

"Okay." Nate followed the foreman's cues. They used a sledgehammer on the boards that were rotten or loose, then Nate held the new section while Nakos nailed them in place. They got a few done before Nate spoke again. "Where's the reservation?"

"Between here and the Thunder Basin National Grasslands." Nakos pointed due north. "Arapaho tribe."

Nate had never heard of it. He and Justin had served with a guy who was part Cherokee, but that was the extent of Nate's knowledge on Native Americans. "What's that phrase you say to Olivia every morning?"

"*Hebe?* It means hello." The foreman grunted as he nailed a board in place. "The elders are trying to teach new generations the tongue. Only about half speak it now."

Three hours later, Nakos tossed Nate a bottle of water from the back of the ATV and checked the satellite phone. Only two transmissions had come through the radio, but Nakos was hell-bent on watching that, too.

Removing his ball cap, Nate swiped sweat from his brow with his forearm and replaced the hat. "You're awfully protective of her."

Nakos stared at the land and sighed. "You would be, too, if you knew her better."

More than a little shocked the foreman wasn't jumping down Nate's throat at the comment, he crossed his arms. "What does that mean?" Olivia seemed more than capable. He hadn't witnessed her taking any unnecessary risks. Besides, he'd just met her and he'd take a bullet if it meant saving her gorgeous ass. He didn't need to know her any better. The situation was already amped to DEFCON One.

Nakos passed Nate a small bag of chips and dropped to the ground, leaning his back against a post. "She doesn't like to be a burden, so by the time she does ask for help, she's neck-deep in a problem. She cares. About everything and everyone. Too much, which means she rarely pays attention to her own needs."

Nate sat next to the foreman and drew his legs up, resting his elbows on his knees. "Could have worse traits than that."

"No argument there." With a nod, Nakos dug into his chips and chewed. "But add in the fact she's got no one but Mae left, who's watching out for Olivia while she takes care of everyone else?" He tossed his hat by his hip and ran his fingers through the short black ponytail at his nape. "When we were twelve, we went swimming by the creek up at Devil's Pass. She found this deer trapped in the barbed fence and rescued the thing. Once free, it got spooked and kicked her. She tumbled down the incline and broke her ankle. I was tempted to knock her unconscious just to carry her back. Nope. She had to walk herself." His gaze grew distant. "It still gives her fits sometimes, the ankle."

He hadn't really said anything Nate didn't already know about her personality, but he was getting a glimmer of their dynamic and how far back it went.

In the military, Nate had to depend on and trust his unit or men died. Sometimes it had seemed like they'd been dropped at the ends of the earth and left there. But he'd never, not once, had a person in his life that came close to what Olivia and Nakos shared. Nate had been in town for under a month, and he cared about her more than he should. Tack on twenty-one years like she and the foreman had together, and Nate would probably have her in bubble wrap in a locked room. His, the only key.

"I'm not the only one protective of her, either." Up went Nakos's brows. "Are you the pot or the kettle?"

Wiping a hand down his face, Nate huffed a laugh. "Touché. But why aren't you two married with kids? You obviously care about her."

"She never looked at me the way she does you. Yes, I've got eyes." He rose and took Nate's wrapper, shoving both into the ATV bag. "If we went that route, it would be because she thought it was the right thing, not because she wanted to, and that's not happening."

Nate stood and dusted off his jeans. "Nothing will happen with me and her." At Nakos's doubtful scowl, Nate shrugged. "It won't. But, for as long as I'm here, you've got another set of eyes on her."

For the longest time, Nakos studied Nate as if dissecting meaning and calculating odds. Finally, he grabbed his hat and set it back on his head. "The only reason we had this Kumbaya heart-to-heart is because Justin said you could be trusted and your background came back clean. Piss me off, and I wasn't kidding about them never finding your body."

Damn, but Nate wanted to smile. "I can shoot a fly off a donkey's ass from fifty kilometers away."

"Then we understand each other." Nakos bent to retrieve a sledgehammer when the walkie-talkie crackled to life.

"Nakos?" Olivia's frantic wail pierced clean through Nate's chest. "I need you up here. Now."

They both scrambled to get the radio, but Nakos got to the ATV first. Except she wouldn't answer, no matter how many times he cued, and Nate went into panic-mode.

While Nakos tried and failed to get her to respond via radio or phone, pacing all over the field, Nate detached the trailer and started the ATV. "Let's go. You can try her again on the way."

Christ, they were twenty minutes from the house. He'd never heard that tone in her voice and damn if nothing in all his experiences sounded worse. The radio silence was almost more frightening than her frenzied request.

What in the hell could've happened? She was supposed to be in the barn putting on horseshoes.

He drove them as fast as the vehicle would allow over hills and across the prairie, but Nate could almost run faster than the damn

61

thing. Nakos keyed up all the ranch hands on the walkie-talkie, but none of them were closer than they were.

"Hell." Nakos growled. "She's not responding and Mae's not answering the house line."

"I'm going as fast as I can." Not fast enough, though.

Some protector Nate turned out to be. The first time he wasn't within spitting distance of Olivia, and she was in trouble. The most ungodly scenarios shoved through his mind and acid burned a path from his gut to his throat.

Finally, he rounded a bend and parked not far from the barn. Both he and Nakos dismounted and rushed to where Mae had been pacing, her white hair flying around her face in the wind.

She ran over, meeting them halfway. With wide, blue eyes, she pressed her finger to her lips, telling them to be quiet. "Amy stumbled into the barn about an hour ago and collapsed, covered head-to-toe with bruises. We called Hank. Doc's on the way."

"Who's Amy?" Or Hank, for that matter?

Mae sighed, her brows tight in concern. "Kyle's sister and Olivia's best friend."

Nakos, mouth grim, tried to round Mae, but she grabbed his arm. "Listen to me." She made a sound of duress. "After we phoned the doc, Amy's husband Chris showed up. With a gun. He has the girls in the barn. I called Rip, but he's thirty minutes out on a traffic problem."

Nate's heart stopped so fast, it left skid marks.

Obviously having heard enough, Nakos stalked to the ATV, pulled a revolver from the bag, detached a rifle from the back, and handed the smaller piece to Nate. "You go in the front. I'll head around back. We'll cover both sides."

Nate checked the chamber, finding it loaded, and nodded. He glanced at Mae. "Wait here."

He strode to the open barn door, his heart firing on all cylinders. Unable to catch his breath for fear of Olivia being hurt—or worse—he ducked his head inside the structure and forced himself to rely on training over emotion.

Olivia sat on the floor halfway between the front and back exits, a dark-haired woman sprawled in front of her, head in her lap. A walkie-talkie was in pieces and partially under a stall. From what he could tell, the entire right side of what he assumed was Amy's face was puffy. Bloody nose, eye swollen shut, cut lip. She barely seemed conscious.

The husband stood off to the side, too close for comfort, with a 9mm aimed at the ground. His jogging pants were dirty and his sweatshirt didn't fare much better. The stench of beer engulfed soil and hay, burning Nate's nose. The prick was a scrawny bastard, too.

Rage pounded Nate's temples, and he tried to dial it back to think clearly. Only a sad sack hit a woman. Assuming this was a domestic case, which it appeared to be. And then to bring a weapon into the mix, involving someone else to boot, made this prick not worth the shit Nate wiped off his shoes.

Nakos poked his head around the door on the other side, nodded at Nate, and lifted the rifle. "Drop it, Chris."

The guy flinched and pressed the barrel to Olivia's forehead. She closed her eyes on a whimper, a tear trickling down her too-pale and soiled cheek.

Oh, hell no.

Nate lifted his revolver, bracing the bottom with his other hand. "He said drop it."

Chris turned his head and stumbled to the side, sending Nate's pulse toward stroke-level. "Who're you?"

Great. Slurring his words, barely on his feet, and drunk off his ass. This situation just kept getting better.

"Lower the weapon or you'll never find out." Slowly, Nate stepped deeper into the barn.

Nakos followed suit until both of them had Chris trapped.

"This is a private matter." Chris shoved the barrel at Olivia so hard, her head snapped back.

She sucked in a harsh breath, trembling.

This fucker's balls were going to become intimate with Nate's boot. And his fists. Soon as the gun was out of play. "Private is what your jail cell will look like." Right after a very long hospital visit. "Drop. It. Now."

"Nate." Nakos's determined gaze flicked to his and back to Chris. "I don't see a fly, but there's a donkey's ass right there."

Nate's words from his conversation with Nakos back at the fence. Got it. But Chris's trigger finger could twitch before Nate got things handled. "You sure?"

"Positive."

"What in the hell?" Chris spun, jerking the barrel away from Olivia...

And there was the opening.

"Olivia, baby. Don't move." Nate fired a shot, hitting the brim of the prick's tan cowboy hat and spinning it off his head.

Neighs rent the air. Hooves stomped dirt inside the stalls.

While Chris reeled and dropped the weapon, Nate strode forward, shoved his revolver in his waistband, and planted Chris face-first in the dirt. With a knee between his shoulders and a firm hand on the back of his neck to hold him, Nate toed the gun farther from them.

He whipped his attention to Olivia. "Did he hurt you?" Christ, say no. He visually scanned her for injuries, finding nothing. But that didn't mean...

She shook her head repeatedly, tears leaving tracks on her dirty cheeks. Her gaze dropped to Amy. "She's pretty bad, though."

Nakos set his rifle behind him and squatted next to the women. "You've looked better, Ames."

She tried to smile, but it reopened her lip and sent blood trickling down her chin.

"Mae!" Nakos ran his hands down Amy's arms, her legs. "Do you think anything's broken?"

She shook her head and closed her eyes.

"Hank's here." Mae ran into the barn, quickly scanned her surroundings, and knelt beside Nakos. "Rip is just pulling in, too. We'll get you all fixed up, sweetheart."

"Let me up!" Chris squirmed, but got nowhere for the effort.

Nate dug his knee deeper into the bastard's spine. "You ever want use of your legs again, you'll shut up and stay still."

Turned out, Hank was a two-hundred pound, fifty-year-old woman with black hair down to her ass. She walked in carrying a doctor's bag circa the 1900s with one hand on her hip.

"Well, give her some room." She set the bag down, opened it, and knelt on Amy's other side, shining a penlight in her eyes. "Where'd he hit you and with what?"

"His fists." Amy struggled to draw breath and winced. "Kicked my side. Punched my face."

"Nothing on the back or neck? Did you fall at any time?"

"No." Amy closed her eyes.

"She needs an ambulance." Nate had to shove his homicidal rage back into a hidey hole at seeing her curvy form mottled with injuries. Flashes of Darla swam before his eyes and he involuntarily squeezed Chris's neck. The guy cried out, and Nate loosened his grip.

"Closest hospital is in Casper. We've got it handled." Hank sighed. "Olivia, you got a room for her? I need to better examine her."

"Yes." She glanced at Mae. "We can put her in the extra guestroom."

"All right." Hank stood. "Nakos?"

"Yeah. I've got her." With an arm under her knees and behind her back, he lifted Amy and cradled her to his chest. At her wince, he froze. "I'm sorry. I'll go slow."

A forty-something man with a Fu Manchu and brown officer's uniform waddled into the barn, favoring one leg. He ran a hand over his thinning brown hair. "I apologize for the delay. The Hendersons decided it was a good idea to plow their minivan into the Garrison's ditch and take out a mailbox in the process." He glanced from Nate to Chris to Amy in Nakos's arms, then finally, Olivia. "Looks like you got it covered."

"I'm taking Ames up to the house." Nakos strode out, Mae and Hank on his heels.

Chris squirmed. "I didn't do nothin', Rip."

The sheriff lifted his thick brows. "Doesn't look like nothin' on your wife's face. She run into a wall all by herself? A hundred or so times? Is that your story?"

Nate gritted his teeth. "He had Olivia and Amy at gunpoint when Nakos and I got here."

"And who might you be, son?"

"Nathan Roldan, retired U.S. Army and her new...handyman."

Rip swiveled his attention to Olivia. "That true?"

"Yes." She rose unsteadily to her feet, looking like a gentle breeze could topple her.

Nate shook his head and gnashed his molars into a fine powder. "Could you slap some handcuffs on him, please?" He needed to take care of Olivia before the adrenaline crash fully hit her. He shook with the urge to drag her against him and simultaneously comfort them both.

Silently, Rip pulled cuffs off his belt and secured them on Chris's wrists behind his back. "Sit up, now."

Chris, with a petulant scowl, did as he was told.

Nate rose and stretched, then collected the guns. He held up the rifle. "Nakos's." The revolver. "Mine." And the 9mm. "Douchebag's."

"Give me the short version." Rip took the 9mm, put it in a bag he pulled from his pocket, and stared at Olivia. "We'll get into details later at the station."

She ran a shaking hand across her forehead while Nate set the remaining weapons on the floor. "I was here with the horses when Amy stumbled in looking like..." Her voice hitched and her eyes welled. "Looking like that. She collapsed. I guess she'd walked all the way here, though I don't know how. She didn't say much. Chris showed up. He held the gun on us. Nakos and Nate came. And..." She shrugged. "They diffused the problem."

"Good enough. Let's go, Chris." Rip hauled the guy to his feet. "Tell Amy I'll come get a statement from her tomorrow, if she's up to it."

Olivia nodded. Once Rip left, she closed her eyes and let out the most God-awful sob Nate had ever heard.

And that was it. The straw that broke the soldier's back.

He erased the short distance between them and pulled her against him. She pressed her face to his chest while he wrapped his arms around her tight enough to crack ribs. He breathed for the first time in an hour and struggled to bank the need to kiss the shit out of her in sheer relief. She trembled, and he kissed the top of her head, letting his lips linger in her rain-scented hair.

He ran his hand down her braid and closed his eyes. "You're all right. Everyone's safe." A few thousand more times, and he might get his heartbeat to believe the words.

"Safe," she muttered against his chest and went eerily still. Her fingers fisted his tee as she slowly lifted her head. Her cornflower gaze swept over his face, wide and unblinking. "Safe," she repeated as if in afterthought. A small wrinkle formed between her brows like she'd come to some sort of conclusion while he tried to figure out what the equation was in the first place.

"Oh God." She unfurled her fingers from his shirt and stepped away so quickly, he got whiplash. "I did it again and..." She waved her hand, indicating them. "I'm sorry. I can't..." Turning, she jogged toward the exit.

Damn it. "Olivia."

But she was gone.

Chapter Seven

After the doctor left and assuring herself Amy was okay in the guestroom, Olivia took a shower and made her way downstairs. Comfy in a pair of loose sweats and a tank top, she figured she'd heat a cup of tea and crash. Her limbs were as useless as Jell-O and, any second, she was going to collapse.

The house was quiet and dark, but a light shone from the direction of the kitchen, along with the murmur of muted voices. Heading that way, she found Aunt Mae, Nakos, and Nate at the table drinking coffee. They all looked up at her and started talking at once.

Olivia waved her hand. "I helped Amy get washed up. She's trying to relax. Her brother Kyle's with her now." She leaned against the doorjamb and rested her head. "Hank says she doesn't think any ribs are broken, just bruised. Same with her face. She gave Amy a shot for pain and a script. I'll fill it tomorrow when I grab clothes from her house."

"Think she'll eat something?" Mae rose and went to the fridge. "Soup?"

"Sure. That's soft to eat, too."

Nakos stood. "I'll take it up to her. How are you doing, little red?"

"I'm..." She didn't know. Confused. Guilt-ridden. Shaky. "Fine. I had no clue Chris had become violent. Did you?"

Nakos and Mae shook their heads. Nate stared at her like he was about to snap.

"Me, either. I mean, he's always had a short fuse, but I've never seen her with bruises or..." Dang it. And here she thought she'd finally stopped the waterworks. "Lord, what he did to her." Barely able to speak through tears, she clutched her chest. "I should've known. I'm her best friend and how could I not..."

Mae wrapped Olivia in her arms and smoothed her hair, damp from a shower. "This might've been the first time, baby girl. And if it wasn't, Amy only showed you what she wanted you to see. You know her. Stubborn as a mule."

With a laugh-sob, Olivia pulled away and wiped her eyes. "I'm sorry. I think I just need some air."

Nakos, bowl of soup in hand, stopped by her on his way out. "You need to eat something, as well. You look like a ghost."

She sent him an I'm-not-hungry look, which he countered with an ask-me-if-I-care. She glanced around him to the table. Yep. Nate's jaw was still clenched and he had murder in his eyes. More guilt coagulated in her belly for her behavior in the barn. Crying on him the way she had and all but clinging to him.

Lord. Shaking her head, she focused on the cowboy hat beside his arm. It wasn't Nakos's and Nate only ever wore a black baseball cap. "What's that?"

Nakos turned and grinned. "That would be a souvenir for great shooting." He looked at her and sobered. "Truth. Are you all right?"

The incident in the barn came back to her in quick flashes and rapid spurts. Amy's battered body. The insults. The press of cold steel against Olivia's forehead. Heart pounding, she stared at the cowboy hat, a hole clean through the brim. Because Nate had shot his gun. To protect her. After Chris had...

Dizzy, she tried to clear her throat and whined instead. "I'm going outside for air."

Against the male protests, she strode out of the kitchen on shaky legs and through the living room to the front door. On the porch, she sucked cool air and dropped her hands on the railing, leaning into them.

Everything was fine. Just as Nate had told her earlier. She was...safe.

Like it had before, her mind and heart tripped over the word. Safe.

Funny, she'd never considered the term in regards to herself. Certainly not as anything she'd been lacking. Aside from her parents' death, she'd had an uneventful childhood on a beautiful spread of land, with food in her belly, and a roof over her head. Aunt Mae had been there for whatever Olivia and Justin needed from hugs to band-aids on a scraped knee. Nakos had been and still remained at her side like a guardian. Amy filled the female gaps and they'd formed a long-ago bond of girl power in a friendship of genuine affection.

So why, then, when Nate held her, did she get an overwhelming sense of security? A virtual stranger, he should not fill her with a sense of peace. One she hadn't realized she'd been lacking. Yes, he was big and strong. Yes, he was irrevocably tender considering his size. But he had dark, ugly shadows behind his stricken gaze that told her he was anything but safe.

She attempted to recall the last time she'd felt this way and couldn't conjure one instance. Not the insane attraction or chemistry, nor the sheltering calm he inflicted when they were in contact. It was the craziest combination that would've had Freud banging his head.

Every person in her life had a purpose, a special gift they brought to the table. And in walks Nate, throwing everything off kilter. He didn't even seem to like her presence, contrary to what he'd said in the kitchen a couple weeks ago.

The screen door snapped shut, and she knew without looking who stood behind her. Nate had an energy, a hum about him. She swore she could feel his gaze on her, no matter the time or place. Since he'd arrived, she was in a constant state of awareness and it wasn't unpleasant.

"Mae said she was heading to bed. Nakos is upstairs with Amy and Kyle."

Nodding, she stared at the quiet ranch as nerves danced in her belly. "You got stuck as the designated babysitter."

"You don't need a babysitter and no one asked me to come out here." His boots scraped the wooden planks as he drew closer. "What are you thinking about?"

Right. They should talk? If only. He'd erect more walls if she told the truth.

She turned to assure him she was fine, but he frowned and crowded her against the porch post. Fieldstone dug into her spine as her breath caught. He traced his rough fingers over the bump on her forehead with such tenderness, her heart lodged in her throat. His hand shook as he dropped it by his side.

He let out a quiet, uneven breath. "Scared me to death. I saw that asshole standing over you and I was scared to fucking death."

Lord. And then there were the rare instances like this when he let his guard down and she wanted to crawl inside him. For a guy who wore layers upon layers of armor, his give-a-shit was showing. And not for the first time.

"You didn't seem scared." At all. He'd taken charge and handled the situation with a frightening level of calm.

"Trust me. I was."

Somehow, he seemed to need reassurance instead of her. "You and Nakos saved me, saved Amy. Doesn't matter how scared you were. What matters is what your actions were when afraid."

He stared at her and shook his head. "How do you do that? Twist things around and try to take care of me? You're the one who was held at gunpoint."

"And I'm standing here because of you."

Closing his eyes in a languid, frustrated blink, he sighed, then glanced at her bump again. "You're starting to decompress, aren't you?" At her questioning glance, he tucked a strand of hair behind her ear. "Decompressing. Adrenaline wears off and the tremors start. You feel hot and cold. You want to close your eyes and sleep, but your brain shoots images at you of what happened."

Nailed that on the head. It made her wonder how many times he'd experienced this. She was a few hours in and could barely stand being in her own skin.

"Come take a walk with me." He stepped away and held out his hand. Patience and understanding shone in his eyes while he waited.

"Where are we going?"

"Not far." He waggled his fingers and she slipped her hand in his.

He led her off the porch and around the side of the house, his thumb stroking the back of her hand as if to console her. She wondered if he realized he did stuff like that because she'd grown to crave the small signs of consideration.

Such a conundrum, Nathan Roldan. Grizzly bear on the surface, teddy underneath.

They strolled in silence with the stars overhead and gravel crunching under their shoes. A breeze swayed the grass in the distance, creating a crackling in the air and leaves. Though the temperature was still mild, she hadn't been prepared for the outdoors. Goosebumps skated over her bare arms and she shivered.

Without a word, he unzipped his hoodie, took it off to reveal a black tee, and stopped walking to hold the sweatshirt out for her.

Moved, she slid her arms in and turned around to face him, her cheeks hot. Hopefully, the darkness hid her blush. Before she could do it herself, he zipped the hoodie, reclaimed her hand, and started them in motion again.

He stopped outside one of the barns and slid the padlock from place, then pulled open the carriage doors. Quietly, he watched her as if waiting for her to do something.

She stared inside the dark structure. The moon's illumination from the skylight was the only thing chasing shadows. Silver light reflected off the gated stalls. The scent of soil and hay and horse fur filled her nose. Familiar. Yet, her heart pounded and her chest grew tight. Dots blurred in her peripheral.

"I know a little something about PTSD."

Her gaze jerked to his. "But nothing happened to me."

He took a step closer. "You found your friend bloody and bruised right here, then had a gun aimed at your head." His jaw ticked. "Something most certainly did happen to you."

She focused on the barn again. She'd been in there more than a billion times. It was just straw and dirt and wood. Her precious horses. Nothing scary. Her stupid pulse throbbed against her neck, though. "What went down today can't be nearly as horrible as the things you've seen."

"Look at me." He ducked his face close to hers. "This isn't a competition. You stared down the barrel of a gun and had your life threatened. Trust me on this. The longer you deny it, the harder it'll be. Go inside. I'll be right here with you."

Eyes ahead, she drew a deep breath and did as he asked. But the sound of her shoes hitting dirt ricocheted around her head and she froze.

His warm hand skimmed up her spine and down again. "Right here, baby."

Baby. He'd said the term earlier, seconds before he'd fired at Chris.

She'd never been one for endearments, but Nate's wrapped around her and squeezed. Comforting. Unique. Special.

Using that as leverage, she put one foot in front of the other until she stood in the center of the barn. Right where it happened. The stench of beer. Chris slurring his words. The sharp smack of metal against her skin.

73

Warm hands cupped her cheeks and Nate's face blurred in front of her. "Close your eyes. That's it." His hoarse, low tone caressed her ears. "Think of a happy memory. Something that happened here."

Justin's grin immediately came to mind. Once, they'd been brushing down the horses after a ride, and he'd nailed her with a stream of water from the hose. Except, her cocky brother hadn't paid attention to what he was doing and tripped over a bucket. Lord, she'd laughed so hard her side ached.

"There you go." Nate grabbed both her wrists. "Keep your eyes shut." He guided her a few steps forward and moved behind her. Taking her hand, he set it on something soft. "Touch is a sensory. Keep that memory while you're doing it." Under his direction, he had her…pet whatever was beneath her palm. "Open your eyes."

They were standing in front of one of the stalls. Leia, their youngest gelding, held her nose close to the gate, enjoying the attention like the princess she was named after.

Smiling, Olivia stroked her again. "How'd you learn to do that?"

"Therapy. It was forced on me after the injury." His breath teased her hair.

"Well, it worked." For her, anyway.

His hands fell on her shoulders. "You may have to repeat the process a lot." He stilled as if contemplating something, then swept her hair to the side. "Memory replacement is another technique." Gently, he massaged her neck with his thumbs. "The object is to return to a scene and substitute the bad feelings with good ones."

Oh God. His hands were freaking amazing. And talented. Firm fingers, soothing motion. "Substitute feelings?" she breathed.

He dipped his face near hers, their cheeks brushing. The rasp of his beard grazed her skin and sent every nerve in her body on fire as he pressed closer, cradling her against him. "Are you scared right now? Panicked or upset?"

"No."

"Do you feel good?" His hot breath fanned her jaw.

She moaned and tilted her head back, fully leaning on him. "Yes." So, so good. Her breasts ached and her panties grew damp. "Yes," she repeated. Pleaded.

His hands moved from her shoulders to her collarbone and slipped under her sweatshirt. Chest rising and falling in a rapid pant, he brushed his nose against the shell of her ear, then pressed his lips there. "I don't understand how you do this to me. But hell, you make me feel good, too."

Reaching around, she grabbed the backs of his thighs, earning a low, rumbling groan. His thick muscle was tense under the denim, yet his touch was tender. His fingers delved lower, tracing the outline of her shirt while his mouth moved to her neck. Feather-light kisses and unspoken words fluttered against her skin, and her legs buckled.

He instantly wrapped an arm around her waist, holding her to him. "I'm sorry. I shouldn't have…" Face pressed in her hair, he sighed. "I forget to think when I'm close to you."

He wasn't the only one. And why was that a bad thing?

She turned in his arms and he gripped the stall bars above her head, leaning into them. His lids fell closed as—guilt?—furrowed his brows. His scent of soap and warm male filled her nose, surrounding her because of the sweatshirt and his nearness. It was beginning to become familiar and she wanted to bury her face in his neck, breathe nothing except him.

This attraction was about more than just the two of them. It had grown and cultivated. She was caged by bulging biceps and a fortress of a chest, in a place where, hours ago, something awful had happened. Yet all she could do was focus on how badly she wanted him. All he seemed capable of doing was denying it. With everything he had.

"I don't understand." She pressed her lips together, rolling them over her teeth.

He opened his eyes, gaze trained heavenward. "Ditto."

"No. I mean, you said you couldn't do this, that it wasn't right and—"

"I know what I said, Olivia." He still refused to look at her, his position stiff and unrelenting.

"I gave you space." She pushed the hair away from her face with both hands, growing frustrated. "I stayed away from you because I thought that's what you wanted. Forget what happened were your words."

His biceps flexed as if he'd fisted the bars tighter. His jaw ticked to the beat of her pounding heart and his nostrils flared like a confined bull.

"Is it what you want? Do you want me to forget?"

He shook his head, turned it away, and set his chin near his shoulder in a clear move that proved he was ready to snap. Veins and tendons popped on his neck and his tat sleeves came to life with the ripple of muscles.

"You claimed to not be the right guy for me. But one minute you act like being near me hurts you, and the next you're touching me as if you want to be that man." His only response was a steady increase in his respirations. "If you don't want to try—"

"I do," he growled and shoved off the bars. He stalked away and came back. "Everything I said was true. But you make me burn, Olivia." He fisted a hand over his heart. "I don't understand it and I'm doing my best to fight. You are this strange anomaly that's become an obsession. So, yes, I want to try. Can I? No."

A cold sense of unease wove around her and chilled the blood in her veins. Not from his livid mood or his prowling, but because something was very, very wrong if he had to deny himself something he wanted. She scrolled through the fragmented conversations they'd had and latched onto the one thing he'd said that fit.

"Why are you unaccustomed to touch?"

Cursing a wicked streak, he set his hands on his hips and glared at the floor as if expecting it to swallow him.

There. An answer without him saying a thing. "Does it hurt? When I touch you, I mean?" Holy Lord in Heaven, please tell her this wasn't due to an abuse situation from his childhood.

"No."

"Does it make you uncomfortable?" There had to be a valid explanation. The few times they'd been in contact, his mouth said one thing and his body another. She didn't know which to listen to.

"Christ," he muttered and pinched the bridge of his nose. "No, no, and more no. I'm not feeding you a line here. It's me, not you." He strode forward two feet, right up to her until their chests bumped. His golden brown eyes were dialed to say-a-prayer and dilating darker by the second. His irises were nearly swallowed by his pupils. "No one's ever touched me."

76

What? "You can't be serious."

His unrelenting expression didn't waver.

And her heart cracked. Right in two. "Ever? I don't—"

"Foster care, Olivia. Since infancy, I got moved around from one place to the next. Cuddling wasn't part of the system's M.O."

He was killing her. Killing. Her.

She exhaled a turbulent gust and rubbed her forehead. "After you aged out?" Surely, he'd had sex. Partners. Something.

"Minimal." He pointed at her as if reading her mind. "Uh-uh. No, I'm not a damn virgin and I'm *damn good* in the sack. Doesn't mean I'm up for fondling and everything else."

Then he'd never been intimate, truly intimate, with anyone, woman or otherwise. Had he not been…hugged? Held? She couldn't fathom it. For crying out loud, the poor man had never been loved. Did he matter to anyone?

"And we can call this exercise a rip-roaring success." He gestured toward the exit. "Let's go. You need to sleep and I need a drink."

She knew exactly what he needed and it wasn't alcohol. But she didn't think he'd allow her to show him.

Chapter Eight

The ceiling above Nate's bed creaked for the eight-hundredth time from Olivia's incessant movement. He rubbed his eyes and glanced at the dog next to him. "You should've slept with her instead of me tonight."

Bones set his head back down, tail wagging.

Two hours since they'd returned from the barn, and it appeared neither was going to get any rest. Hell, she needed it bad, too. After her ordeal, she'd be no good to anyone as a zombie. Yet, she paced. And paced. He wondered if it was what he'd said that made her restless or if it was the day's events. Which was worse?

And...great. The image of her on the ground and a gun to her head materialized again. Nothing would erase it. Swear to Christ, he didn't think he'd ever been so scared shitless. If he had, he couldn't recall.

Perhaps it was his connection to Justin, Nate's time on the ranch, or his unfettered attraction to her, but his sun rose and set with Olivia Cattenach. Try as he might, he couldn't explain it and he didn't see a way out. It only got stronger as the seconds ticked by. Guard. Defend. Worse, and entirely new to him, was the urge to let her in. Mind. Heart.

He'd been protective of Justin, as well, just not to this degree. When Nate had first met the fellow soldier, he'd been unable to understand the instant connection. The kid had grated his nerves in an adorable way and, no matter what they'd seen overseas, Justin had forever kept his optimism. He and Olivia were so alike it was uncanny. Compassionate, sincere, forgiving.

Hell, Nate missed the little shit so much the loss was a cavern. It was his cross to bear. He had no right calling Justin a friend and certainly had no business lusting after Olivia.

The door at the top of the stairs just outside his room opened, and Nate flung the covers aside to shove his legs into a pair of sweats. Her footsteps padded on the creaky boards and he rushed to cut her off at the pass, intuition telling him her motives. Waiting for her in the doorway to his bedroom, he leaned against the jamb while Bones sat dutifully next to him.

She descended into view and paused on the last step, her gaze raking over his naked chest and bare feet. Biting her lip, she swallowed and focused on his arm. Why, he hadn't a clue, but even with the dim light at her back, he saw her pupils dilate. And hell, a blush worked up her neck and infused her cheeks.

What she saw in him, he had no idea. Like he'd done with her brother, Nate had been pleasant and distant, and like her brother, she'd shot holes through his Kevlar to get underneath. Body builder physique aside, Nate wasn't exactly the kind of man someone like her should be attracted to. Inked, scarred, and unattainable. Yet here she stood, her desire a living thing and trying to sink its claws deeper into him.

Her auburn hair was on top of her head in a messy knot and she wore the same damn...nothing from that night in the kitchen a couple weeks ago. Criminally tight shorts that barely covered her ass and a tank top which played a groan-inducing game of peek-a-boo with her ample breasts.

"I couldn't sleep." Her quiet voice was a combination of uncertain and come-hither, which did nothing to eradicate fantasy number seventy-four rolling around in his head to take her right on the stairs.

"Figured as much. You've been wearing the finish of the floorboards for a couple hours."

She glanced at the ceiling. "I'm sorry to keep you awake. I'll just go check on Amy and head to bed. I promise."

Just as he suspected. "I was already up and Amy's resting. Kyle's in with her if she needs something."

She pouted, part adorable and fully sexy, though he was pretty positive that wasn't her intention. "She's okay? I'll just peek and—"

He stepped forward, cupped her shoulders, and turned her around. "She's fine. No sense in disturbing her. She needs rest and so do you. Upstairs. Go." When she glanced at him over her shoulder with a look of sheer helplessness in her eyes, he sighed. "I'm coming. Go on." He'd make her a cup of tea and let her talk to death. That should do the trick.

A weary sigh, and she climbed the stairs. He followed with her tight ass in his direct line of sight and his pulse hammering. At the top, Bones trotted inside after Olivia and Nate quietly closed the door.

He glanced around and grunted in surprise. "You've got your own little pad up here." There was a tiny kitchenette big enough for an elf that bled into a living room. Hardwood floors, like downstairs, except she had drywall instead of paneling. Off to the side was a doorway which he assumed was her bedroom. "To the couch. I'll be right there."

Dutifully, she listened and sank onto the plush yellow cushions, wrapping herself in a blanket.

He pivoted toward the two-burner stove and filled her kettle with water, setting it to boil. "Where's your tea?" He knew she drank the stuff because Mae tended to make her a cup after dinner.

"Check the cabinet next to the fridge. There might be some."

He found a box of chamomile and another of cocoa. "Got anything one-hundred proof up here?"

"No, the good stuff's downstairs. I have Bailey's in the cupboard right below you."

Blech. Hot chocolate instead of tea for her, then. He checked the date on the bottle, assured it was unopened and not expired, then poured a generous amount into a mug. When the kettle whistled, he mixed the cocoa and brought her the steaming cup.

"Drink," he ordered and nodded when she took a sip.

From over the rim, her gaze landed on his chest and traveled across his abs, then his arms. Since there was appreciation in her eyes and he...liked it, he moved to the wall to study her photographs. Several contained her and Justin at various ages. A few were of the two of them with what Nate assumed were her parents.

"You look like your mom." Gorgeous auburn hair, fair skin with a dusting of freckles, fragile frame, and a smile that could stop the earth from rotating on its axis.

"All but my eyes. Got those from Dad."

Cornflower and very expressive. Yeah, he'd have to be blind to miss those baby blues. Too many times, he'd gotten sucked in with one glance.

They were a good-looking family. Or had been. Wholesome. Happy. It was as foreign to him as touch, but his chest pinched imagining what it would've been like to have someone, anyone, give a damn. Maybe he might've turned out different, been a guy worth the admiration in her eyes.

The other wall had nature photographs. Blades of grass, up close, with sunlight reflecting off dew. Another of a horse's snout, steam billowing from its nostrils, and snow as a blurry afterthought in the background. Well-worn wooden planks with a ladybug front and center.

"These are good." Impressive, actually.

She nodded. "Amy took them. She calls it fooling around, but I keep saying she should be serious about it. I haven't seen her pick up a camera in a long time."

"That's a shame." Not that he knew anything about art, but he knew crap when he saw it and these didn't qualify. He went to turn when a corner cabinet caught his attention. Behind glass were several shelves containing figurines of... "The Loch Ness Monster?"

She was a trip. He would've pegged her for butterflies or horseshoes or something. Who collected an ugly mystical figure? Where would one even buy such a thing? Then again, she only had about ten total.

"We Scots call her Nessie." She smiled and sipped her cocoa.

"That's right. Cattenach's a Scottish name." Grunting, he claimed the seat on the other side of the couch, giving her a wide berth. "Makes sense with your coloring."

Bones curled up on the rug in front of a coffee table and promptly closed his eyes. Smart dog. Which reminded him...

"What kept you awake? Talking it out will help." He crossed his arms, wondering how many branches of the crazy tree he'd smacked his head on when he'd fallen. He'd typically take a second coming of the bubonic plague over conversation.

"Because talking worked wonders for you, seeing as you're so well-rounded." Blink, blink, blink. Grin.

Sarcasm and he were intimate bedfellows, and hearing it from her lips, combined with that sassy little smile he wanted to kiss off her mouth, had him struggling to breathe. Issuing a mental *down boy* when his dick twitched, he sighed. "Don't make me regret coming up here. I'll take the cocoa back."

The grin amped and lit her eyes. "I drank all of it. Too bad." She set the mug on the table. "It had enough Bailey's to bring down an Irishman."

He laughed and... Damn her. He actually laughed. The sound was rusty, even to his own ears, but something unfurled in his chest. Strangest shit, right there.

"Be still my heart." She brought her bent arm to the back cushion and rested her cheek. "He's capable of laughter. Sigh."

Who said the word sigh out loud? Honestly. It was cute as hell.

"Okay, okay. I'll stop poking fun." She adjusted the blanket in her lap and sobered. "I was thinking about Amy. That's why I'm awake. It's driving me crazy, wondering how long Chris's behavior has been violent and why she didn't tell me."

He ran his hand over the rough stubble on his jaw as visual reminders of today's events seared his retinas. "You won't know the whole story until you can talk to her tomorrow. There's no sense in beating yourself up over it." Not that she'd stop simply because he suggested the notion. She wore her heart on her sleeve and carried everyone's burdens on her shoulders. He'd tell her to quit that, too, but the world needed more bleeding hearts. "Besides, regardless of how long it's been happening, you can't make someone accept help if they don't want it."

She studied him a long beat. "And you don't want help. Is that it?"

"We weren't talking about me."

Her lips curved. "In case you missed the topic change, we are now."

A wise man would get up and concede the loss. He'd never been smart, though, and he couldn't make his body follow his brain's orders. In fact, nothing was computing at the moment because...

She was at it again. Her gaze dipped to his torso. Roamed over him with interest and fascination in the cornflower depths. Lips slightly parted, she drew a barely audible inhale and, with a flutter of her lashes, met his gaze once more.

The air crackled between them the longer they stared.

He'd never been particularly sensitive about his body, but the way she looked at him left him exposed and unnerved. And turned-on. Stranger still was the array of emotion in her eyes when she focused on what was above his neck. Half the time, he couldn't keep up. Right this second, he could've sworn she was shoving aside shadows in his mind and checking corners for secrets.

Finally, she nodded as if she'd discovered something. "You said earlier you've never been touched."

His heart puttered and quit pumping. She didn't have to use her hands for him to feel her. Her gaze was enough. And where was she going with this?

"You like it when we do. I can tell." Her eyes narrowed a fraction. "However, you claim you can't be with me. Logically, if you enjoy it, you should be curious. But you deny yourself the opportunity. What does never having been touched before have to do with refusing to try now?"

"I said that so you'd understand why I acted the way I did when we were close." And so she'd get it through her stubborn skull she hadn't done a damn thing wrong. It wasn't that he hated being near her. The opposite. He craved it.

"As far as non-answers go, I give that four out of five stars." Patience in her eyes, she lifted her brows, letting him know he wasn't off the hook.

"I told you before, Olivia. I'm not the right guy for you."

"Shouldn't I get a vote? Decide for myself?"

No. Because if she knew him at all, she never would've let him in her home, never mind close enough to share the few moments they'd had together.

He turned his face away and dug his fingers into his eye sockets. To give her even a shred of the truth would mean opening the door to a past he'd sealed closed. And revealing the detrimental issue of what was on the other side—her brother and the reason he was dead.

"I'm not a good guy." Nate forced himself to look at her, nail home the point for her and himself. "Everything I touch turns to shit. Getting involved with me will bring you down to my level and you'll never climb out. I'm not the hero or the white knight, and that's the man you should be looking for."

Unblinking, she stared at him. "When you say things like that, it makes me want to..."

"To what?" He knew a trap when he saw one, but he stepped in it, anyway. Common sense got drunk and giddy when Olivia was on the premises. Maybe he should just raise a glass, too, and dub reason a lost cause.

"Prove you wrong." She tossed the blanket aside, got on her hands and knees, and crawled across the sofa until she knelt in front of him on the cushion. "Sometimes the hero's a beast or a frog or an ogre. Maybe I'm not looking for a knight."

He couldn't fucking breathe, damn it. "Olivia—"

She climbed on his lap and straddled his thighs.

Oxygen? Depleted.

His head hit the back of the couch. Panting, he stared at her, hands fisted at his sides and his dick throbbing to the jack-hammering beat of his heart.

And then she killed him dead. She set her hands on the top of his head and splayed her fingers. When he didn't move, she caressed his scalp like he was a cat, and he thought about purring to reward her. It was difficult to tell who was getting more pleasure out of the situation. Though her cheeks were flushed and her lids were heavy, she seemed more interested in his reaction.

Trying to swallow and failing miserably, he gave into temptation and dropped his gaze. The swells of her breasts were inches from his face and the nipples had peaked to hard little buds through the thin shirt. Her toned thighs had his caged, and the tent in his pants was within thrusting distance to her heat. If not for her clothes, he feared he'd have already taken her. Another time, place, or woman, and this would be a done deal. She'd be screaming with orgasm number two by now.

But this was Olivia. The proof was in their position and the basic, essential fact that she had her hands on him. He'd never ceded control a day in his life. Yet, for this tiny, fair-skinned, combustible redhead, he'd wave a white flag. Actually, he wasn't sure he had a choice.

Her hands descended slowly, skin shushing skin, over his ears to his jaw. She held his face and brushed her thumbs across his lips. Her lust-saturated gaze followed the movement and he groaned at the carnal interest blowing her pupils. Her fingers trailed lower and the urge to touch her became a feral warrior cry inside his head. Gently, she stroked his neck, his throat, and he nearly snapped.

Grabbing her wrists, he ceased her movement. "You have no idea what a dangerous game you're playing, baby."

Before he knew what hit him, she leaned forward and brought her lips to his. She stopped short of an actual kiss and they shared air, barely connecting. Hovering. Drifting.

"Game, you say?" Her warm breath teased his lips as she spoke. While he shook from restraint, she tilted her head the other way, brushing their noses. "Scrabble? Monopoly?" Her breathy whisper and the joking reply made him groan again. "I know. It's spin the bottle."

Screw this. A man could only take so much. She'd been rattling the cage of his restraint since the episode in her kitchen. She wanted to play? He'd play.

Grabbing the back of her head, he threaded his fingers in her hair, dislodging the knot, and held her millimeters from his mouth. "War, baby." And then, he plunged.

Except, instead of ravaging her mouth and staking a claim, he got confused by the softness of her lips and her tender response. Christ, he'd never been seduced before, but sure as shit, that seemed to be her counter offer. He could trace every red blood cell that swam through his veins. He was that hyperaware, that...lost.

Delicately, she parted her lips, swept them against his, and kissed first his top, then the bottom. Letting her lead, he pinched his brows together and held still. She didn't come at him with fire. She told him a story. And he'd be damned if it didn't start with *once upon a time* like she were proving he was some kind of hero. Specifically, hers.

Sliding her arms under his, she gripped his shoulders from behind. He inhaled—hard—at the overwhelming sensation of her warm hands on his bare skin. Her fingers moved across his biceps, tracing the dips and grooves of his muscles while she tilted her head and opened for him.

His insides incinerated to ash the moment his tongue stroked hers. A taunt and a coax. An endearment and a promise. She tasted like Bailey's and cocoa, and it was so sweet, he figured he'd grown an affinity for it after one sip. Addicted, he went back for more.

Christ, it was like she was everywhere. The scent of rain in his nose. A caress against his flesh. Lightning in his gut. Lava in his blood. He didn't normally care for kissing all that much. It was too intimate, too personal. No one had ever taken the time to show him they gave a damn, that he was worth the bother of learning. His body or mind. One kiss, and Olivia almost had him believing he could be a man worthy of her.

He wasn't.

He went to pull away, but she had other ideas. She pressed closer until she was all but lying on his chest, crushing her breasts between them. Out of instinct, he grabbed her hips, and immediately knew it was a mistake. Because now he had his hands on her. A saint would've committed several carnal sins to be in his shoes.

She amped the wattage and explored his mouth with languid, deep strokes of her tongue. He matched her best he could, sinking into the hot, wet cavern of her sweetness. A mind of their own, his hands settled low on her back and slid up the curve of her spine until his fingers were buried in her soft strands.

This kissing thing had merit. Fucking hot and more tame than what he was accustomed to. Foreplay. Seduction. He was utterly lost and heading for oblivion when she eased away. A lazy lift of her lids, and his fingers clenched her strands. Damn, but her eyes were a sucker punch. Especially saturated in longing.

"Tell me again we're all wrong," she whispered. "Try to convince me we shouldn't explore what's happening, that you don't want this."

He didn't know up from down and she wanted him to speak? Rationally?

Her smile was the be-all, know-all to an ultimate game of wits. "That's what I thought." She climbed off his lap, and he wanted to weep. "To be continued. Goodnight, Nate."

Good...What?

He glanced at his raging hard-on, then her retreating form as she disappeared into her bedroom.

Chapter Nine

While Hank examined Amy early the next morning for a follow-up, Olivia figured it was a good time as any to grab her friend some things from her house. Nakos and Nate had teamed up on her, though, and now she had a rigid Nate next to her in the passenger seat along for the ride. Heaven forbid she go anywhere alone.

"I find breathing is a necessity most days." She glanced at him and back to the two-lane highway. "You should try it." Poor guy was tense enough to give concrete a run for its money.

"I'm breathing."

"In and out? In succession?"

He turned his head with a baleful narrowing of his eyes. "I'd breathe a lot easier if you hadn't tried to sneak off this morning to the house of the very man who put that bruise on your forehead."

Hooray. Another Nakos. On steroids.

"I'm fine, Nate. Chris is locked up and I didn't sneak."

Returning his attention ahead, he offered nothing more.

They had other things to discuss, anyway. "Wanna talk about last night?"

"No."

Too bad. "Why not?"

"Because I'm still fucking hard." He muttered a curse and jerked his gaze out the side window. "Pretend I didn't say that. You shouldn't have kissed me."

"Why not?"

He hadn't exactly put up a fight. And...wow. The man could kiss. Every cell in her body remembered his hot mouth and deft tongue. The hard planes of his muscles while his hands were irrevocably gentle. She suspected it had taken restraint on his part, judging by the tension he'd radiated and the way he shook. His initial response still had her reeling. Like he had no clue what to do with her. He'd let her lead and, she swore, he hadn't known what the act of kissing entailed.

She'd spent the remainder of the night aching and dissecting every moment. The only conclusion she'd drawn was that he wanted her and hated himself for it.

When he didn't respond, she glanced at him again. "Why not?"

"Because I want to do it again."

Her throat tightened at his quiet declaration and the gutting tone. Just what had happened to him to make him think he wasn't worthy of basic human essentials? Relationships. Connection. Happiness. He behaved as if he was punishing himself.

Unsure what to say, she drove the rest of the way to Amy's little two-bedroom ranch and used her spare key to get inside. Olivia stopped short in the living room and gasped. Nate stepped beside her, jaw tight.

The place was completely overturned. Tables tipped onto the threadbare carpet. Lamps broken. A hole in the drywall. Clutter everywhere. What Amy must've gone through... Then Olivia's gaze dropped to the floor by the TV stand, and she cried.

"No. Oh God, no." She knelt next to Amy's broken camera. Her printer/scanner machine littered the floor beside it, in pieces also. "She saved for two years to buy these."

Damn Chris. Damn him to hell.

Nate squatted next to her and examined the camera, gaze dialed to homicidal. "It's shot, but maybe we can salvage what's on the memory card."

Heartbroken, she rubbed her chest. "I'm going to kill the bastard."

Chris had always been a selfish jerk, but she'd not known he could be cruel. And to someone he supposedly loved. He and Amy had only been married a few years. He worked at her parents' hardware shop in town and was relatively new to Meadowlark, having only arrived in the area and dated Amy a couple months before they'd wed.

"Jump in line." Nate pulled out his phone and snapped a picture of the camera, then the printer. "I get first dibs on rearranging his face." He rose and shook his head. "Go get her some things. I'll take pictures and clean up a bit."

Since there was nothing else she could do, she nodded and headed to the bedroom. There, she pulled a suitcase out of the closet and packed several outfits, pajamas, and undergarments for Amy, then grabbed a smaller suitcase for cosmetics. Figuring she'd want them, Olivia put a few photos of Amy's family in the luggage to bring, as well. If she needed anything else, Olivia could always come back. For now, it would do.

Upon returning to the living room, she found everything righted and Amy's equipment gone. Olivia went into the kitchen and spotted the missing items on the table. This room was unscathed, though the checkered linoleum floor and oak cabinets needed updating badly.

Nate was at the sink, washing dishes. With his back to her, she watched him, suddenly fighting tears. Such a simple act, him cleaning up, but it meant a lot. Very thoughtful. When Amy was well enough to return, if she wanted to, then at least she'd come back to a clean house.

Not a good guy? Bull.

A fitted gray t-shirt molded to his torso and muscles shifted as he moved. Graceful. Efficient. For such a large man, he was quiet as a mouse and unimposing. His well-worn jeans hung low on his hips and she tilted her head, enjoying the way his butt filled the denim. He'd forgone the black baseball cap he usually wore. She studied the back of his bald head, wondering why he shaved it. Not that she minded. He rocked the look.

"Do you need my help carting something or are you just watching me for the hell of it?"

Busted. "The hell of it. You're easy on the eyes, Nate."

He paused a moment, his spine stiff, then finished rinsing the last of the dishes. Shutting off the water, he reached for a towel and turned to dry his hands, studying her. His expression gave nothing away, but the longer he stared, the more weary his eyes grew.

His lids had a soft, almost feminine curve to them. Like a puppy, really. Long lashes. Golden flecks in the irises to keep the dark chocolate from being too engulfing. His mouth, though? Full and just shy of pouty.

With a sigh, he tossed the towel on the counter and, his gaze averted, cleared his throat. "You ready to go?"

"Yes. We just need to grab two suitcases from the bedroom."

He shoved off the sink. "I'll get them and meet you outside."

She swore, the harder he fought her and the simmering attraction, the more she wanted to push. She'd never considered herself forward, but something about him had her taking the initiative. Sometime, somehow, she'd get him to snap. And their sparks would catch to create an inferno. It was inevitable. Maybe then he'd let her in a little. To help. To trust. See himself how she was beginning to and not whatever image he'd put there.

Nathan Roldan had been hurt. No doubt. Just how badly and for how long was yet to be determined. But he was not a lost cause. He'd shown more courtesy and compassion toward her in a few weeks than most had her whole life.

For now, though, they went to the police station and gave Rip an official statement. Olivia tried to ignore the stench of burnt coffee and sugary pastry, and the fact Chris was just down the hall in a cell. Nate, from his phone, emailed Rip the pictures he'd taken of Amy's house.

As they were getting ready to leave, Rip gave Nate a once-over. "You interested in a job?"

Nate flinched. "Here? In law enforcement?"

"Yeah, son." Rip smoothed his Fu Manchu. "You handled yesterday like a pro. I could use another man. I've got two other deputies, but they're worth spit most days. County's not that big. Not much happens around here. Former Army, you said?"

As if confused, Nate nodded. "Medically discharged with honor."

"Got a criminal record?"

Nate paused, and Olivia's heart tripped rhythm. He glanced at her out of the corner of his eye and back to Rip, shoving his hands in his pockets. "A juvie record."

Rip's eyes narrowed. "For what?"

Yes, for what? A chill raced up her spine. Justin had never said anything about Nate being arrested. The breath caught in her throat. She wondered if her internal radar had suddenly taken a crap.

"Dealing." Nate's jaw ticked.

"Weapons?"

She darted her gaze back and forth, stomach in knots.

"Cocaine."

Rip nodded slowly. "You clean now?"

"I never took drugs." Nate shifted to his other foot. "I did what I was told and ran packages to specific locations. I served eighteen months in a facility, aged out, and enlisted. End of story."

"And that will check out?" Rip crossed his arms.

"Yes. I can give you someone's name inside the system and my captain's recommendation."

"In that case, do you want a job, assuming those folks tell me what you just did?"

Nate studied him a long beat, then pulled his phone out of his back pocket. His thumbs went to work while Olivia tried to process. "I sent you an email. Jim Foggerty was my juvie parole officer and Ken Wainright was my captain. Their contact info's in there." He rubbed the back of his neck. "As for the job, I'll have to think about it. Talk it over with…" He gestured to Olivia, gaze down.

A minute later, they walked to her car, and Nate gently stopped her with a hand on her arm before she could climb in. "Nakos didn't see the arrest in my background because I was a minor and the record was sealed. I can be packed up and off the ranch in under three minutes, if that's what you want."

She took in his haggard, concerned expression and tight mouth. Her first instinct was to grab him to keep him put. Now that she'd had a second to accumulate the facts, her stomach settled. She didn't know the circumstances, but he'd been a kid when this incident had happened. By all accounts, he'd seemed like a solid guy since.

"Why didn't you tell me?"

He glanced heavenward. "It's not exactly something I'm proud of, Olivia."

That spoke volumes. And he didn't give excuses, either. "How old were you?"

He stared at their feet, sunlight reflecting off the skin on his head. "Sixteen. I got mixed up in shit I didn't understand and had no way to get out. I was stupid." He stared at her, desperation clear in his eyes. "That's all you need to know except I would never, *ever* do anything to hurt you or compromise the ranch." He paused, and she swore he stopped breathing. "Just say the word and I'm gone."

Panic clutched her airway, giving her the answer. She no more wanted him to leave than he seemed to want to. "Go where?"

He shook his head, jaw ticking. "It won't matter."

"Of course, it matters." He had no one. She'd suspected it before, but the notion gelled the more she got to know him.

"I don't…" He closed his eyes and sighed.

"You don't what? Don't matter?" Lord, her stomach rioted. The longer he stood not answering, the hotter her eyes burned. Her heart cracked for the troubled, scared kid he used to be and the broken, misguided man he'd become.

Justin must've known. The realization slapped her in the face like the brisk wind off the mountains. Maybe her brother hadn't had the whole story, but enough to know sending Nate to her was the last gift Justin could give his fellow soldier before dying. Tears clung to her lashes and she closed her eyes.

"I'll do whatever you want, baby. Just tell me."

"Stay." Lunging, she wrapped her arms around his waist and gripped his shirt. "I want you to stay."

He stood frozen for a moment, then his rigid body sagged. One hand in her hair, he set the other low on her back. "I promised your brother I'd take care of you."

No. He had it wrong. Him being in Meadowlark, on Olivia's ranch, was Justin taking care of Nate. She pressed her cheek to his pec, inhaling his scent of soap and warm male. "Then let's go home."

He dropped his chin to the top of her head and lingered a silent beat. "Okay."

When they finally got back, Aunt Mae and Amy were at the kitchen table, drinking tea.

"Hey, you." Olivia gave her friend a tentative one-armed hug and sat down. "No, stay in your chair. It's good to see you out of bed. How are you?"

"I'm sore, but okay. Thanks."

"Where's Kyle? Did you talk him into going to work?"

Aunt Mae laced her fingers and set them on the table. "He and Nakos are reshoeing horses."

"I'll take these upstairs." Nate jerked his chin at the luggage and stepped out.

Amy sighed. "I thought my eyes were playing tricks on me yesterday, but he is that big, isn't he? Dang, Olivia."

She laughed, but the sound was forced after what she'd learned and the attack on her emotions. "He's a nice guy, too." Refocusing on her friend, Olivia's stomach clenched at the day old bruises mottling Amy's face. At least her right eye wasn't swollen shut today. "We picked up your pain meds and got you some things from the house. I'm sorry about your camera."

"Yeah." Amy stared into her teacup as Nate quietly returned and stood in the corner. "That's what started...this." She waved at her injuries. "Chris was pissed I cared more about the camera than him or some such crap. He took a hammer to it. Just like that. Two years of saving dimes from odd jobs, and all that hard work's gone."

Olivia exchanged a worried glance with Aunt Mae. "The printer's toast, too. I didn't see your laptop."

"That would be in the garage. Under his truck tires. It was the first thing he destroyed." Amy closed her eyes. "He stopped paying the mortgage six months ago. The house is in foreclosure."

Before Olivia could respond, Aunt Mae took Amy's hands in hers. "Then you'll stay here. For as long as you want or need."

"I can't impose."

"Don't you ever say something like that to me again." Olivia looked at Amy dead-on. Her folks were hard people and it would be a cold day in hell when they'd let their daughter back into their house, especially after what they'd consider a scandal. She wasn't going anywhere. "You're staying here. Period."

"Thank you. I don't know what to do around here, though. It's not like you need the help. There's no jobs available in town."

Aunt Mae shrugged. "You can cook, can't you? Clean? When you're up to it, you'll give me a hand, and there's nothing more to it."

"You're the best. Thank you. I'll figure something out soon for the long haul." Amy ran her fingers through her cocoa hair and winced. "I think I'll take that pill, Liv. If you don't mind?"

"Sure." Amy was the only person who called her Liv. She wasn't fond of the nickname, but her friend wasn't up for a reminder. Not that she'd listen.

Aunt Mae rose and opened the pharmacy bottle Nate had set on the counter. She poured a tablet in her hand and passed it to Amy. "Olivia will take you upstairs, get you unpacked. You should rest."

Amy swallowed the medicine with a healthy gulp of tea. "I can't thank you guys enough." She looked at Nate. "And you, charging into the barn like you did? That was amazing."

He stared at her, seemingly uncomfortable, but when he spoke, his tone brooked no argument. "It was necessary and anyone would've done the same."

"I'm not so sure about that. Thank you, anyway."

His gaze slid to Olivia's and back again. "Get better. That's thanks enough." He shoved off the wall. "I'll see if Nakos needs a hand." He glared at Olivia. "Don't leave the house without telling someone."

When the door closed behind him, Amy blew out a breath and fanned her face. "Dang. Is he always that intense?"

"Yes," Aunt Mae and Olivia said together.

Olivia laughed. "Imagine Nakos's protection gene and multiply it by ten, then give him military training."

"Huh. I hope you're getting some. He's hot, Liv."

Up went Aunt Mae's brows. "Just what I've been saying."

"And that's my cue." Olivia rose. "Come on. Let's unpack."

Once upstairs, Amy climbed in the full-size bed and curled up on the yellow comforter while Olivia folded clothes and put them in drawers. For too long, the only sound was Olivia's feet on the hardwood floors. Silence had never been their thing.

"How long has the abuse been going on, Amy?"

"This was the first time he hit me, if that's what you're asking." Amy flung her arm over her head and winced, clutching her ribs with her other hand. "I might've been stupid for marrying the jerk, but I'm not a complete idiot. I would've left his ass."

Relieved she hadn't missed signs, Olivia gingerly sat next to her, hating how frail her friend looked. Amy always had the life and gumption Olivia strived to replicate. "What happened?"

"I already told Rip and Kyle."

"Tell me."

Amy sighed and closed her eyes. "I found the foreclosure notice from the bank. He never mentioned things were that bad. He wanted to sell my equipment and I refused. It wouldn't have made a dent, anyway." She glared at the ceiling. "The next thing I know, he's on a tear. Took my laptop and ran it over. Smashed my stuff with a hammer. When I cried and tried to stop him, he turned his tantrum on me."

She turned her head and met Olivia's eyes. "He left. I walked here. You know the rest."

Throat tight, Olivia forced back tears. "I'm so sorry."

Amy shrugged as if it didn't matter. "Chris will be taken to Casper for sentencing tomorrow. He's pleading out. Rip told me today when he got my statement. I need to find somewhere to store my stuff before the bank takes possession of the house. And a divorce lawyer. What a mess."

"You can put your things in our basement. We don't use it for anything but canning in the fall, anyway." Olivia took Amy's hand and wove their fingers together. "As for the rest, we'll deal with it."

Chapter Ten

Nate petted Bones from a living room chair, wasting time until Olivia and Amy proved to him they'd call it a night. Every evening for a week, they'd taken a walk after dinner, and he'd learned to stick around or they'd go without him. Maybe he was paranoid, but he didn't give a damn. Until his heart stopped pounding when he didn't have a direct visual on Olivia, he'd keep being paranoid.

The girls came in from the kitchen and took a seat on the sofa. Amy's bruises were fading to an ugly shade of yellow and green, and every day she moved a little better. The sight of her no longer sent him into a homicidal fit, so there was that. And Chris was probably going to end up serving fifteen to twenty at a prison in Casper. Nate would take it.

Mae passed Olivia a mug of tea and glanced at Nate. "Want anything?"

"I'm good. Thanks." She always asked like it was her job to wait on him. He didn't care for it, but it seemed habit for her. "Are you guys staying in?"

"Yeah. I'm too tired to move. It started raining, anyhow." Amy glanced around and frowned at the box by the fireplace. "What's that?"

"Oh." Mae rose. "I almost forgot. That came for you today."

She went to lift it, but Nate stood and shooed her aside, doing it himself. After all, he knew what was in the package, and it wasn't light. He set it by Amy's feet and reclaimed his seat, figuring it would seem suspicious if he left now.

"For me? From who?" She examined the label, but Nate had made sure there was no return address. "That's weird. It doesn't say."

Olivia helped her open it, and the gasp Amy let out, followed by happy tears, made the past week's bullshit somehow worth it. She took the laptop out, followed by the camera, and stared at both.

"I don't understand." She glanced inside the package. "Oh my God. And a new printer, too." Olivia removed it from the box when it proved too heavy for Amy. "There's no note or anything." Amy wiped tears from her cheeks and looked at Olivia, then Mae.

"Your parents, perhaps? Or Chris trying to apologize?" Mae shrugged.

Amy shook her head. "My folks can't afford this and they never supported my photography. Chris, either. Besides, he's been locked up." She blinked at Olivia.

"Don't look at me."

"Or me." Mae smiled. "Sure was nice of whoever it was, though."

"I can't accept this. There has to be thousands of dollars in equipment."

Five grand, to be precise. Well worth the money see to the dejected look erased from Amy's face. No asshole had the right to break her dreams or put bruises on her body.

Or come within ten feet of his Olivia.

Damn. There he went again. She wasn't his, yet his primal caveman kept trying to surface.

Nate stood. "I'm going to sit outside for a bit if you need me."

With Bones on his heels, he made his way to the rocking chair on the far end of the porch. Just beyond the wrap-around railing, rain beat down. A warm front had come through, keeping the temperature hovering in the mid-sixties and humidity clinging to everything. The scent of wet grass and mud mingled with budding flowers from the corner garden, and he breathed deep, listening to the patter of drops.

After awhile, he grabbed the tin bucket where he'd put his supplies while the dog curled up at his feet. He'd managed to find good use for the boards he and Nakos had stripped from the fence. Instead of being destined to become firewood, the pine kept Nate's hands and mind busy, whittling a little at night after Olivia went to bed. He'd crafted two tiny figurines of Bones, several horseshoes, and a tree that resembled the cottonwood in her front yard. They weren't pretty, but he found it relaxing.

He was just carving the shape of a horse's flank when the screen door snapped shut and Olivia stood there, hands on her hips and tears in her angry eyes.

Carefully, he set his items in the bucket and stood, his heart wrenching ribs. "What's—"

"You," she growled and stalked closer. "You bought her those things."

100

Shit. How did—

She launched herself at him, wrapped her legs around his waist, and cupped his cheeks.

He grunted, stumbled backward, and righted them, grabbing her ass so she wouldn't fall. And damn. This couldn't end well. "Olivia—"

"Don't you ever tell me you're not a good guy." Before he could retort or argue or so much as blink, she pressed her lips to his.

Lights out. Sayonara sanity.

Unlike the night a week ago on her couch, there was no tenderness or coaxing. She ate at his mouth like she was starving. For him. With her hands everywhere—his head, his face, his shoulders—she tilted her head and moaned. She nipped his lower lip and slid her tongue inside to tangle with his. Hot, wet, deep.

"Sweet Christ," he muttered and spun, reaching blindly for something to pin her against. His palm encountered the stone porch support and he eased her back against it, freeing his other hand to explore.

She ground her hips against his growing erection and he barked a sharp cry of surprise into her mouth. But she never let up. Opening wider, she turned a hot interlude into something downright pornographic, sizzling his nerves at the root and making him harder than iron. Swirling her tongue, caressing his, sucking on it.

And her hands. *Uhn*, her hands. The way she stroked the top of his head was the oddest turn-on. Or the firm grip on his neck as if claiming him for her own and daring him to pull away.

He grabbed her slim waist and dipped under her shirt, finding soft, warm skin. While she assaulted his mouth, he kept going until he encountered satin. He'd kill to know what color bra covered her perfect breasts and wanted a look at them more than any sustenance for preservation. He settled for brushing his thumbs over her peaks and groaning when they hardened more.

Mercy, she killed him. Her warm skin. Her hot mouth. Her slender body in comparison to his own. He was a dead man walking and, suddenly, didn't give a rat's ass.

Needing oxygen, he tore his mouth away and latched onto her neck. She heaved air and arched, making his erection painful behind his jeans. He never craved the ache more. Her flesh smelled like a sweeter version of the downpour behind them. Sucking, licking, he worked his way across her throat to the other side.

"I can't believe you did that," she breathed, grabbing his shoulders. "You made her so happy."

He really didn't want to discuss another woman just now, but he lifted his head and stared into her cornflower eyes. The raw emotion there closed his airway. "How did you figure it out, anyway?"

Her thumbs brushed his lower lip, and even that was a mind fuck. "The camera and printer were the exact same brand as the ones broken. It couldn't have been anyone else."

"Don't tell her. Let it be a mystery, okay?" He'd accumulated quite the savings over the years not paying rent or other expenses. He didn't want his gift to be a big deal and she was making it one.

"I don't understand you." Brows furrowed, she searched his gaze.

The fact that she was even trying to understand him was new territory for him. She very well might be the first to attempt the hopeless feat. "It's not worth the frustration of figuring it out."

Eyes wounded, she parted her lips as if to speak, but shook her head instead. She placed her hand on top of his head, her gaze following the movement. Slowly, she trailed her fingers to his forehead, his nose, cheek, mouth, and stopped on his chin. She did the same with the other hand as if memorizing his face, and his heart turned over in his chest.

She was back to the tenderness again and he couldn't take it.

It took him two attempts to speak and, when he did, his voice was gravel. "What are you doing?"

"Touching you." She traced his eyebrows, his lips.

He couldn't breathe. Because he was a man who'd not had an ounce of affection, he didn't know what the hell to do with hers. His chest pinched and blood roared in his veins. He didn't deserve this, deserve her, but he couldn't make himself move. She was both a balm and dick CPR, wrapped into a tidy bundle. The conflict was jarring.

Panting, he fought the push/pull war in his head. "Why, baby?"

She started the pattern all over again as if they had all night and she intended to do only this. "Because no one ever has and I enjoy it." While he grappled with that answer, she kept going like she hadn't just leveled him flat. "I don't care what you say. You are worth it."

Christ. "Olivia—"

"No talking." She nudged his chest and dropped her feet to the porch. "Come with me." She headed for the steps and he called her name. "I said no talking."

"It's pouring." By the buckets.

She crooked her finger and descended the stairs, then waited for him. Immediately, her auburn hair got drenched and the yellow shirt molded to her lithe body. Her skinny jeans, already painted on her long legs, became second skin.

Fuck him. Desire was a living, heaving, clawing thing. More than that, a…passion that went deeper than a physical blow unfurled inside him.

It didn't matter what he did or didn't do. She just kept coming at him. Nothing but fire and brimstone awaited him, and he wanted, with everything inside him, to experience something good first. Just once.

"Trust me, Nate." Her lilting, soft voice carried across the raindrops to him.

And the strangest thing happened. He realized he did trust her.

He stepped into the downpour and followed her to the other side of the house by a copse of trees. The rain lessened to a drizzle as she wove through several oaks until stopping under one with a rope ladder. He glanced up as she climbed and found a treehouse among the branches.

Shaking his head, he climbed up after her. It wasn't any wider than he was tall and had no roof, but the leaves and branches above and around created a type of haven. It smelled faintly of mildew and aged pine, yet the structure seemed sturdy.

"This was my secret spot as a kid. Not because no one knew about it, but because I'd come here and tell my secrets out loud. I always felt better afterward."

He studied her through the darkness, soaked to the bone and getting wetter, and dread settled in his gut. "Some secrets are just too ugly." And she was so beautiful it hurt.

"There's nothing ugly about you." She stepped flush against him and grabbed the hem of his shirt. "Take it off." She nudged the sopping material up until he had no choice but to pull it over his head or get strangled. It landed with a splat on the floor. "Sit down."

"Olivia, what are we doing?"

Despite better judgment, he did what she asked and nearly swallowed his tongue when she straddled his thighs. A hand on his shoulder, she pushed, encouraging him to lay back. She was maybe a hundred and twenty pounds, leaving him to wonder how she became the dominant one between them. Then again, if she requested he bark at the moon, he probably would.

Settling his bent arm behind his head, he hissed at the cool planks against his back. She leaned over him, her wet strands a curtain, and he stopped breathing altogether. The rain had stopped, but droplets fell from the canopy of leaves. Between that and the darkness, she looked like a sexy version of a sprite.

"You taught me something about memory replacement when we were in the barn. I'm going to return the favor." She kissed his jaw and he closed his eyes, confused and fascinated. "Why did you work for people who sold cocaine?"

His eyes flew open. "Olivia. We're not—"

"Answer me and I'll reward you."

He froze, tempted. "Reward me how?" Why the actual hell was he considering this?

She offered a sly smile and splayed her fingers on his chest. Unimaginable heat spread from her palms and he groaned. "Should I keep going?"

Fire licked his skin and he blurted a response, seeking more from her. A necessity. "I had no choice. I'd joined a gang called The Disciples two years prior for protection. Chicago's south side was not friendly."

Just like that, she dipped her head and her hot, wet tongue swirled around his nipple. He choked and jerked toward her mouth. He shoved the fingers of his free hand in her hair and held her to him.

The new, riotous sensation made scrambled eggs of his brain and whatever good intentions he'd arrived with. He'd never been the focus of sexual ministrations before and he shook with uncoiled need. With previous partners, he'd been the one in control, and he hadn't let them...play. This was...she was...

Shit. He was dying.

"Did you like being in the gang?" This time, she asked without lifting her face.

Chest heaving, he stared at the leaves overhead. "At first, but that changed fast. I'd finally belonged to something, but everything came with a price. My time wasn't my own and they stole what little humanity I had left." Knife fights and turf wars. Women were things to be owned and whored into submission. Constantly, he battled to keep a straight face when his stomach rioted at beating after—

She sucked his nipple and sunk her teeth around it, flicking her tongue. Broken bottles and graffiti disappeared. The blood and fear and screams dissolved into nothing but Olivia's sweet mouth and the way she made his heart pound for a different reason. Glancing down his nose at her, he massaged her scalp to encourage her, wondering what was happening to him.

Moving to his other nipple, she paused. "What would've happened if you said no? If you walked away?"

"There was no out once you were in. They would've killed me." Painfully. He'd witnessed it more than a few times. Torture. Stabbings. Carving their symbol on flesh. Boys begging for death—

She ran her hands up his sides while she licked the flat disc of his nipple into a hard peak. Lightning shot through his system and short-circuited everything except her. He ached. Christ, did he ache. For her to keep going, to stop, to quit making him...feel.

"But you're alive. You escaped."

Damn, it was impossible to focus. Cool raindrops leftover from the storm hit their hot skin and he was shocked there wasn't steam. "Once I was thrown in juvie, I became disposable until release. But I joined the Army and never went back."

She kissed her way up his chest and under his jaw. A semblance of reality trickled through his haze. Tilting his head, he threaded the fingers of both hands in her hair and forced her to look at him.

"I did terrible things, Olivia. Stuff I can't erase."

Her somber gaze studied him. "If you could go back and do it over again, would you join the gang?"

"No."

"And do you regret the things you've done?"

"Yes." Every second of every minute of every day.

She swept her fingers over his face as if wiping the past away. "You were just a boy. A scared, helpless boy. The fact that you feel

105

guilty, that it's eating you up even now, should tell you what's in here." She pressed her hand over his heart. "Good people do bad things for all kinds of reasons. Fear, desperation, but that doesn't make you a terrible person."

He shook his head, powerless against her.

"When your mind goes back there, think of this instead." She kissed him, soft and slow and with such aching reverence, he had to close his eyes. "And remember this." She sat up and placed her hands on his pecs. Gaze holding his, she skimmed her fingers over the ridges of his abs. "Allow yourself to feel good, Nate. That's what you do to me."

Christ Jesus. She was…he didn't know.

Gritting his teeth, he gave her a little shake. "You should run, baby. Where I go, pain follows."

She set both her hands on the floor by his shoulders and leaned over him, blocking out everything but her. "You call me baby when frustrated or aroused or scared. Are you aware of that? You don't seem to be."

He stilled, frowning. No, he had no clue he'd been doing that. Pet names weren't his bag. Then again, of all the terms he could've inadvertently used, baby was more of a signal for…possession. A claim she was his as much as an endearment she meant something profound.

"I…" What? He wasn't exactly sorry and, though the path she was dragging him down could only end badly, he couldn't stop desiring her. Christ knew, he'd tried. "Do you want me to stop?" He'd find a way, somehow, to accomplish it.

"No." She leaned in and spoke against his lips. "I like it."

He groaned and, holding the back of her head, pulled her to him the rest of the way. She opened for him immediately as if anticipating what he needed and wanting nothing more than to provide. He'd noticed that in their few interactions before, as well. Her kiss was the mirror of her character. Kind. Giving. Observant. Clever. Sexy. Or, when at her emotional breaking point, fierce.

And she always seemed to be telling him something. Like right now, as she held his jaw and offered slight teases with the tip of her tongue on the top of his, she was in nurture mode. I've-got-you meets it's-safe-for-you-to-fall. It was enough to make a grown man weep.

With an arousing little hum in her throat, she pulled away. "Why do you shave your head?"

He blinked at the abrupt topic change and scratched his jaw. "I got in a fight in juvie. A kid grabbed my hair and one-upped me. Shaved it ever since."

"Interesting. I thought you were going to say something like you were hiding male pattern baldness or a receding hairline."

One second she had him on the brink of madness and the next huffing a laugh. "No. Or, well, that may be the case now. I wouldn't know." He stared at her, wondering if she didn't like the look or something. "Why?"

She shrugged. "Just curious." Again with the hands on his head. Stroking. "It's hot."

"Hot," he repeated, not computing.

"Sexy, attractive—"

"I know what hot means." Damn, but he grinned. She was adorable. "I'm just not seeing how you'd think so." Not for the first time, he wondered what the draw was for her. He wasn't a cowboy or anything all-American, and that was the kind of man he pictured her with.

"Good thing they're my eyes, then."

He gave up. Understanding women, especially this one, was like trying to learn molecular fusion while drinking Jack Daniels. Pointless.

Drawing a cleansing breath, he set his hands on her thighs and rubbed his thumbs over her wet jeans. "If we're done with this torture session, we should head back inside before you get sick."

She rolled her lips over her teeth, fighting a grin.

Yeah, fine. Let her poke the bear for being protective. But she was drenched and the temperature was dropping.

"I don't know what to mock you for first—the torture comment or the fraternal one." Her cornflower eyes lit with humor and settled the last of unease in his chest.

He gave her ass a firm slap and she yelped. "Home, Olivia, or I'll carry you."

Chapter Eleven

Olivia leaned against the stall door in the barn Nakos had just closed and heaved a sigh. "I'm so over today it's ridiculous." She rubbed her sore left shoulder and dreamed of a hot shower. And ten pounds of chocolate. Add a glass of wine, and the day might end on a good note.

Gary, their vet, had been out to the ranch for a six-month visit on the horses. She adored the man, but hated check-ups. Some of the horses spooked easily when it came to exams and it was a never-ending parade of in-out, in-out. When things had begun running late this afternoon, she'd barely had time to jog up to the house—on Nakos's insistence—to grab a sandwich for an early dinner because she'd skipped lunch.

"You okay?" Nakos dropped his hands on his hips and frowned, gaze assessing.

"Yeah. Just a stunner, I think. Firestorm jerked when Gary gave him his shots. Tugged my arm a little." For a thoroughbred, Firestorm was a big baby. Then again, he was a male.

Nakos nodded. "Let's get you home, then. You can take something for the pain and soak in the tub."

"Good plan." If she made it that far. The bale of hay in the corner was looking perfect.

They locked up and headed down the path in the fading daylight, rounding a pile of shingles from the third barn. Nate had been tasked with stripping the roofs and re-shingling, something she'd been meaning to hire someone to do. When he'd caught wind, he'd insisted he could do it for her.

"He got a lot done, didn't he?" She nodded her approval and breathed a lungful of humid air as they walked. Spring was finally settling in and she was grateful. Winters around here were long.

Nakos grunted. "He's efficient. I'll give him that."

She studied him in her peripheral. "You guys seem to be getting along better. I haven't heard death threats in at least a week."

He stopped and faced her, short black ponytail catching the breeze under his cowboy hat. "Anyone who puts himself on the line while a dickwad threatens your life is solid in my book."

"He wasn't the only one who came to our rescue. Have I thanked you?"

A corner of his mouth quirked. "Only eighty times. And it was a knee-jerk reaction. I'd do it again."

"I know." And that was why he was one of the best people she'd ever had the pleasure of having in her life. She sighed, fondness tightening her throat. "I'm going to hug you and you're going to let me."

In answer, he opened his arms and she stepped into them. She pressed her cheek to his chest and closed her eyes a beat as he enveloped her.

"I love you." She inhaled his scent of hay and sunshine. He'd always been there for her and she didn't have a clue how she'd get along without him. "I don't say that enough."

"Ditto, little red." He tugged on her braid, something he used to do when they were kids.

"I'm sorry about what I said a few weeks ago." It had been eating away at the lining of her stomach, and it was high time she faced her mistake.

"I understand, but listen to me." He pushed her away and held her shoulders. "I would've taken you up on that offer or made one of my own years ago if I thought it's what you really wanted. But that's not the case and we're fine. We'll always be good, just as we are. I've known for a long time I'm not the right man for you."

"That seems to be a mantra." She pouted.

"Let me guess. A certain ex-military, Harley-riding individual is trying to keep his attraction leashed?"

She laughed. "Yeah." And she knew why, too. Or she had an inkling, anyway. She didn't know how to relay to Nate that she didn't care about his past, other than to slowly chip away at him until he heard her. "Does it bother you? Him and me, I mean."

"It shouldn't matter what I think. But no, it doesn't bother me." He offered a contemplative smile. "Know why? Because if you feel half as much for him as his eyes say he does for you, then *that's* the person you should be with."

Well, damn. "When did you get so wise?" Except, she wasn't so sure about Nate's feelings. It seemed like mostly lust on his end. If there was something more, it was buried under a heap of other emotions he refused to acknowledge.

"I've always been smarter than you."

Laughing again, she walked with Nakos the rest of the way to the house. Bypassing everything and everyone with an exhausted wave, she headed up to her suite, popped a few ibuprofen, and sank into her bathtub full of steaming water. By the time she emerged, Mae and Amy had retreated to their rooms, so Olivia hunted down Nate on the porch.

She eased the door open and stepped partially out, propping the screen with her shoulder. In the corner rocking chair with Bones at his feet, Nate stared out at the dark ranch with a tranquil ease to his expression she'd not seen often. His thumb idly tapped his jean-clad thigh as he laid his head back, and she took a moment to watch him.

More than anything, she hoped he was getting a semblance of peace his past hadn't seemed to allow. She'd been accumulating broken fragments of his history, and what she'd gathered made her heart ache. And memories were obviously eating away at him. For a man who looked as beautifully strong as him, he sure didn't appear to think very highly of himself.

Her gaze wandered over the tattoo sleeves covering his corded forearms to his bulging biceps until they disappeared under his tee. She outlined the hard ridges of his abs and pecs through the fitted shirt, remembering the feel of his hot skin under her hands. The way he'd reacted had her wet and achy, even now. He'd been so responsive.

A day's worth of outgrowth shadowed his jaw and she smiled at the fullness of his lips. They said the damnedest things, those lips. Sometimes a heart-stopping memory, often a dry or witty comment, and on rare occasions, something so utterly alpha-sexy she had to clench her thighs. They'd been few and far between, those remarks, but when he let his hunger rise to the surface, she was one-hundred percent lost. His.

No one had ever spoken to her like that before—with guttural, commanding need.

Since he seemed to be enjoying the quiet, she went to go inside, but he turned his head and looked at her. Trapped by his gaze, she froze in the doorway, surprised by the lack of censure in his eyes. He'd allowed blips of openness when she could tell what he was thinking, but those had been atypical. Not like now.

No guards. No walls. Just...him. And his many contradictions.

111

Desire and loathing. Affection and repentance. Optimism and despair.

This wasn't the first time he seemed to crave. Seeking, almost. Her, maybe, or perhaps something on a deeper level he couldn't trust himself to go after. Her heart beat in shallow flutters behind her ribs, because she wanted nothing more than for him to reach out and take. He was able to uproot so many responses from her, often without trying, but she could only do so much if he wouldn't believe he deserved something good.

And they could be so, so good together.

"I won't disturb you." She offered a smile and nodded her goodnight.

"You're not disturbing me, and what's wrong with your arm?"

She hadn't realized she'd been absently rubbing her shoulder again. "Just a muscle strain."

He paused, staring as if contemplating a reaction. "Come over here." He leaned forward and patted Bones' head. "Look out, boy." After the dog rose and moved to the other side of the chair, Nate pointed to the floor between his legs and looked at her.

Letting the screen door close behind her, she made her way over. His gaze took in her shorts and tank top, his jaw tight. He seemed to have a love/hate response to her PJs every time she wore them. At his nod, she sat on the porch in front of his chair, her back to him, and flanked by two solid thighs. She mentally bitch-slapped the happy bubble in her chest that he'd initiated interaction this time.

Two large, warm hands settled on her shoulders and she inhaled. His thumbs dug into the muscles of her neck, working their way down across her shoulders and back again in a circular motion.

Her eyeballs thunked the back of her skull. "Oh my God. Don't stop."

A quiet chuckle, and he dipped under her shirt straps to keep massaging. Lord, his hands were amazing. Rough, slightly calloused, and huge. There was nothing sexual about his touch, but her skin heated and her nerves sizzled, even as her muscles went lax. The strain and tension from the day drained out of her in five seconds flat.

She moaned and he stilled. "Too hard?"

"Lord, no. Keep going. I'm going to be comatose soon."

Another low chuckle, and he continued his ministrations. "Never done this before. Let me know if I'm hurting you."

A pang hit her belly. Not only had he made the first move and asked her to join him, but he went outside what was obviously his comfort zone in order to try and make her feel better. His own sweet, clumsy way of taking care of her. She wondered if he realized the amount of character he displayed with the simple act.

Closing her eyes, she rested her cheek on his knee, giving him better access to the side that hurt. He smelled good. Denim and grass and soap. He had this way of surrounding her, either by his size or his scent or his presence. She'd been raised in wide-open spaces and with plenty of breathing room, so she was shocked being around him didn't cause suffocation.

"You're not falling asleep, are you?"

"I might." She hummed as he worked the upper part of her arm and back to her shoulder. "You're freakin' awesome at this." Bones set his head in her lap. "Someone's jealous I'm getting your attention." With a grin, she scratched behind the dog's ears.

Nate grunted. "Where I go, he goes. Strange how he follows me everywhere."

"It's not strange. He likes you." She sighed and breathed in a lungful of humid air. A slight breeze wafted and, in few hours, the temperature would probably drop. For now, it was a perfect night. "Are you sleeping better since he can come and go from your room?"

"Yes, actually." The low rumble of his voice made her shiver. So yummy. "Are you cold?"

"Nope. Your voice is sexy."

"My voice is..." He stilled an extended beat as if processing. "What?"

"You heard me. Sexy. Continue what you were saying."

"I forgot what we were talking about." The confusion, amusement, and shock in his tone made her laugh.

"The dog in your room," she cued.

"Right. He's caught me on the cusp of a bad dream several times and I've been able to go right back to sleep."

Lord, that was music to her ears. "Repeat after me. You were right, Olivia. I shall listen to you about everything from now on."

Gently, he cupped her jaw and tilted her head back until she stared at him upside down. With his face inches from hers, his somber, dark eyes swept over her face like a caress as his thumbs stroked her cheeks.

After a careful assessment, he sighed. "You are downright adorable sometimes. It's maddening."

She grinned.

He grunted and kissed her between the eyes, then brushed his nose against hers. "You were right, baby. I shall listen to you—within reason—from now on. Better?"

"Define reason."

A grin split his face so fast she doubted he even realized he'd done it. Holy damn. It changed his whole appearance, infused the golden flecks in his eyes, and gave her a full-body tingle. From the inside out. His hardened edges disappeared, transforming sully and brooding into charming and approachable.

"I was right," she breathed. "Your grin is panty-melting."

He flinched, his brows furrowing.

"Boo. And there it goes." She shrugged, feeling the loss all the way to her toes. "I'll bring it back eventually."

He shook his head. "What in the hell am I going to do with you?"

"Anything you want." At the narrowing of his eyes and flare of his nostrils, she smiled. Seemed a certain unmentioned male's armor could be breeched. "Oh, you meant that rhetorically. My bad."

He growled, snapped his eyes shut, and released her. "Go to bed, Olivia."

Satisfied she'd chipped away at him a bit, she rose to her feet and stretched. The pain in her shoulder was mostly gone. "Do you like sci-fi?"

"What?"

"Sci-fi. The genre?" Teasing him was becoming her favorite pastime. She gestured between them. "Resistance is futile."

"Christ." He pinched the bridge of his nose. "And she quotes Star Trek. What next?"

She turned to leave when something in the corner caught her eye. "What's that?"

He glanced at the tin bucket and back to her. "Something to shut my brain off before I go to sleep."

Okay, now she was curious. Kneeling, she dragged the bucket over and peeked inside. There were a few tools that looked like extravagant ice picks, along with a couple knife-like things. She removed a large freezer bag and paused.

Figurines. Interesting.

Opening the bag, she smiled as she pulled out a carved replica of Bones, no bigger than her thumb. "You did these?"

He nodded, strumming his fingers on his thigh.

"They're good." Another one of her dog, a horse, a tree, and a few horseshoes were also inside. She remembered the box he'd crafted containing Justin's things and looked up at him. "That's some talent, Nate."

"Hardly. Like I said, whittling shuts off my mind."

She tilted her head. "Amy said that about her photographs, too. That she was just fooling around. She's wrong and so are you."

He only stared at her in response, and she got the impression he was carefully measuring his breathing in order not to react. Why? Had no one paid attention to see he was really great at this? Complimented him? Noticed at all?

Suddenly sad, she glanced at Bones. "Look, it's you." She showed the dog the figurine and grinned when he barked. "Bones likes it."

"He licks his own ass and sniffs crotches, too. Pardon my lack of enthusiasm."

She rolled her eyes. "Can I have this?"

"You can have them all if you really want them."

"I do." Rising, she put the items back in the bucket to grab later and set it aside. Hands on the arms of Nate's chair, she leaned close. "I'm going to kiss you goodnight."

He offered a lazy blink.

"What? No argument?"

"I've stopped fighting you. There's no point. I just go around in circles." His throat worked a swallow. "The same reasons for not doing this still apply, Olivia. We shouldn't. Period."

His struggle was waning. She could tell in the slight amusement in the curve of his lips and the lack of tension in his frame. She was getting to him. Good. He'd had her interest since day one. But he wasn't at the point where he was ready to grab what he wanted. Until then, she'd keep at this pace.

"Are you saying I make you dizzy?" She brushed her lips against his and he watched her through narrowed slits. The few times they'd kissed, he'd kept his eyes open, too. For a few beats, anyway. She wondered why.

His fingers tightened on the chair arms, turning his knuckles white. "If by dizzy, you mean frustrated as hell, then yes."

She smiled against his mouth and climbed sideways in his lap, earning a sharp inhale. Holding his jaw, she added pressure to his lips.

A furrow of his brows, and he closed his eyes. His mouth widened, spreading her lips so he could dip inside, and she moaned at the first shallow stroke of his tongue. As if holding back, he remained rigid, searching only with a kiss for her reaction.

He drew a rapid breath and pulled away to look at her. Gaze seeking, burning into hers, he shook with something she could only call unfettered energy. Instantly, like the decision had been made for him, his arm covered her to keep her against him while the other slid up her spine and into her hair.

Then, he tilted his head and sealed the gap, devouring her with fierce lashes of his tongue. His fingers fisted her strands and his groan rumbled from his chest to hers like his control was a thin tether. His kiss turned angry, harsh, and her arousal consumed. Every cell awakened—a part of herself that had been asleep, unaware this kind of heat existed.

He took and took and took from her everything she had left, only to seemingly give back pieces of himself in exchange. Punishingly, he urged her jaw wider, thrust deeper, and need raked her raw. Unrefined power vibrated from him, but he wouldn't snap the leash. Just tugged until...

Panting, he pressed his forehead to hers, eyes pinched tightly shut. "I'm sorry." His ragged breath fanned her face and he shook his head. "Christ, I'm sorry."

"For what?" And why? Please, whatever that was, he needed to do it again.

"That was no goodnight kiss. It wasn't even human."

She buried her face in his neck and closed her eyes. That was more passion than she'd ever known, and he wanted to apologize? "I'm only sorry you stopped."

"Damn it, Olivia." But the curse was a half-hearted muttering. "I don't do that very often."

She lifted her head, confused. "Do what?"

"I don't do intimacy. Making love, sex, foreplay? Not at all. Kissing included." He frowned with that look in his eyes, telling her he wished he'd never brought up the subject. "Forgive the term, but I fuck. That's it."

Understanding dawned. She'd suspected as much after the first time they'd kissed, but hearing it from him was...a reality slap. "Do you enjoy it when we're together?"

"I nearly swallowed you whole and you're asking me that question?"

She offered a reassuring smile. "I repeat, I'm only sorry you stopped. Let's make a deal. If you push too hard, I'll tell you. If you need time with an aspect of us being together, you'll do the same."

"This is wrong, you and me. I don't care how right it feels." He cinched his arm tighter to draw her closer to him and, after a moment, set the rocker in motion as she put her head on his shoulder. "I thought you were going to bed."

The gentle sway of the chair, combined with his warm body cradling hers, had her drugged and headed toward oblivion. "I'm working on it." She yawned.

"Your ethic needs improvement."

She smiled against his skin and hummed. It was the best she could do, considering.

He kissed her temple. A hearty sigh, and he dropped the back of his head to the chair.

With his thumb stroking her arm and fingers of the other hand lightly running through her hair, she gave in to the sweet darkness pulling her under and the safety he invoked.

And she woke in her own bed the next morning with the figurine of Bones on her nightstand.

Chapter Twelve

The temperature had barely hit the upper forties today and, with dusk an hour off, it promised to drop. A chill laced the breeze and the scent of snow clung to it. Nate had grown up in the Midwest where all he had to do was blink and the weather shifted, but Wyoming was a whole different level of bipolar.

With all three barns stripped of shingles and one roof completely redone, he descended the ladder to call it quits. By tomorrow, he should have most of the job finished. He could punch out another thirty minutes, but his arms were jelly and Olivia didn't like him working alone late in the day. Besides, he didn't care for the look of the feud brewing between Olivia and Nakos in the gated pasture.

Feet on the ground, he wiped sweat from his brow and headed over as Olivia climbed on a horse. "What's up?"

"I'm riding over to Dead Man's Pass to bring Kyle and George a coil of barbed wire."

Nakos's jaw clenched. "You know I can't go with you and it'll be dark in under an hour. It'll take you thirty minutes just to ride out there."

Olivia's cornflower eyes dialed to castrate. "Beating a dead horse, Nakos. Enough already."

Nate held up a hand for peace. "Why can't you ride with her?"

"Someone has to guard the front and watch the radios in case of an issue, plus gate the horses as they come in for the evening." Nakos glared at Olivia. "We have the buddy system here for a reason and safety measures in place. *Your rules*, which I whole-heartedly implement, and you're breaking code."

Nate scratched his jaw. "I can ride with her."

"No. You've been working all day. It's just a quick drop-off mission. I'm fine." Olivia turned her horse and glanced over her shoulder. "I have the equipment and a revolver." She leaned forward and nudged the horse into gear, taking off at a brisk pace.

"Damn her, anyway." Nakos whistled for the dog and pointed when Bones trotted out of a barn. "Follow Olivia, boy. Go."

When both dog and woman disappeared over a ridge, Nate faced Nakos. "Never seen her that mad." It was hot. All that fire simmering under the surface to match her hair.

"She only gets like that when you tell her she can't do something."

Sounded about right. "Want me to chase after her? I can hop on an ATV."

Nakos sighed. "Tempting, but no. We'll never hear the end of it and she's right. The guys will ride back with her."

Studying the foreman's tense expression, Nate's gut started to shift with concern. "But you're still worried."

"Anything can happen out there. It's why we have precautionary measures in place. The closer to dusk, the higher the bear activity. Especially at Dead Man's Pass. And that's only one scenario."

Well, shit. "Couldn't the barbed wire wait?"

Nakos removed his black cowboy hat, scratched the top of his head, and replaced it. "Yes, but it shouldn't. Kyle said a whole section was missing by the creek. It keeps the wildlife out and the sheep in. We could lose some if they wander that far southeast."

Not liking the sudden unease in his chest, Nate glanced at the barn, then to where Olivia had disappeared. "I think it's time you taught me how to put the horses away and man the radios."

"Yeah." Nakos looked at his feet and closed his eyes a second. "Now's not opportune, but follow me. I'll give you a quick run-down to get you started."

Just inside the main barn's door was a wall of cork and dry erase boards. A giant map of the entire ranch was tacked above a row of clipboards. Nate had seen the info before, but hadn't paid much attention.

"The ranch is divided into four sections based on direction, but each has several sub-areas." Nakos pointed to a spot southeast. "This is where Olivia's heading." He ran his finger along a blue squiggly line marked Devil's Creek. "The embankment is steep there and, due to proximity of the mountains, it gets its share of wildlife."

Nakos jerked his chin toward the dry erase board. "We've got ten full-time men, broken up into five teams. Their assignments are posted daily on the chart. They radio in a minimum of twice a shift, sometimes more if reporting an issue. No one rides alone and they return thirty minutes before dark, unless something major's going on. Signal is crap out here. Each team has a gun, a satellite phone, a first aid kit, and a walkie-talkie. You can always find who and where and what right here."

They were organized, that's for sure. Each phone number was posted, the guys' names, their locations, and what task they were doing. And Nate had to give them credit for safety guidelines. It was obvious both Olivia and Nakos cared about the people who worked for them.

"Sometimes Olivia or the guys like to take a ride alone on their time off. They have to sign in and out so someone knows where they are. This is the route we deemed secure." He pointed to a large area south of the house. "Home base phone and radio are kept on me or whoever stays back. Any concerns reported go on this board so I can dole assignments as needed." He showed Nate a mini-office where files were stored, along with emergency contacts. "We need a chart for you. I wouldn't know who to call if something happened."

"I don't have any family." Or friends, but he slid a blank employment form across the tiny desk and quickly filled out the appropriate former work, education, and skills boxes, listing Jim as his contact. Nate only talked to his former parole officer once in a blue moon to catch up, but the man had been good to him through the years. He probably should be notified if Nate got hurt. "There you go."

Nakos frowned at the scarce info, but said nothing.

The teams started returning twenty minutes later. They seemed to have it down to a science. One man stored equipment while the other groomed horses or parked ATVs. Nakos inspected hooves for injury, then stalled and fed the horses. Once finished, he checked the guys off on his board.

Every time Nakos glanced at the barn opening, Nate's gut clenched. The two of them may have gotten off on the wrong foot, but the foreman knew his shit and obviously cared about Olivia a great deal. If he was worried, Nate should be, too.

Kyle and George rode in, Kyle on horseback and George on an ATV. Both dismounted and started unloading, but Olivia didn't follow.

Nakos eyed the two men. "Where's Olivia?"

Kyle paused with a saddle in his hands. "Isn't she with you? When she didn't show by quitting time, I figured you had us holding off until tomorrow for the fence."

Nakos's eyes turned homicidal. "And it didn't occur to you to check with me first?" His voice boomed off the wooden planks. He pulled a radio from his belt. "Olivia, report in."

George's pudgy face paled. "She never said to wait when she responded by walkie-talkie."

Rubbing his neck, Kyle sighed. "I know. Leave the ATV in case we need it. Go ahead and grab dinner. I'll stay with them."

The bulky man strode off and Kyle's wide eyes met Nate's. "I figured he'd never let her ride that far this close to nightfall. Any of us, for that matter. She's fine, though. I'm sure she—"

"Report now, little red!" Nakos stalked the barn opening as Nate's stomach landed near his knees.

Finally, the walkie-talkie crackled and emitted Olivia's voice. "I'm good. I finished rewiring the missing section. It wasn't as bad as I thought. I'm saddling in a sec and on my way back."

Nakos's shoulders sagged as he let out a hefty sigh. His breath expelled in puffs from the cooling temperature as dark descended. "You better cue up every five minutes. Do you hear me?"

Kyle put the saddle back on the brown horse he'd been riding. "I'll keep him ready, just in case." He petted the horse's flank. "Last fall, Rico and I were out at Blind Man's Bluff. We split up to save time and he got hurt. Dislocated a shoulder. Luckily, I wasn't too far from him, but Nakos flipped out. Accidents can happen easily, you know?"

Heart pounding, Nate nodded. Ice water swam in his veins as the fine hairs on his arms grew erect. He should've followed her, regardless of her argument. Thousands of what-if scenarios riddled his mind and his stomach revolted the sandwich he'd eaten for lunch.

"I'm gonna kill her." Nakos growled and brought the mic back to his mouth. "Olivia?" When she didn't respond, Nakos looked at Nate and shook his head. "She's pissed off and won't listen to me."

Kyle crossed his skinny arms across his chest, looking like the spitting image of his sister Amy when trying to put on a brave face. "I'm sorry, man. I didn't know she was meeting us. But she'll be all right. She said she's on her way."

Twenty minutes passed, then thirty, and every tick of the clock sent Nate's pulse hammering harder and dangerously close to stroke level. They waited outside the barn, a horse ready and ATV standing by. He could only hope to hell they were being paranoid. But if she was merely a thirty minute ride's distance, she should've been back by now. While he stayed put, joints locked in anxiety and gaze trained on the black horizon, Kyle held his horse's reins and Nakos paced tread patterns in the dirt.

At thirty-five minutes, Nakos tried reaching her again. No response.

"I don't care how mad she is, she wouldn't make you sick with worry going radio silent." Kyle adjusted his hat and looked at Nate. "Maybe you should try."

Nakos passed over the walkie-talkie and Nate called her name into the speaker. Nothing.

"Olivia, baby. Please." Acid ate the lining of his gut and threatened to burn a hole clean through his esophagus. Kyle was right. Even if she was spitting nails, she wouldn't purposely scare them. Something was wrong. "We're going after her."

Nakos nodded and faced Kyle. "Stay here. Radio if you see or hear anything. We'll use Hero's Trail up to the ridge. That's the most direct route and the one she'd likely take. Give Mae a call at the house and tell her what's up."

As Nate mounted the ATV and Nakos the horse, Kyle scanned the horizon. "Be careful."

Nate followed Nakos across prairie grass, over a few hills, and onto a beaten path. The complete darkness made navigation difficult and the new moon wasn't helping for illumination. Nate could barely see twenty feet in front of him. A cold wind stung his cheeks and freezing air grated his lungs. From the time they left the barn until they were almost to the location, the temperature had dropped at least ten degrees. Olivia had been wearing only jeans and a light coat when she'd ridden away.

Damn, but his chest was tight. Panic clutched his airway and nausea swirled in his gut. He despised this shitstorm inside him and had no idea what to do with the riotous emotions. Barring very few exemptions, he'd never had to worry about anyone but himself, and this was twice in a handful of weeks Olivia had him terrified out of his mind.

Nakos drew up short by a scattering of trees and quickly dismounted, taking off somewhere to their right.

Nate cut the engine and followed, having no idea what had lit a fire under the foreman. Snow tinged the air. The trickle of running water blended into the background noise of wind and leaves crackling, and he realized it was probably the creek. But he didn't see or hear...

His gaze landed on a horse grazing on grass by an oak. The horse she had been riding, in fact. But there was no Olivia.

Nakos fumbled with the sack on the horse's flank and pulled out her radio, then her phone. "Crap." His head whipped around, gaze narrowed to slits as he scanned their whereabouts. "She tied Firestorm here, so she's got to be close. Olivia!"

Nothing but nature answered and Nate's heart stopped. A strip of barbed wire fencing lined a row of trees and, just beyond that, starlight glimmered off the creek. It didn't look any wider than a hundred feet, nor very deep, but the embankment was rocky. The incline alone was nearly a sheer twenty-foot drop.

"She wouldn't leave the horse here." Nakos used his radio. "Kyle, you got anything?"

The walkie-talkie crackled. "No. She hasn't returned. Mae's here with me."

Nakos stared at Nate as he lifted the mic again, frenetic worry in his eyes that barely held a match to the sickening dread in Nate's gut. "We found Firestorm. No sign of her yet. Have Rico meet you and get a couple ATVs ready. I'll radio back if I need you."

"Rodger that."

"Olivia!" Nakos turned a full circle. "Olivia!"

Nate couldn't breathe to save his life. Wind burned his eyes and a hot ball of fear lodged in his windpipe. Swear to Christ, if she wasn't okay...

"Bones is with her. Wouldn't he go for help?" Hell, the dog was brilliant and severely protective of not only Nate, but Olivia as well.

"No. He'd stay with her and stand guard." Nakos shoved his hat off his head and fisted his ponytail. "Goddamn her. Okay, I'll head north, you go south. Keep your radio on and follow the fence line."

Nate ran to the ATV, grabbed the walkie-talkie and a gun, then took off in the opposite direction of Nakos.

124

"Olivia!" Nate altered his search from the trees and creek on his left to the pasture on his right, but it was damn impossible to see much. Utter isolation and deafening silence met him. "Olivia!"

Christ Almighty, let her be okay. Hand to God, he'd never let her out of his sight again. Anything, he'd do fucking anything just to know she was breathing.

Five minutes in, and he was going apeshit. There was no damn sign of her. He let out a roar, shaking with fury and panic, and stalked faster. He started calling for the dog instead, hoping to get any kind of response.

He'd just hit a slope where the tree line ended and the creek bed incline became less drastic when two sharp barks rent the air. He froze.

"Bones! Olivia!"

Again, two barks, far in the distance. That was what the dog had done to wake Nate from a nightmare, too. He ran toward where he thought the sound had come from, finding Bones between the rocky creek edge and a gentle hill. Next to the dog was...

Oh, shit. *No, no, no.*

Nate dodged boulders and descended the hill, his boots sliding on wet grass. He skidded to a halt by Olivia's prone form lying face-down, her lower half in the water. Dropping to his knees beside her, he rubbed his chest as his breath hitched. A sharp, desperate cry passed his lips and he clenched his fists.

Don't be dead, baby. Don't be dead.

Hands shaking, he felt for a pulse on her neck and nearly wept when he got one. Slow and weak, but there.

"Olivia?" Hell, she wasn't moving. Carefully holding her head, he rolled her to her back. A gash, still actively bleeding, marked her forehead by her hairline. It was a mere couple inches long, but deep. "Olivia, baby? Open your eyes." Please, Christ.

She moaned and her lashes fluttered. It took her a few attempts, but finally those baby blues met his. "What happened?"

He choked. "You tell me, baby." Christ, she was pale as goddamn snow.

"I was rinsing my hands and..." She frowned. "I don't know. When did it get dark?"

"About an hour ago." Her speech wasn't slurred, but she was talking slower than normal. He could barely hear her through the roar of blood in his eardrums. Grabbing a bandana from his back pocket, he dipped a corner in the creek. "You smacked your head pretty good." He swiped blood from her cheek and temple, then pressed the bandana to the cut.

She winced.

"Sorry." He tried to swallow to clear the rasp from his throat, but couldn't manage. "Nakos and I have been looking for you. We were scared to death. You wouldn't answer the radio..."

Shit. He grabbed the walkie-talkie off his belt. "Nakos, I've got her. About a ten minute run from our original position. She hit her head. She's barely conscious, but she's all right." He glanced at her glazed expression and blue lips. "Possibly hypothermic. Bring the blanket from the ATV and follow the tree line."

"On my way." Nakos keyed up to Kyle, telling him to call the doc.

"Bones, get Nakos. Go on, boy. Get Nakos."

The dog barked once as if he understood, then loped up the hill, disappearing from view.

Nate refocused on Olivia. "Does your neck or back hurt?" She shook her head, so he ran his hands down her arms and legs. Her clothes were soaked. "Do you feel me touching you?"

"Yes." Her teeth chattered.

No spinal injury, thank Christ.

"We need to get you warmed up." She was in shock and, in another couple minutes, hypothermia could stop her heart like fear had done to his. Only she wouldn't recover.

With an arm around her back and the other under her knees, he lifted her and cradled her to his chest. Carefully, he carried her up to the top of the hill and set her on the grass.

She smiled. "Told you. I was...right. You're...a hero."

Shaking his head, he gave her a brief kiss. Her lips were ice. "Stop talking and save your strength." This hero nonsense needed to stop.

"Twice now, you've...rescued me." Her teeth were clacking, she shivered that violently.

"Shit, baby. Forgive me." But he had to get her body temp up or she'd be in real trouble.

He shrugged out of his coat and took off the hoodie underneath, then removed her jacket and tee. Tossing the sopping clothing aside, he put his sweatshirt on her. Ignoring his own trembling hands, he unbuttoned her jeans and slid them down her legs. Methodically, he ignored her slender curves and translucent skin in order to take care of her. But hell, it was hard. Even hypothermic and bleeding, she was beautiful. He put his own socks on her feet after discarding her shoes, then slipped back into his. He laid his coat over her legs and briskly rubbed them to get some circulation going.

"Finally, you got...me naked. About...time."

"Hilarious, baby." He could hardly execute basic oxygen exchange and she was cracking jokes. He pulled her into his arms to share heat and breathed in her scent. Held her. Almost expired in relief. A semblance of a normal heart rhythm returned, but the organ would never be the same.

"You shaved ten years off my life." Having the very real feel of her in his arms offered a measure of calm, but it might take fifty years to wash the memory of cold terror from his mind.

Footsteps pounded. Nakos jogged into view, Bones right behind him. "Is she okay?"

"I'm...good." She buried her cold nose against Nate's neck.

"Excellent." Nakos knelt next to them and glanced at her cut. "I can kill you now that I know you're still breathing."

She offered a weak smile. "Love you, too."

Nakos helped her into the jacket, put the hood over her hair, and wrapped the blanket around her legs to replace Nate's meek covering. "I'll get her clothes. You good carrying her?"

Like he'd let go of her now that he had her.

"Yeah." Nate lumbered to his feet and headed toward where they'd started. "Is the doc coming? This cut will need stitches and I'm certain she has a concussion." She should be going to a damn hospital, but it seemed one needed an appendage chopped off around here to even bother making the trip.

"Hank should beat us there. Mae's drawing a hot bath."

Nate could use a scalding shower himself. Now that the frigid claws of fear had retracted, he was no longer numb to the elements. She wore most of his clothes, but him being cold didn't matter. Only her.

When they finally made it to the ridge, Nakos mounted his horse and grabbed the reins of the one Olivia had ridden. "Follow me."

With Olivia in his lap, he started the ATV. "Hold onto me best you can." She didn't respond, and he glanced at her, finding her asleep. "Baby, stay awake."

"I'm awake." She didn't open her eyes, though.

"Olivia." Finally, her lashes lifted, and damn if his eyes didn't burn. Trust and affection stared back at him through her cornflower gaze. He sucked in a breath and shook his head, wondering how he thought he'd ever stood a chance of not getting wrapped up in her. "Stay with me. Keep your eyes open."

Chapter Thirteen

With evil trolls drilling into her skull and her tongue plastered to the roof of her mouth, Olivia pried her eyes open. Sunlight scorched her retinas and she winced. Moaned.

Clothing rustled. "*Hebe*. Welcome back, little red."

She moaned again and squinted at Nakos. "Hi." Head pounding, she glanced around, trying to focus through the heavy dregs of sleep. Her bedroom. Okay. How'd she get here? Why was she in bed? "What time is it?"

"Noon." The mattress dipped with his weight. Sitting by her hip, he swept his concerned gaze over her. "You've been out cold for a couple days."

"What?" She tried to sit and a wave of nausea churned in her belly.

He set a hand on her shoulder, heavy and warm, easing her back. "Relax. You've got eight stitches in your head and finally broke a fever last night. That's not accounting for the concussion."

That's right. She'd hit her head by the creek. She had a vague recollection of Hank visiting, plus a steady stream of Aunt Mae, Nakos, and Amy waking her repeatedly. But...two days?

She eased onto her elbows. Her limbs were dead weight and her back ached. "I need to sit."

Cupping her shoulders, he helped her up. "Doc said you could have Tylenol when you woke." He passed her two pills and held out a glass of water.

She forced the medicine down her dry throat, relishing the water. Lord, she was thirsty. "Thanks." She blinked, still a little foggy.

He set the glass on the nightstand and sighed. "You're a sight for sore eyes. You gave everyone quite a scare."

"Sorry." She pressed a hand to her forehead and tentatively touched the bandage by her hairline. "Could we hold the lecture until the room stops spinning, please?" Knowing him, he'd reiterate, ad nauseum, how she shouldn't have ridden alone. The fact he was right was beside the point.

Her skin felt sticky and her pajamas were plastered to her body. That must've been some fever. Who did she have to threaten to let her bathe? She could only imagine what she looked like. Nakos, of course, was dressed as always in a tee under a flannel and jeans. He was sans a cowboy hat, though. His black hair was pulled into a low ponytail as he stared at her. Hard.

"I'm not going to lecture you." He took her hand and pressed it between his, the darkness of his olive skin a stark contrast to her fair tone. "My world would cease to rotate without you in it. Plain and simple. You've been my friend as long as I can remember and I think I cared about you before we ever met. You're family."

Lord. Sinuses prickling, she attempted to blink back tears. "Nakos—"

"Not done." His dark eyes zeroed in on her. "So imagine how it felt when you didn't answer your radio and we had to desperately search for you in the dark, in the cold, praying you were alive, only to find you bleeding, unconscious, and freezing to death. Another thirty minutes out there, and you'd be right next to Justin in the cemetery."

Hot tears clung to her lashes and dripped onto her cheeks. Guilt and shame coagulated in her belly as her chest cracked open.

"No, little red. I'm not going to lecture." He squeezed her hand. "I'm going to make you a promise. If you ever do something so stupid and stubborn again, I will hog tie you and throw you in the barn for all eternity. Understand?"

Nodding frantically, she collapsed against his chest and fisted his shirt. "I'm sorry."

He ran his hand down her hair. "I know. Stop crying. You're already dehydrated." His chest rose and fell with a deep breath. "Since my chat is out of the way, you should prepare yourself for when Nate realizes you're awake."

Lord, poor Nate. He'd pulled her out of the creek and put his own clothes on her to keep her warm. Again, he'd come to her rescue. And by what little she could remember, he'd been distraught beyond measure.

"He's mad, too, huh?" Sniffing, she straightened and wiped her cheeks.

"Mad's not the word I'd use." He handed her the water glass and nudged his chin in a silent order to drink. "He spent the first twenty-four hours in that chair right there by your bed, refusing to eat or sleep. On day two, we talked him into showering, but he only agreed if he could use your adjoining bathroom. Heaven forbid he move more than thirty feet from you. This morning, he finally crashed after Mae forced him to eat, but the couch is as far as he'd distance himself."

Nakos jerked a thumb over his shoulder and she glanced out the open bedroom door to the giant man on her living room sofa.

Nate was sprawled on his back, an arm over his face and one foot on the floor as if ready to spring into action. His chest rose and fell in even, deep breathing while Bones sat at attention, staring at him.

Like Nakos, Nate was a little too protective of her. But had he really stood sentinel for two days at her bedside? Hardly eaten? Slept?

"Nope. Mad's not the right word." Nakos's brows rose as she glanced at him. "Obsessed. Fixated. Concerned. Take your pick. Personally, I think crazy as shit fits." His lips twisted. "Little red, you brought the guy to his knees. And he hasn't gotten back up."

She looked at Nate again, not sure what to think. Half the time, she assumed the draw for him was solely a physical one. But the more time they spent together, the weaker that argument became. Twice now, she'd pushed him, trying to get him to snap and take what he wanted. And he'd jerked the reins as if he needed to show her respect. Achingly gentle, actually. That's what he'd been, proving size didn't always mean strength.

Such a conundrum, Nathan Roldan. He could be sarcastically funny and equally intense. Sometimes he seemed amused by her and other instances he appeared enthralled. She swore, it was as if no one had looked at him, really looked, before her. Judging by what he'd told her, that was no doubt the truth.

Forcing her gaze away, she refocused on Nakos. "He doesn't have any family."

"He told me something similar the other day."

"Honestly, I think Justin was the closest thing he had to a genuine friend." She stared at Nate again, her heart heavy.

"If that's the case, he probably has no idea what to do with attention." Nakos glanced over his shoulder at Nate, then back to her. "And confused about how to handle his feelings. Good thing it's you who got under his skin. There's no one more patient than you."

She smiled. "Except you."

"He's not my type." Nakos flashed a grin. "You're his type, though." He lowered his tone to mimic Nate's. "*Olivia, baby.*"

"Shut up." She laughed, then winced at the dull throb in her head. "Ow."

Nakos sobered. "That medicine should kick in soon. After you eat something, you'll feel better."

"Yeah. I need a shower first. I feel like something scraped off the barn floor."

"Look like it, too."

"Ha-ha." She tugged off the blanket.

He cupped her shoulders and stood as she edged to the end of the mattress. "You sure you're okay to get up?"

"No, but I'm doing it anyway." Slowly, she rose on shaky legs.

The room immediately turned into a disco ball with a caffeine chaser, and she reached out for something to grab to steady herself. The edges of her vision grayed and nausea flipped her stomach upside down. She teetered.

Footsteps pounded on the floor planks and she took a face-plant against something solid. And warm. And that smelled like soap. Arms came around her and hauled her closer. She closed her eyes as the topsy-turvy sensation eased and safety surrounded her.

"Why didn't you tell me she was awake?" The wall vibrated against her cheek and Nate's voice filled her head. Low. Rough. Yummy.

"Because it just happened and you were asleep." Nakos sighed. "You okay, little red?"

She hummed, more stable now. "I'm taking a shower. Be back soon."

"The hell you are." Nate eased her away and stared down at her, hands gripping her waist. "You can barely stand."

"A bath, then." At his frown, she rolled her eyes. "This isn't negotiable."

Jaw tight, he glared at Nakos. "Can you ask Amy to come up and help her?"

132

"Amy's at an appointment with the divorce lawyer. And, before you ask, Mae's with her since Olivia was incapacitated. Why do you think I'm up here and not working?"

Wait. She rubbed her forehead. "Amy wasn't supposed to meet the attorney until—"

"Thursday?" Nakos dropped his hands on his hips. "It is Thursday. You've been out a couple days, remember?"

Right. Damn, she was supposed to be standing beside Amy through her difficult time and Olivia had dropped the ball. "I'm a sucky friend."

"No, you're not." Nate tilted her chin until she met his gaze. "You are a crappy patient. Get back in bed."

"Not happening." She didn't care if her ranch hands sold tickets and put stadium seating in her bathroom. She was washing the filth off. "If you insist on a chaperone, you can come in with me."

Nate tensed, his wide gaze flicking to Nakos as if beseeching aid.

"Don't look at me."

Exhausted already, she snapped her fingers to get Nate's attention. "You've seen me naked. Nakos hasn't. I'm going, like it or not."

"I'm out of here." Nakos jerked his chin toward the door. "Mae left soup in the fridge for you. I'll heat it up and leave it on the stove. You will eat it without argument. I'll call Hank and tell her you're awake, have her come check on you."

"Thanks." She slid out of Nate's arms and, when dizziness didn't swamp her, she made her way to the dresser at a snail's pace.

Once the door closed behind Nakos, Nate stepped behind her. "I really wish you'd wait for Amy or Mae."

She pulled out a pair of gray sweats and a white tee. They could be twins, since Nate had on the same thing. "It's nothing you haven't seen before, but stay out here if you want." She was tired, achy, and pretty sure she smelled. The last thing she cared about was Nate's discomfort with her body.

"Undressing you while you were partially unconscious to avoid hypothermia is entirely different than watching you bathe, Olivia."

"Then close your eyes." Snatching a clean pair of panties, she shut the drawer and turned. The room spun again. "Wow. It's like being drunk, but not as fun."

He growled and took the items from her. "Stubborn as shit woman. And you're lucky I'm so relieved you're awake that I'll give you whatever you want." He wrapped his arm around her waist. "Come on."

They walked into the bathroom and he set her clothes on the toilet lid. While she grimaced at herself in the mirror, he started filling the tub. He studied the products on the shelf, then dumped in half a bottle of bubble bath.

He did a double-take at her grin. "What?"

"Nothing." Adorable man. She refocused on her image and wished she hadn't. "Lord, I look like crap." A bandage covered a good part of her forehead, her hair was matted and stringy, and she could fill a grocery cart with the bags under her eyes.

"At the risk of sounding like a sap, having your eyes open and you out of bed is the best thing I've seen in days."

"Aw. Be sappy more often."

"Scare the shit out of me less often and I'll consider it."

She met his gaze in the mirror, weary and worried, and her shoulders sank. "I'm sorry. It was obviously an accident, but I'm sorry."

Saying nothing, he stepped behind her and, with his hands on her waist, gently turned her around to face him. He raised his arms and framed her face with his bulging biceps to get at her bandage.

"Doc said this could come off, but you should try to keep the stitches dry." Dark gaze on his task, he peeled the tape away and removed the pad. The bandage fell from his fingers into the sink and he froze. "Christ," he muttered and, with a shaking hand, ran his fingertips over her eyebrow, gingerly inching closer to her hairline. After a moment, his throat worked a swallow and he blinked.

"You have really pretty eyes." His lids were soft, downturned, kind of like a puppy. Sometimes, like now, the color looked like chocolate. In the sunlight, golden flecks swam in his irises. And at night, they were as dark as the sky and twice as haunting. Adding to the punch were his long, thick lashes that only managed to draw more attention to the potency. "I like looking at them."

A wrinkle formed between his brows as he met her gaze. He swept a strand of hair from her face and let his hand linger on her jaw. "You're one to talk. There isn't a name in the color spectrum for yours." He shook his head as if dumbstruck. "And it's really good to see them again."

Now that she got a good look at him, she realized the level of worry he must've been under. "You look exhausted."

"Yeah, well, I haven't slept much." He skimmed his fingers down her arm and removed a bandaid on her inner arm she hadn't noticed.

"What's that from?"

"Doc put in an IV yesterday. Fluids and an antibiotic."

Lord, she had been out of it. "I don't normally get sick. Must've been a doozy."

"Falling in a creek and spending hours in the elements will do that." His gaze flicked to hers as he tossed the items in the garbage. When he looked at her once more, there was utter submission in his eyes. "You spiked a temperature we couldn't bring down. One hundred and four at its worst."

Wow. "I—"

A knock came at the door. "Olivia? It's Hank. Can I come in?"

Nate leaned over and shut off the bathwater, then opened the door.

Hank eyed Nate and flung her long black hair over her shoulder. "Nakos said you were up and at 'em. How are you doing?"

"Good. Better, thanks."

Nate leaned against the doorjamb and crossed his arms. "She can barely stand. Got dizzy and almost went down."

Nodding, Hank kept her focus on Olivia. "That's to be expected." She set her black bag on the vanity and opened it. She held up a pen light and flashed it in both Olivia's eyes. "Equal and responsive." She checked Olivia's pulse and blood pressure next, then took her temp. "All normal. How's the headache?"

"It's there. Nakos gave me Tylenol. It's better."

"Good. Any nausea?"

"A little."

Hank put her supplies back in the bag. "That should resolve after you get food in your belly." She examined the stitches. "I'll come by next week and take those out. In the mean time, no strenuous activity for a week. Avoid bending at the waist and lifting anything heavier than a gallon of milk the next couple days. Have someone with you if you're going to navigate stairs. Lots of fluids and stick to a light diet today. If you experience vomiting, have them call me right away."

"Okay. Thanks, Hank."

Nate cleared his throat. "Could you help her with..." He waved his hand at the tub.

Hank winked at him. "Sure thing."

He looked at Olivia. "I'll check on your soup." He closed the door behind him, his footsteps padding away.

"Thought I was gonna need to give that guy a sedative." Hank jerked her thumb at the door. "Climbing the walls, stalking like a caged lion. Nakos wasn't much better."

"I heard." Olivia rubbed her eyes, feeling bad enough. "And Nakos always worries."

"Not like your giant soldier. He kept saying, *I thought she was dead, I thought she was dead.*"

"Oh God." Her throat closed and she choked on a sob. She had no idea it had been that bad. Nakos and Aunt Mae must've been out of their minds, too.

"Thought you should know." Hank squeezed Olivia's arm. "Come on. Let's get you cleaned up. You'll feel more human."

With Hank's help, Olivia stripped and climbed in the bathtub. She moaned at the hot water against her sore body and closed her eyes. "Heaven."

Hank laughed and passed her a washcloth. "Put that over the sutures. We'll wash your hair."

After they finished and Olivia was dressed, Hank walked her out to the kitchen table and checked her vitals one more time. "All good. Mind my orders and I'll peek in on you tomorrow."

The doc had no sooner left and Nate set a bowl of chicken noodle soup in front of Olivia, along with one of the Gatorades he was so fond of drinking. "Eat. Drink."

She eyed him as he sat across from her. "You should, too."

"Don't worry about me."

"Someone should." When he only gave her a blank stare, she chewed her lip. "Nakos said you refused to eat and—"

"I just had a bowl while you were in the bath. I'm fine." He pointed to her soup.

Once she'd taken a few bites, he seemed appeased and set his elbows on the table. Head in his hands, he pressed his palms to his eyes. He had such big hands to go along with the rest of him. His tattoo sleeves moved with the shift of muscle and his fitted white shirt accentuated the hard planes of his pecs. Tension knotted his frame and, by the time he lifted his face and scrubbed his hands over his bald head, his expression was just as tight.

"I really am all right now, thanks to you."

He rubbed his lips, studying her. His gaze darted back and forth between her eyes, the edges of concern lessening. "I didn't do anything but stand around feeling useless."

"You carried me out of the creek, kept me warm, and brought me back home."

His eyes slammed shut so quick she was surprised there wasn't an aftershock vibration. "I don't need the reminder." His lids lifted and he pinned her with an agonizing display of helplessness. Exposed, vulnerable, he shook his head. "Please eat. And the drink will help restore the fluid you lost, balance your electrolytes."

There he went again, taking care of her. He was obviously crawling out of his skin, but his focus was all her. She glanced at her bowl. The sooner she did what he wanted, the quicker she could try to settle the turmoil inside him.

Finishing the soup and sports drink, she stood. "You need a nap."

Ignoring her, he walked her bowl to the sink and tossed out the bottle. He kept busy putting the leftovers in the fridge and washing their measly couple of dishes. Then, as if hitting the end of his patience, he gripped the sink and leaned into his hands, hanging his head.

Her heart cracked in half. Nakos had been right, as were her suspicions. It seemed Nate never had anyone in his life he cared about and, when faced with genuine emotion, he hadn't a clue how to handle it. What had happened to him, this gentle giant? How could a person go their whole life completely...alone?

Worse, she wondered how she was going to repair that kind of damage.

Chapter Fourteen

Olivia's warm, tentative hand slid up Nate's arm and he pinched his eyes tighter, gripped the edge of the sink in her suite's kitchen harder. He tensed at the pleasure/pain combo her touch forever instilled and hunched to defend himself. Or her.

For going on three days, he'd watched her lying in bed, pale as a corpse, and sick to his gut with abject fear she wouldn't wake up. Every concussion check by Mae or Amy or Nakos that first night had been goddamn torture until she'd briefly opened her eyes, muttered a few syllables, and drifted off again.

And mercy. That fever? The need for an IV? Her drenched in sweat and hotter than the damn desert he'd escaped? He'd thought he'd die. Shit, death would've been preferable. He'd almost redecorated her bedroom by punching holes through the drywall upwards of a thousand times.

None of his experiences had prepared him for that. Nearly starved as a child in foster care...subordinate to countless violent acts in that gang as a teen...holding Justin's hand while he'd slowly, painfully slipped away. Christ. Nate would gladly relive every second of his crappy life if it meant he wouldn't have to spend one more second at her bedside like he'd done the last couple nights.

Powerless to do a thing. Utterly...fucking...helpless.

There had been no outlet for the mutinous assault then and there wasn't one now. Insects burrowing under his skin. Knives piercing his chest. A vise squeezing his lungs. Sandpaper grating his throat. Images upon countless images strobing through his mind.

If this was what caring about someone was like, what the hell was he supposed to do? Because he couldn't handle it, couldn't live like this.

She ducked under his arm and stepped between him and the sink.

He didn't dare move, not even to open his eyes. "Olivia, baby, I'm at serious risk for coming unhinged."

Her arms wrapped around his waist and she brought herself flush against him. While he struggled with depleting oxygen levels, she rose on her toes and pressed her face into the crook of his neck.

Warm, soft body. Her scent of rain. Her hot, shallow exhalations caressing his skin.

Funny, he'd always thought he was headed straight for hell, but Olivia Cattenach was everything that embodied heaven, minus the wings. She probably had those stored away somewhere for future use.

"You're okay," she whispered.

Why the hell was she telling him the platitude when it was her who'd been sick and injured? Why would—

"You're okay," she repeated. "You're safe."

Shit. Because it was the exact thing he'd needed to hear, that's why.

Filling his lungs with much-needed air, he wrapped an arm around her back and shoved his shaking hand in her hair. Holding the back of her head, he pulled her close enough the holy ghost couldn't have come between them and...

Yes. Finally. His heart stopped relocating ribs and something close to normal respirations returned. The knots in his gut unraveled. His shoulders released the steel strain encasing his muscles.

Once he figured he could speak, he leaned back and looked at her. "Are you feeling better now that you ate something?"

"Yes. Come take a nap with me. You need to rest and I'm tired, too."

She'd been unconscious two days and wanted more? "Sleeping together is not a good idea."

"Not this again." She rolled her eyes with an impish smile and walked her fingers down his back. "I meant actual sleep. But if you're—"

"So did I." He reached around and halted her hands before she got to his ass. "I don't trust myself not to accidentally hurt you while I'm still experiencing nightmares."

"Oh." Blink, blink. Pout. "Are things out of place when you wake up? The room destroyed?"

"No."

"Is Bones still catching you before they get too bad?"

"Yes." He narrowed his eyes. She was trapping him again, but the idea of lying next to her was too damn tempting. Especially now that he was blessedly calming down and she was out of the woods.

"I can crash on the couch if you promise not to roam around while I'm zonked out or get yourself into trouble."

"You can monitor potential naughty behavior from next to me." She ducked under his arm and moved around him, only to stop short and grab her head. Swayed. "Note to self. Don't do that anymore."

Christ. He picked her up and carried her to the bedroom, depositing her on the bed. He climbed in after her and covered them with blankets. The dog trotted in, jumped onto the mattress, and curled up by their feet.

She rolled on her side to face him. "You changed my sheets."

He grunted. "While you were in the bath. Figured you'd want clean ones." He brushed a strand of hair away from her stitches, noting the swelling had gone down and the site looked less angry. An ugly bruise surrounded the area, though. "Go to sleep, baby."

With a sigh, she closed her eyes, and he propped his head in his hand to watch her. Because he liked the calm it brought him, he lightly ran his fingers through her auburn strands.

Her jaw and cheekbones had a fragile quality to them, especially while she slept. He'd noticed while endlessly monitoring her the past couple days, but he was much closer now and it punctuated the point. Little button nose. Full lips just this side of sulky and with a naturally dark hue. She didn't need a swipe of cosmetics to be lovely. In fact, he couldn't remember seeing her wear any.

"Stop staring at me and go to sleep."

He smiled. "How can you tell with your eyes closed?"

"Because you know my eyes are closed, that's how." Her lips curved in a wistful ghost of a smile. "Besides, your lashes are criminally long and create a tornado every time you blink."

A laugh pushed past his lips. "Is that right?"

She hummed. "Seriously, Nate. I'm fine. You're fine. The dog's right there."

If she said it a zillion more times, he might believe her. Yet, he was exhausted and the adrenaline crash was wearing off.

He rested his head on the pillow and draped his arm over her waist. He'd never slept with anyone before and found he didn't mind. There was no suffocating sense of smothering or lack of privacy he'd expected. She wouldn't be a bad thing to wake up to first thing, either. He glanced at her injury, the sutures and bruise, and that was enough to speed his pulse all over again.

Her facedown on the creek bank. All that blood. Blue lips and chattering teeth.

She'd inadvertently replaced awful PTSD images with worse ones and hadn't realized it. There wasn't an hour that went by where Justin's face didn't shove to mind, followed by crippling guilt. And now her with a gun to her head or bleeding and hypothermic on the ground added to the mix.

The Cattenachs were kryptonite. Had to be. Both siblings had wormed their way in and burrowed so deep he'd never extract them. He didn't know whether to be pissed off or grateful.

She opened one eye. "Do I need to call Hank for that sedative after all?"

"What?"

"Hank offered to knock you out with drugs." When he couldn't find something to say, she inched closer until their noses brushed. "*I thought she was dead.* Hank said you kept repeating that."

Damn. He sighed, at a loss.

She lifted his arm and pressed his palm to her chest. "Feel that? My heart's beating."

Proof didn't erase memory. "I feel it." He felt her every-fucking-where and all the time.

"Close your eyes. Do it." He complied, and she slipped her thigh between his, then idly traced patterns on his pec with her fingers. "Remember the first time we kissed?"

As if he'd ever forget. "On your couch in your living room."

"And it's a good memory?"

He lifted his lids and was rendered mute by her cornflower eyes, the cajoling touch of her fingertips, and her rain scent.

"Was it?"

He cleared his throat. "Yes." He didn't have many good things to hold onto or drum up from memory at will, but kissing her was at the top of the short stack. Not just because it had been hot as hell, but it had been one of the only instances where he'd done anything so intimate. Or wanted to. "Scary and frustrating, but good."

At some point, he might even get used to the way his brain detached from his mouth around her. The crap she continuously got him to admit was downright humiliating.

"Close your eyes, think of that, and go to sleep." She...kissed his nose and resettled. Her lids drifted shut as if an exclamation point to her rhetoric.

Fine. Securing her against him with an arm around her back, he pressed his lips to her forehead and closed his eyes. When he opened them, her room was dark, night had fallen outside her window, and he was hard.

She had her face buried in his neck like she so often preferred to do and every supple curve of her was molded to him. Still on their sides facing each other, they were a tangled knot under the sheets. There was no way to extradite himself without waking her.

How long had they been out? He glanced at the alarm clock, shocked as shit it was past midnight. Ten or so hours. No nightmares, either.

Something pinched inside his chest. Not altogether unpleasant, but a new sensation nonetheless. He couldn't recall ever being interested in...snuggling. Or whatever it was they were doing. Stranger yet was the fact he didn't want to move.

The dog had other ideas. Bones stood at the end of the mattress, stretched, and hopped onto the floor to curl up in the doorway.

Olivia made a mewling noise and stirred. Her hand, trapped between their bodies, slid from his abs and dipped under his shirt. Fingernails traced his ribs and up to his chest.

He couldn't tell if she was asleep or screwing with him, so he kept quiet and unmoving until those goddamn wonderful fingers started to descend again. "Olivia, what are you doing?"

"If you can't tell, I'm more out of practice than I thought."

Christ, her voice was almost as coaxing as her touch. Sultry and unhurried. The tone made his dick twitch. And she was injured, damn it.

With a hand over hers, he ceased her torture before she could hit the waistband of his sweats. He forced a swallow. "How are you feeling?"

"Great until you stopped me. Or, I should say, *you* were feeling great."

"Not exactly what I meant." He sucked a harsh inhale when her tongue darted across the tendon in his neck and lit a path of fire straight to his balls. "Olivia," he warned.

"Nate," she mimicked. She eased him onto his back and sprawled over him, resting her chin on his breastbone. "You have a tattoo on your chest. It's not like the patterns on your arms."

He grunted, trying to follow her change of topic when his very erect, very throbbing dick was pressed against her belly and she was positioned between his legs.

While he was still processing, she inched the shirt up to his chin and glanced at the ink in question. She couldn't possibly see very much considering the only light was a glow from the lamp in the living room, but she traced the intricate wings that spanned his pecs and stopped above his navel.

"Why an eagle?" She tilted her head, studying the tattoo.

He had a branded mark The Disciples made him get and had wanted to cover it up. "Got it when I enlisted. It was my first. A sign of home or something."

She nodded and sat up, only to remove his shirt completely and resettle in her original position. Why he let her, he didn't know, but it seemed whatever Olivia did while touching him made him a willing participant.

She tossed his shirt on the floor. "And the others? The ones on your arms?"

He'd enjoyed the pain. Or, it had started that way. After one tribal design on his shoulder and bicep, he'd kept going over several sessions until he was as ugly on the outside as he was inside. A decent portion of people liked ink, found it sexy, but he'd never been one of them. It was a constant reminder to himself that his sins weren't redeemable.

"Nate?"

He sighed, not wanting to lie to her. It was getting harder to hold things back where she was concerned. "Punishment, I guess."

"For?" A wrinkle formed between her brows. When her gaze lifted to his, genuine curiosity morphed into understanding. "Lord, Nate. You were just a kid."

The last thing he wanted was to get into this again. It seemed she'd have an excuse or absolve him of anything. Except she had no clue he was the man responsible for her brother's death, and that was unforgivable. That he was even allowing her to get this close was probably the worst sin he'd ever committed.

144

To keep her talking, he struggled with a topic. "Do you have any tattoos?" He might reconsider his view on them. Then again, the thought of anything marking her perfect skin made him ill.

"No. I've thought about it, though."

Not wanting to push his opinions on her, he feigned interest. "Like what?"

She smiled. "I don't know. Maybe Nessie on my lower back or something." Her brows wiggled.

Caught up, he laughed. "What's with your interest in the Loch Ness Monster, anyway?"

"The myth's part of my ancestors' culture." She shrugged. "I like the idea of there being a mysterious creature lurking about no one's discovered."

"Like Bigfoot?"

"Don't be ridiculous. He's living in sin with Elvis on Atlantis. And I can find a seven-foot hairy guy anywhere near the mountains."

"Christ." He ran a hand down his face, laughing until his gut hurt. "You are something else." Sobering, he skimmed his thumb under her jaw. Damn, but she was beautiful. Even battered and coming off a fever, she made him not have the desire to look anywhere else.

"Are you ticklish, Nathan Roldan?"

"Uh…" He didn't really know. "Maybe. Why?"

"I want to hear you laugh again." She grazed her fingers up his sides. "I thought your grin was panty-melting, but your laugh singes them to dust."

Again with the compliments. He grabbed her wrists and pinned her arms at his hips. "If I were to check said panties, would I prove you're lying?" Heart pounding, he stared into her eyes lit with humor and heat, wondering how she'd careened him from laughing to desperate-to-have-her in five seconds.

She wiggled her arms in a request to be set free and straddled him when he complied. Her lips hovering over his, she stared down at him. "Go ahead. Find out."

Great. A challenge.

Placing his hands flat on her back, he thrust against her and hissed. Christ, he wanted inside her, but not so soon after her ordeal. He could, however, pacify her itch.

"Baby, are you dizzy, nauseous, or have a headache?" He licked the seam of her lips and groaned when she parted for him.

"No." She nipped his lower lip. "I do have this awful throbbing sensation, though." She ground against his shaft and kissed him. "Would you like to know where?"

"I know where." He closed his mouth over hers and drove inside, stroking her tongue with his. And as soon as she was one-hundred percent, he was going to be inside her in every imaginable way. He'd put up a fight, but she'd knocked him down for the count. "I know exactly where, baby."

He rolled her beneath him and leaned on one forearm, keeping his lips fused to hers. Shoving his hand under her shirt, he splayed his fingers and was surprised, yet again, by how tiny she was in comparison. His hand nearly spanned the width of her waist.

She moaned into his mouth, urging him on. He eased his hand into her pants and cupped her mound. She jerked her hips and grabbed his head, taking the kiss so deep he'd require oxygen therapy afterward.

"They're not singed, baby. They're drenched." Wet and hot. She had barely any hair and her swollen little nub was begging to be teased by the way it poked his palm. He panted against her lips, his dick aching, his skin on fire. "How wet can I make you?"

In response, she spread her legs and hooked one behind his thigh.

He groaned his approval, needing to hear her voice. "You want that?" He added pressure to her clit.

"Yes." She opened her eyes. Blown pupils all but swallowed the blue of her irises and lust saturated her gaze. "More, Nate. Please."

It was the please that sent his heart jack-hammering. But his name on her lips was his undoing. He spread her folds and slid a finger inside. Shit, she was tight. And hot. And soft. She immediately clenched around his digit, seeking more. He added another and dipped his head to kiss her neck, lick her thumping pulse. Her breaths rasped and her hips undulated.

But then she turned the tables and cupped…him. Through his pants, she stroked him from base to tip and squeezed.

He choked. "You, baby. Not me."

She didn't let go. She worked her hand past his waistband and gripped him.

Skin to mother-effing skin.

"Holy shit." He thrust against her, not caring about anything but her firm hold and how she seemed to know the perfect amount of pressure without any direction.

To reciprocate, he coated his fingers with her slick heat and pumped inside her, nudging her clit with the heel of his hand with every pass. She matched his frantic pace and ran her thumb across his slit.

Goddamn, he was going to come in his pants like a teenager.

As if reading his mind, she jerked his sweats past his hips, and took him in hand again. Stroking, pulling, teasing his head. He pumped faster as his lower back tingled in warning. To avoid a mess, he rolled them to the side, facing each other, neither ceasing the desperate ministrations.

He screwed her hand while his fingers screwed her and took her mouth again in a kiss that seared reason. Seconds later, her walls clenched him and she trembled. Stilled. Cried against his lips. Her forehead wrinkled in a close resemblance to concentration and her lips parted wide. Shit, she was even more stunning when she came.

He followed, unable to withstand it, and released jet after jet with a shocked bark. He withdrew his fingers from inside her and grabbed her ass, needing to touch her. Rigid, shaking, he opened his eyes to find her watching him as he finished. Something about her expression, having her so close, made the act less about need and more about…connection.

Heaving, he came down, unable to look away. Time passed. Hell, it could've been a decade for all he knew. But he stared at her in complete awe and wondering what happened. He'd sought women and he'd screwed his brains out. Nothing he'd done was anything like…

"Olivia." He skimmed his knuckles across her flushed cheeks. "Not really sure what to say."

She smiled and reached behind her for some tissues on the nightstand. Then, she…cleaned him off and reset his pants. Too confused to argue, he let her.

Afterward, she set her head in her hand and grinned. "I want it reflected for the record that I love your hands."

147

"You'll get no complaint from me about yours." He ran his gaze over her face and stilled when he encountered her stitches. "Are you okay?" She was supposed to be taking it easy.

"No."

His gaze jerked to hers as his stomach bottomed out.

"I'm great." A slow, steady smile split her face. "Besides being hungry, that is."

Chapter Fifteen

While Nate cleaned up in her bathroom, Olivia slowly made her way to her kitchenette to forage for something to eat. After sleeping solid for so long and the extremely pleasant way she'd awoken, she was ready to devour her own hand. Or her own cooking.

She found a small platter of fresh fruit in the fridge Aunt Mae had probably put there and a plate of brownies on the counter. Perfect. Chocolate was the most important food group. She took both to the couch as Nate emerged from her room.

Lord, he was gorgeous. Sweats low on his hips and nothing else. Bare feet, bare chest. She even loved his bald head without his usual black cap. Before him, she'd not had an opinion one way or the other on tats, but he'd turned her on to them. Big time. Especially with his naturally dark skin and muscles.

He took a seat across from her with his version of an amused smile. "Brownies and pineapple?"

"And strawberries." She popped one in her mouth, chewing as she studied him. "Hungry?" She waved the plate at him.

"I'm good, thanks."

To her knowledge, all he'd had was a bowl of soup and that was hours ago. "I screwed up our sleep schedule, but there's nothing wrong with midnight snacks."

"I only eat at designated times."

The censure in his tone didn't sit right. He had weird food quirks and she'd been dying to ask him about them. "Is that because of the military? Habit?"

His gaze drifted away. "Partly."

"And the other part?" What wasn't she getting here? Was it a discipline thing because of a training regimen? Judging by his facial expressions when she'd watched him, he didn't care for eating with others. He acted as if food in general was a displeasure and, for a guy his size, he consumed very little.

He turned sideways to face her and crossed his arms. "I don't know how to explain it to you in a way you'd understand."

And there went those warning knells in her head. "Try."

"I'd rather not."

She forced herself to swallow the pineapple she'd been chewing as her stomach suddenly took a dive. "When you say cryptic stuff like that, I form my own conclusions and—"

"Growing up the way I did, meals were a privilege. I never developed an affinity for indulgence like others. I eat when I'm hungry. Okay?"

No, not okay. "What does that mean? Growing up the way you did. Do you mean foster care?"

He glanced heavenward as if seeking patience. "Yes."

"And what do you mean by privilege?" Because that sounded an awful lot like he hadn't gotten fed routinely.

Closing his eyes, he let out a slow, even breath, then looked at her. "It was hard getting used to new families all the time. Everyone had a different way to cook even the simplest of things. I've consumed fifty alternate versions of meatloaf."

Yeah, that made sense. It was sad, but it's not as if that was something fixable. In a way, she'd taken Aunt Mae's recipes for granted, which was something Nate had never been allowed. And he hadn't exactly answered the question, just dodged it.

"Explain privilege." When he merely pinched the bridge of his nose in frustration, she shook her head. "Were you...starved?"

Again, he took a deep breath like he was fortifying himself. "That's a strong term, but I suppose it's accurate in a couple cases. Most of the families I was placed with were nice. Some used food as punishment. Withholding it and so forth. It wasn't unusual for me to get ginked from one location to the next with zero warning. I never knew what I was walking into."

Lord. The fruit churned in her belly and threatened to come back up. What kind of person withheld food from a boy? "I'm sorry you had to go through that."

"Over and done. Doesn't matter."

"It does matter."

"Olivia." He sighed. "You keep doing that. Reversing the clock hands, dragging me back to the beginning. Why? It's in the past."

"Because it made you who you are." His expression indicated he was through discussing the matter, but he had to understand his childhood wrongs weren't his fault. They were the monsters, not him. "Justin and I were one living relative away from winding up in the system. If these things had been done to me instead of you, would you feel the same? Would you blame me like you do to yourself?"

He stared at her long and hard, his jaw ticking. The powerless torment in his eyes said he was pulling memories, inserting her instead, and it was ripping him open. When he finally spoke, his voice was barely a whisper and riddled with emotion. "I would never wish any of it on you. Not one second."

"You're not responsible for your past. Only how you choose to live in the aftermath." Her throat grew tighter because she knew, *just knew*, she'd only nicked the tip of the iceberg that was his suffering. "You can't run from it, but you can move beyond it." He shook his head, yet she kept at him since she assumed no one had ever bothered before. "It doesn't matter how much you resist. I have enough faith for the both of us."

He froze, eyes wide and nostrils flared as if he'd never heard of such a thing. "It's not up to you, nor is it right for me to look to you to absolve my pain."

"Take a good, long look. See me? This is what caring looks like. I realize you probably don't recognize it, but make a mental note for future reference. And don't think for a moment that I don't know what it means to hurt. Despite my size, I'm not fragile."

"That's exactly my point." He growled and scrubbed his hands over his head. "You've been hurt enough. I'm not adding to that."

"Too late. That's what people who give a crap do, Nate. I'm not interested in absolving your pain. Only you can do that for yourself. But I can climb inside and share it, lessen the burden. My actions are not your decision. It's done. Get used to it."

"Christ, Olivia." Bit by bit, the fierce warrior shrank into the background and his expression softened. The guy who'd tended to her with wrenching gentleness returned as if he'd lost his will to fight. His throat worked a swallow. "Justin said you were stubborn, but I think that might be the world's largest understatement."

She grinned. "Now you're beginning to understand." She cleared her throat as her gaze dipped to his body. All the grooves and ridges, the ripples and contours. Her skin grew hot. "Terrible as foster care was for you, at least it taught you discipline. If you want to put a positive spin on things, glance in the mirror."

His lips twitched like he wanted to smile. "I suppose it prepared me for the Army and MREs, too. Since I often had to eat things I didn't like as a kid, I lacked the ability to appreciate taste."

"What's an MRE?"

He scratched his jaw, rough with stubble. "Meal, ready-to-eat. Individual field ration in a pouch."

She gagged. "Ugh."

He laughed, grated and low. "Your brother initially had the same reaction. You get used to it. Some of the guys called them meals, rejected-by-everyone."

Since he'd brought it up, she followed the topic change to keep him talking. "What was it like over there? Were you with Justin's unit a long time?"

He nodded. "Met him on my second tour. We did a couple more together." He glanced away, his dark gaze distant. "Most of the time, it wasn't so bad. I think your brother had a hard time adjusting at first, but he was a go-with-the-flow kind of guy. Everyone loved him. Talked a mile a minute."

She laughed. "I think he had to in order to get a word in. He grew up with two females."

"True." His smile slipped. "Nothing much got him down. He had an infectious grin and was quick to use it."

"Yeah." She sighed, missing her brother with a fierce pang of longing. "I think I miss that most. His cheesy grin." And one wrong move by a commanding officer meant she'd never get to see it again. "We knew there was the possibility he might not come home, but I never let it gel in my mind. It hit me hard when the soldiers showed up at our door to deliver the news. I kept thinking it was a mistake. Misguided delusion, I suppose."

"A coping mechanism." He rubbed his chest as if it hurt. "I did the same thing every day recovering in the hospital." With a sharp inhale, he slammed his eyes shut and shook his head. Once he opened them, some of the distress was gone. Not all, though. "You want me to put that away?"

She glanced at her plate, having lost her appetite. "No, thanks." The things he'd mentioned about food and foster care sprang to mind, then how he'd said he didn't appreciate taste. Perhaps she could do something about it. "I'll be right back. Don't move."

Heading into her bedroom, she snatched a sleep mask from her nightstand drawer and returned. "Experiment time."

The color drained from his face. "I'm not wearing that, if that's what you're thinking."

She tilted her head. "Do you trust me?"

"You know I do, but I'm not—"

"Comfortable? Taking away your eyesight might force you to bring internal images to mind?"

Mouth firm, he narrowed his gaze. "Yes and yes. The last time we did one of your *experiments* I wound up flat on my back in a treehouse with your mouth driving me out of my mind."

She hummed her approval. "And when you think about your teen years, about the gang, are the memories as terrible?"

He opened his mouth as if to argue and quickly shut it again.

"Precisely my point. Experiment successful. You shouldn't have taught me coping mechanisms if you didn't want me to try them."

"*For you.*" He leaned forward. "They were supposed to help you."

"They did. And now they will in your case." She climbed on his lap and straddled him. "Complaining yet?"

He dropped his head to the back of the couch and closed his eyes, his shoulders sinking in defeat. "Would it matter if I did?" He looked down his nose at her, seemingly hesitant but curious.

"Nope." She ran her fingers over the white silk mask, giving him a minute. "It's the middle of the night, everyone's asleep, we're alone, and nothing bad is going to happen."

Up went his brows. "Who are you trying to convince?" He took the mask from her and put the band around his head, then slipped the material over his eyes. "Do your worst, baby."

No, she'd do her best, but she grabbed her plate and set it next to them on the cushion in silence. Then, she leaned forward, crushing her chest to his, and kissed him. She ran her fingers across his wide shoulders, down to his biceps, loving the soft skin over hard muscle.

He tensed, but eventually participated and set his hands on top of her thighs, thumbs stroking the deeper he sank. His touch was as tender as the kiss, surprising her. They'd had brief moments where passion hadn't kicked in the door, but not like now where he seemed more interested in showing her a part of himself rather than telling.

Drawing a ragged breath, he pulled away. "If this is the point where you bust out handcuffs and—"

"Wrong kind of experiment."

He grunted. "I can't tell if I'm disappointed or relieved."

Laughing against his lips, she reached for a piece of pineapple. "Open your mouth."

He hesitated, then did as she asked.

She traced his lips with the fruit. "Take a bite."

Breathing irregular, he sank his teeth into the pineapple and chewed. A drip of juice fell onto his chin and he went to wipe it away, but she used her tongue instead. Licking a slow path up to his mouth, she paused as he groaned.

"What does it taste like?"

His brows furrowed. "Pineapple?"

"Describe it." While he appeared to be thinking, she kept her fingers moving. Over his throat, collarbone, to the hard discs of his nipples. The longer she caressed, the more his erratic breathing escalated. "Tell me."

His fingers clenched her thighs. "Uh...sweet. Juicy?"

As a reward, she kissed him again, deep, and ground her hips against his thickening erection. Back during their interlude in her bedroom, she'd learned he was big *everywhere*. Nine perfect inches covered in velvet skin. And she wanted all of him. Soon. He wasn't ready yet, though. He still wasn't taking much initiative.

A harsh inhale, and he cupped her jaw, his need apparent as he pulsed between her legs. "Damn, Olivia."

"More?" She reached for a strawberry and brought it to his lips.

This time, he bit into the fruit without wavering. While he chewed, his hands trailed to her throat. Lower. He teased the neckline of her shirt with his callused fingers. "Tastes like summer." He dipped his head and kissed her neck, setting off a thunderous tremble from deep within her core. "Let me amend that statement. Summer and rain. You make everything taste better."

Which meant he *was* tasting. Not just seeing food as a basic necessity, but as something pleasurable. She broke off a small piece of the brownie and waited for him to lift his head.

He took it from her, but immediately stilled as if perplexed. "I haven't had dessert in...I can't remember." He swallowed. Before she could respond, he tore the mask off and stared at her. Confusion. Interest. Surprise. His dark eyes searched hers. "Never really cared for sweets."

"Why?"

His gaze skimmed over her face and he shrugged. "Didn't have them often, I guess."

"And now?" She broke off another chunk and held it out for him.

He glanced from the brownie to her and back again. As if unsure, he gripped her wrist and brought her hand to his mouth. Gaze locked on hers, he sucked her fingers, swirling his tongue.

Dang, nothing was sexier than that move right there. Erotic and intense. She wondered who was playing whom all of a sudden. Her lungs struggled to cooperate while her pulse thumped, her heart pounded, and her panties grew damper by the millisecond.

He swallowed, still watching her as he eased her fingers out of his mouth. "I could learn to like it." A battle waged in his expression. For what, she hadn't a clue, but then he blinked like he was attempting to focus. "I could more than like it."

An exhale, and he rested his head on the back of the couch. He gingerly swiped a strand of hair from her forehead, tracing the stitches with his fingertips. Chocolate gaze on the movement, full lips twisted in thought, he looked like he was a million miles away.

"I did think you were dead." His gaze slid to hers. "Hank was right, though. I don't remember saying it aloud."

"I'm not. I'm right here."

"Since you instigated this twisted heart-to-heart, I'll be honest." He offered a slight shake of his head. "When I found you, I swear, my heart stopped. It hasn't beat right since. I don't know what you're doing to me or why you're hell-bent on trying to fix me, but..." He shook his head again as if at a loss for how to finish.

"Fixing you implies that you're broken." With a heavy heart, she wondered if it was possible to undo a lifetime of damage. "There's nothing wrong with you, aside from a misguided sense of guilt."

He gave her a frustrated, not-this-again look and glanced away.

She gripped his chin with her thumb and forefinger to make him face her. "Tell me something good about yourself that you do well. And don't say fucking."

His lashes fluttered in a rapid blink as if shocked by her curse.

"Yes, I swear." She smiled. "I don't do it often, but I'm capable. Fuckity fuck-fuck. Now, tell me something good about yourself."

Affection warmed his eyes as humor curved his lips. "I'm great at reading people."

Interesting. "Maybe you should take Rip up on his offer of a job, then. Police work would suit you." She inhaled his scent of soap and warm male, wanting to burrow into him. She absolutely adored him all gooey around the edges as much as the alpha side he tried to cage. "Read me, Nathan. What do you see?"

His hands settled on her waist. "I see a woman who was so intent on making her little brother feel secure after their parents died that she grew a fierce independent streak and forgot altogether how to put her needs first." His thumbs stroked her ribs over her shirt. "She's breathlessly beautiful and knows it, but doesn't have a vain bone in her body and gets suspicious when someone's attracted to her. She uses humor to put people at ease, even if she's uncomfortable herself, because she doesn't have an inkling how not to be selfless." He paused. "How am I doing so far?"

How was he doing? Dang. "Forget Rip. You should work for the FBI."

He nodded, expression serious. "And the way you look at me sometimes, like right now, with warmth and adoration, indicates you're slipping into dangerous territory. The more time we spend together, the deeper you embed, and it's wrong. I don't like it."

"I think you do like it. Too much. Which scares the crap out of you."

Unflinching, unblinking, he went stone-cold still and stared. "You're a square peg and I'm a round hole, baby. We don't fit."

"Then we'll build our own world in the shape of us."

Closing his eyes, he pinched the bridge of his nose, then exhaled and dropped his forehead to her shoulder. "Christ, you have an answer for everything."

"Not everything." She might be getting through to him on a surface level, but she'd failed to penetrate. Regardless, she wrapped her arms around his head and held him to her. "Life is scary, more so if navigating alone."

"Justin used to say that." His low admission was slurred since his face was pressed against her, but his tone was contrite.

"It's one of Aunt Mae's phrases."

He turned his head, kissed her neck, and rested his temple on her shoulder. "He talked about you all the time. I thought you were twins until he corrected me."

"We were as close as twins. Looked enough alike, too."

He grunted. "Felt like I knew you long before I arrived in town or saw your face, but I was wrong."

Taking that as the compliment she hoped he intended it to be, she thought about Justin's letter and the mention of Nate. "Did he know? About your past, I mean."

"I told him about juvie, but not how I ended up there. And that I was a foster kid."

That cemented the footprints of suspicion in her mind. This whole "watching over her" promise Nate had made to Justin never sat right. Her brother knew very well she could handle herself. Perhaps part of him wanted someone to take care of her for a change, but it wasn't about her so much as it was for Nate. To give him a home and a family and support and purpose.

Everything he'd never had in his short thirty years.

He ran his hand up and down her back. "I call it verbal diarrhea. Ten minutes with him and he'd get me talking. Pissed me off." He lifted his head, brows raised. "Not unlike another redhead I know." He smiled, full and wide and like a punch to her abdomen. "You're much better to look at, though."

Chapter Sixteen

Beside Nakos, Nate hoofed it from the barn up to the house and rolled his head to stretch his neck. After the stressful search and rescue for Olivia, followed by a week of reroofing and learning the ropes from the foreman, Nate was ready to dive into a bottle of tequila. Or Pepto. Either would suffice.

Their boots crunched on gravel as a stiff wind pushed from the north. Pine tinged the air and he wouldn't be shocked if it snowed tonight, considering the drop in temp since this morning. Dusk was playing cat and mouse in the cloudless sky, though.

Nakos halted near the mudroom and faced him. "Can I give you a piece of advice?"

Studying the man's cowboy hat and flannel under his wool coat, Nate shrugged. "Sure." Didn't mean he'd take it.

"Olivia has never desired or asked for much in all the time I've known her. Yet fate has kicked her repeatedly on the few occasions she has wanted something." Nakos shifted to his other foot and set his hands on his hips. Near-black eyes leveled on Nate. "She wants you. Don't be another disappointment."

What next? It was taking his all to resist Olivia. Add pressure from another front and he'd be sunk. And would take her down with him.

Nate scratched his jaw. "You don't know anything about me. What makes you think—"

"I know enough." Nakos tipped his hat and did an about-face, walking away. "For instance, I know you want her, too." A few feet apart, he stopped and turned. "And I know you'd rather eat a bullet than see one hair on her head harmed. Works for me. Now, man up."

Shaking his head, Nate watched the guy disappear around the side of the house and tried to dissect the "advice." Nakos had a point, and Nate wouldn't begrudge Olivia anything, but this wasn't a simple case of desire.

In truth, he'd hit his breaking point a week ago. Saying no to her was harder than landing on the moon in a paper airplane. He'd been doing his goddamn best to avoid her for that reason. He just didn't think he had enough...control. He'd never had to be careful or gentle or any other such thing. And she was so slender, so...

Christ. She sent him out of his ever-loving mind with a brush of her fingers, never mind a kiss. How was he supposed to trust himself not to hurt her if he couldn't remember his own name when she merely smiled? To have her naked and beneath him would...

Shit.

He headed inside and to his room, where he showered and avoided dinner. And thought some more until his head nearly split open. An hour passed, then two, with him standing in front of the window, staring out into nothing and Bones sitting obediently by his feet.

Once it seemed like the house was quiet, he stepped into the hallway and glanced up the stairs to Olivia's partially open suite. She'd been doing that for seven days—leaving the door ajar for him. He'd spent every night this week on her couch, slipping in after she'd fallen asleep and sneaking out before she'd woken.

Hank had popped by today to remove Olivia's stitches and had given her the all-clear to return to normalcy. He didn't need to sleep sentinel in her living room anymore. But courtesy of her concussion and fever, if he wasn't within spitting distance, he climbed the walls and wore tread patterns into the floorboards.

Since he didn't hear her roaming around, he ascended the stairs, Bones at his heels, and stopped short in her kitchen at finding her standing in front of the coffee table. She wore those damn pajamas that covered absolutely nothing and her auburn hair was up in a loose ponytail. Wisps had escaped, framing her face as she stared at something in her hand.

"Close the door, Nate." Her voice was so quiet he had to strain to hear and, for some reason, she refused to look at him.

"I was just—"

"Checking on me? Sneaking in to sleep on my sofa?" She lifted her head and stared at him. "Close the door, Nate," she repeated, this time slowly and with unerring calm.

Confused, he did as she asked and walked to the threshold separating the rooms, stopping feet from her. Spidey sense had the fine hairs on his arms standing at attention.

She held up one of his carved figurines, the one he'd left her this morning. "What is this?"

Right. Well, he wasn't Michel-fucking-angelo or anything, but it wasn't that bad. "Your Nessie." She *did* have a thing for that stupid mythical creature. What was the problem?

Slowly, she nodded. "And the others?"

Damn. She was leading him into another trap. He just couldn't tell why. "They would be your Nessie also." In various positions.

"Every night this week, you've come up here after I've fallen asleep and left one of these on my nightstand."

Yep. A trap, all right. "Consider them kindling if you dislike them that much. You wanted the crap I whittled, so I brought them to you." He'd needed something to do so he wouldn't go into her bedroom, slip under the sheets with her, and finish what they'd started. Thus, the stupid things. And she'd placed them everywhere—the fireplace mantle, the end tables, the windowsill. "I won't be offended."

"Dislike them. *Dislike them?*" The higher her voice rose, the harder his heart had to work. "You spent time making me something I love, that's very difficult to find in stores, and I'm supposed to make firewood out of them?"

What the actual hell was going on? Because if he'd been gifted an instruction manual and a Google map, he still wouldn't be able to figure it out. "Olivia—"

"I've been patient, given you time." With more care than was required, she set the figurine down and crossed her arms. Tapped her tiny, bare foot.

Uh-huh. "Olivia—"

"Quit saying my name like that."

"Like what?" Forget instructions. He was going to need God Almighty to come down from On High to explain this one.

"Like I'm speaking Vulcan." She starting talking a mile a minute, checking items off on her fingers. "First, you travel across the country to hand-deliver a letter from my dead brother when you could've dropped it in the mail. You shot a hat off a man's head to save me and my BFF from a guy who'd gone off the deep end. Bought said BFF thousands of dollars in photography equipment. Taught me coping mechanisms so I wouldn't go insane from the trauma. Massaged my neck when I'd pulled a muscle. Carried me to bed when I'd fallen asleep..."

On and on she went, ticking off her points, with him standing in front of her like a stupid idiot who'd just had a high-five to the face via a chair. And when she ran out of fingers, she paused, blinked, and started all over again with her thumb.

"Call me baby all the time. Pulled me out of a creek and nearly froze to death to prevent me from going hypothermic. Sat vigil at my bedside while I was sick. Said I was beautiful. And," she held up her pinkie, "carved me personalized trinkets like some woodsman version of Cyrano de Bergerac minus the buffer." She huffed, re-crossing her arms.

He held up his hands in surrender. "You lost me somewhere around Vulcan and picked me up at Cyrano. I have no idea who that is, by the way. It sounds like you're listing nice sentiments as if I had admirable traits, but what does any of that have to do with the damn Loch Ness Monster?"

And...shit. He'd gone and said the wrong thing.

She bared her teeth, her gaze dialing straight to maim. He should've known better than to mess with a third-generation Scottish-American whose temper was turning as fiery as her hair. She'd obviously been straddling the fence of intolerance before he'd made it up here, but she was clear on the other side now.

"*As if* you had admirable traits?" She marched up to him and poked his chest. "Your words of warning about being the Big Bad Wolf are moot when your actions constantly contradict the claims. Truth time. What do you want, Nathan?"

Was his sanity too much to ask? How about a rewind button?

Gaze challenging, she took several steps in retreat and hooked her thumbs in the waistband of her shorts. "What do you want?"

Then—*holy Christ*—she slid the shorts down to her thighs with a shimmy of her hips that sent him from zero to hard faster than a rev of his Harley's engine.

"I only have so much restraint, baby. For the love of humanity, keep your clothes on."

Ignoring him—because when did she ever listen?—she stepped out of the boy shorts and dangled them by one finger. "That's what I'm talking about. Restraint. You show entirely too much of it." She unceremoniously dropped the material with a whatcha-gonna-do-about-it lift of her brows.

162

Chest heaving, he fisted his hands at his sides. His gaze followed a path up her calves, past her toned thighs, and to the thin strip of—*fuck him dead*—black lace. One yank and he could rip them off her perfect ass, have them sailing across the room.

"I'm not delicate. I don't need you to be careful or cautious or anything other than yourself." She fingered the hem of her tank top, putting him into cardiac arrest. "Know what I want? I want the dirty-talking guy in my kitchen from weeks ago. I want the man who devoured me with a kiss on my porch. Snap, Nate. Forget restraint. Take what you want."

No air, no air, no air, no air...

Up, up, up went her shirt. It hit him in the face.

He jerked the material off, threw it aside, and ground his molars into a fine powder. His heart shifted ribs and red blood cells boiled in his veins.

Effing beautiful, that's what she was. And completely unashamed of her body as she stood with her hands on her hips. Slim waist and taut belly. Fair skin dusted with freckles. Tiny, pert breasts and rosy nipples begging to be sucked. A growl of need raked his throat.

Pivoting, she strode into the bedroom and reemerged in under three seconds. She tossed something at him and he caught it against his chest. He didn't even need to glance at the item. The foil packet crinkled in his hand and was familiar to every Y chromosome-carrying male.

His dick twitched. "Olivia, baby..."

She wiggled her fingers in a daring come-hither. "I don't just want you to come. I want you to come undone. Take what you— "

He had them across the room, his mouth fused to hers, and her back to the wall before she could even conjure the end of her taunt. She shoved his shirt up, blinding him and severing the kiss for a second, then tossed it aside and he was right back at her. He grabbed one of her wrists and pinned it above her head, holding the condom between her pulse and his palm. Then he did the same with her other arm and groaned as the position thrust her breasts against his chest.

Bruisingly, he kissed her with violent tongue strokes and enough pressure to cause suction. She hummed and matched his every lash with one of her own. She tried to roll her hips as if seeking relief, but he trapped her to the wall with his, aligning every delectable inch of her with him and crushing his raging erection into her belly.

She'd wanted him to come undone? He was there.

Tearing his mouth away, he glared at her. Vibrating, he struggled with the last tether containing his willpower. "This wasn't the smartest move you ever made, baby."

"Promise?" Her lids lifted slowly, nailing him with cornflower eyes drenched in lust with a defiance chaser.

His pulse tripped out of control. He stared at her, giving her a last silent warning.

She merely looked back in challenge.

Gaze on hers, he let go of one of her wrists to dip his fingers into the waistband of her panties. And ripped them clean off with one swift jerk.

Her breath hitched and she arched against him.

Discarding the lace over his shoulder, he worked his hand between them and parted her folds, finding her slippery and wet and ready. And so, so hot. Her teeth sank into her lower lip as her eyes begged him for more. For everything.

Releasing her other arm, he shoved his sweats to his ankles, kicked them aside, and bit the foil open. Her wide, interested gaze lowered to his erection as he rolled a condom down his length. Desire coiled with anticipation and a trace of concern in her depths. He'd take care of all three right now.

He grabbed the backs of her thighs, spreading them and lifting her so she had no choice but to wrap her legs around him. Then, he pinned her in place with his chest and held her ass to keep her steady. All but panting, she searched his gaze and dug her fingers into his neck like a brand.

Christ. He didn't think he'd ever wanted something or someone so badly in all his life. She'd been rattling his cage since their first encounter. The push/pull of animal versus man warred inside him, stalked his skull, and he gave up. Beast for the win.

He crushed his mouth to hers, searing her with a kiss that detonated reason and obliterated thought as he knew it. When he couldn't take the tension any more, he aligned himself and thrust inside her. Hard. Fast. And almost collapsed as her tight, hot, supple walls fisted him.

The fit was pleasurably....excruciating.

Her cry shot into his mouth, her nails sinking into the flesh on the back of his neck.

He froze. "Did I hurt you?"

She shook her head in a vicious denial.

One hand on her ass, he slapped the other to the wall for balance and brushed his lips against hers. Her eyes were pinched tightly closed and her uneven breaths mingled with his.

"Olivia, baby, look at me." Hand to God, he'd slice open an artery if he found any sign of pain in her eyes.

Her lashes fluttered and her lids lifted to reveal...

Desperate. Blinding. Need.

"Don't stop," she breathed. "Please." She flattened her hands on top of his head. Her gaze wandered over his brow, cheeks, mouth, and back to his eyes. Her gorgeous auburn strands were already a chaotic mess and loose around her face. "Please, Nate."

His lungs stalled. No one had ever said his name during sex, and hearing it from her lips sent his pulse into sporadic meltdown. Something lodged in his throat. His heart, perhaps. She'd had it in her slender, capable fingers since the first time he saw her.

Watching her, he pulled out slowly. As if to fight him, her walls gripped him tighter and cold sweat formed on his skin. She issued a fraught noise and held his face, her body vibrating against his. Halfway, he stopped. Her breaths soughed while his quit altogether.

"You, baby." His eyes darted back and forth between hers. "You asked what I wanted and it's you." Damnation forthright, but there was the honest truth.

Then, he thrust into her with enough force that she slid up the wall a few inches.

And nothing, *nothing* had ever or would ever feel as fantastic, as right, as being inside her. Safety and anarchy. Balance and instability. Sweetness and sin.

"Yes." She spread her arms and slapped her palms to the wall in a save-me version of holy order. As if unsure how to handle what he was doing to her body, she clenched his shoulders. "Nate."

Knowing what she needed, he gripped her wrists, stretched her arms high overhead, and laced their fingers together. Caging her face with his biceps, he drove inside her. Over and over. Again and again. Their stomachs slapped and their chests grazed and her scent of rain swirled around them.

She rolled her hips with each plunge, moaning, seeking. His muscles strained, struggling to keep the pace, a delicious burn he felt from head to toe and every nerve path in between.

He kissed her with all the control of a buoy in a hurricane and then dipped his head to suck on one of her rosy, erect nipples. The hard little bud puckered in his mouth and she squeezed his fingers, indicating she enjoyed it. Moving to the other breast, he repeated the motion, in awe of her.

Responsive. Passionate.

She had more strength than most people he'd encountered, but her appearance belied the personality. Petite. Slender. Even her breasts were small enough to fit in his hands and still leave room for more. And she was utter perfection.

Tingles coursed down his spine and wrapped around his balls. He pistoned faster, determined to set her off before he blew. Judging by the way she dug her heels into his back and her flushed cheeks, she was nearly there.

"Come on, baby." He nipped her neck and flattened his tongue against her thumping pulse, loving the sheen of sweat and salt on her skin. "Christ, the things I want to do to you."

Repeatedly. Forever.

She trembled, her fingers a death grip. If possible, every part of her wrapped around every part of him, even though they were already so entwined a crowbar couldn't have pried them apart.

Throat tight, dick pulsing, muscles burning, he drove into her with everything he had. Each shallow withdraw of his hips made him more greedy to return. The over-sensitization was unbelievable. And each thrust home had her tight, hot flesh cushioning him, welcoming.

It seemed like eons passed the longer they rode the current. Her needy, breathy whimpers of encouragement and his grunts of sheer bliss. Pain and pleasure unlike anything he'd ever known. Yet it didn't seem like enough. No amount of time buried inside her would ever be enough.

"Nate..."

A careening cry, and she shuddered. He crushed his mouth to hers and swallowed the sound while she fell apart in his arms. She contracted around him, milking him, killing him with agonizingly sweet torture. She threw her head back, his lips dragging across her jaw.

Halfway through a string of muttered curses, he opened his mouth wide against her cheek and slightly adjusted his stance to keep them upright. While aftershocks rippled through her and against him, he came with a guttural, primal roar that locked his jaw. Stole his oxygen. Punched his heart.

"Holy..." He jerked, bucked, and died right where he stood.

Jarred to the bone, he heaved air and released her hands. Her arms fell limp at her sides and she dropped her head to his shoulder like he'd screwed her unconscious.

Christ. He'd killed her, too.

Using the last amount of energy he had in reserve, he shoved off the wall, wrapped his arms around her, and stumbled into the bedroom. He collapsed on the center of the bed, her under him, and forced himself into the bathroom to dispose of the condom.

When he returned, he halted dead in his tracks in the middle of the room and...

Died a second time. Or third?

Arms and legs sprawled, she laid with her eyes closed and shallow breaths pushing her breasts toward the ceiling. Stubble burn abraded her cheeks, her neck, and a blush was fading on her chest. Her pale, long lashes left shadows under her eyes. Her skin was as fair as the white sheets, but the small triangle of auburn hair on her mound matched the strands on her head. A fire and ice combination meant to cut him off at the knees.

The strange lump wedged in his throat again. His heart ticked a maddeningly rapid beat and something caused his sinuses to sting.

She moaned. "I feel like I should say *the power of Christ compels you* or something witty like that."

He tried to swallow and failed. "What?"

"It's from *The Exorcist*." One eye peeked open. "The movie?"

"I've seen it." He was only slightly more surprised she could quote the film than the fact she'd compared him to demonic possession.

What they'd done slammed through his mind. Rather, what he'd done *to her*. Shoving her against the wall. Holding her down. Driving into her with brutal strength. He *was* a monster who never should've touched her. His chest hitched.

167

He rubbed a shaking hand across his jaw. "Did..." Christ, his voice was gravel. He cleared his throat and tried again, barely managing a whisper. "Did I hurt you?"

"Lord, no." She turned her head and smiled, oblivious to his distress. "How are you still standing? Moving my eyes is too much effort."

He had no idea, but he sat by her hip and ran his gaze over her. Carefully, he lifted her arm and skimmed his fingers across her wrist, not finding any redness or marks. He leaned sideways and did the same with her other arm, then checked her hips. By the time he got to her throat and face, his hands were shaking uncontrollably.

She stretched. "What are you doing?"

"I..." He sighed. "Checking for bruises." Of all his sins, and there were many, this was the absolute worst. "I'm sorry, baby."

Chapter Seventeen

Checking for bruises? And he was...*sorry*?

Olivia leaned on her elbows and took in Nate's distraught expression. It was apparent he thought he'd been too rough. Though she appreciated the sentiment, disappointment churned in her belly. She'd figured once she got him to finally let go, he'd push past this mindset of not being good enough and the constant need to hold back.

Guess she was wrong.

She tried to school her voice calm when tears threatened. "Twice you asked if you hurt me and twice I said no." Yes, his first initial thrust had caused a minor ache due to his size, plus she hadn't had a lover in awhile. But it had also been amazingly intense. Within seconds, the slight twinge had dissolved and she'd never been more desperate, more turned-on in her life.

His throat worked a swallow. "You deserve better than that, than to be taken like an animal."

"Did you hear me complaining?" She sat up, wanting to cover herself, but refrained. He didn't respond, keeping his gaze trained on her throat, and her irritation mounted. "I didn't hear you complaining, either."

His gaze flicked to hers. "This isn't about me."

"Exactly. It's about you and me. We agreed if one of us wasn't onboard with an aspect, we'd say something." She studied him, but couldn't tell if he was even listening. "I taunted you, got you riled. I all but ordered you to take what you wanted. I'm still reeling from the orgasm and you're...*sorry*?"

Insulted, she climbed from bed and started for the bathroom, but he grabbed her wrist to stop her.

A battle waged in his eyes as he stared at their hands, then his gaze slowly lifted to hers. "Don't be angry with me for being concerned. It's not something I have any control over and it's an entirely new emotion for me."

Her shoulders slumped. "That's not why I'm upset. I love that you care, Nate. What I don't like is that you regret what we did."

"I don't..." He closed his eyes a beat. "I should regret it. I really should. My past mistakes are a constant reminder why we're wrong, but all my instincts are screaming for something else. For you." He glanced away, the look in his eyes telling her he thought he'd said too much.

"I've never had passion like that before. There's a time and place for lovemaking, but there's nothing wrong with what we did, too. It was...barbaric." And Lord, she'd loved it.

"Barbaric," he repeated quietly. "I don't know any other way." His expression indicated he wanted to learn, to try. He opened his mouth to say more, but shook his head instead.

After a moment, his hands settled on her waist and he drew her closer to stand between his knees. Then, he dropped his forehead to her stomach, and tears threatened a second time. This side of him was hard to contend with, hard to face. He seemed to constantly fight his nature for caring.

A thought drifted in and out of her subconscious. Too fast to take root and she dismissed it immediately. Still, she brought it up, regardless. "Was it disappointing for you? Was I...unsatisfactory?"

She was no idiot. She knew when a man was enjoying himself, and Nate had been as into the sex as her. It didn't hurt to throw the notion out there, though. Considering his history, maybe she wasn't enough for him long-term.

His head jerked up so fast, she got whiplash. His seething glare had goosebumps rising over her arms. "No," he growled. "No, no, and no."

Well, okay. That settled that.

He sighed, his features relaxing. He stared at her a beat, then wrapped his arms around her and planted her on the bed sideways to face him. Reaching up, he smoothed her hair from her face. "Don't be mad anymore."

Lord, this man. "Quit assuming facts not in evidence and I won't be."

"All right. As long as you don't ever label yourself unsatisfactory again." His lips curved in a pained smile and he lowered his tone. "It's never been like that for me, either."

She smiled back to erase the little remaining tension. Tracing his stubbled jaw with her fingertips, she took in his golden-brown gaze and melted. He had such an expressive face at times and his puppy dog eyes were this side of aw-shucks. Soft, down-turned lids that contrasted the sharp line of his brows. Criminally long lashes.

Dropping her attention to his full lips, she pressed a kiss there and lingered. He smelled so good, like warm male and soap, and she wanted to burrow into him. There was something innately settling about being wrapped inside his embrace. More so knowing she was probably the first woman he'd held in that manner.

"Now what, baby?" He brushed his nose against hers and tilted his head, giving her a barely-there kiss. He moved over her cheek, feather-light, and stopped at her ear. His breath caressed the shell and she shivered. "I'm not sure what comes next. Typically, this is where I get dressed and leave."

"Well, we have two options." She ran her hand across his pec and down his rippled abs, earning a sharp inhale. "We can go to sleep or..." She caressed his growing erection with the back of her hand.

He groaned, sucking her earlobe into his mouth. "Or what, baby?"

"Or..." She nuzzled his throat, kissing and licking her way over his neck to the spot she found drove him nuts. Just to the left of his pulse and shy of the tendon now straining. "Or you can show me what other caveman moves you have in reserve."

"I'm liking option two very much." He tilted his head to give her better access and shoved his hand in her hair, panting. "Are you sure? So soon after—"

She rolled out of his arms, reached in the nightstand for a condom, and rolled back. She slapped the foil packet to his chest. "The only thing that hurt me was your behavior afterward. Take me again. Like you mean it this time."

Nostrils flared, he stared at her like he was rearing to snap again. "I meant it the first time."

"Prove it." She traced his gluts and wove around to grab his rock hard backside.

A low growl rumbled from his chest to hers. "Don't you want something slower? Less...?"

"Less like you?" She lifted her brows in question. "We have time for slow later. Right now, I just want you. The real you. I'm here because I want to be."

Still, he resisted. He stared at her, gaze darting back and forth between her eyes, his mouth firm. "I don't want to hurt you."

Dang it. "Nate—"

"No." Tossing the condom by a pillow, he slid his hand around her neck and into her hair, fisting the strands and forcing her to look at him. "I mean afterward. You said I hurt you and now I'm upset."

Breaths heaving, he eased his face closer until they shared oxygen and his determined gaze pinned her immobile. "Let's do this again, baby. I want to hear that sexy little noise you make in your throat when I pound into you. To feel your hot flesh gripping me. To watch your eyes lose focus and your cheeks burn from passion." He nipped her lower lip. "There are an unspeakable amount of things I want to do to you. And when we're done, I won't hurt you like last time. Understand me?"

There. *There* was the man she'd been trying to find and bring to the surface. The one unhindered and unafraid and uncontained.

Every square inch of her skin heated and her breath stalled in her lungs. Her core throbbed and her breasts ached, and she succumbed to it all. To what he could give her. She was putty in his huge, capable hands.

"Yes," she hissed and arched toward him, needing him on a level she'd never realized was possible. His lost to her found. His seeking to her waiting. A destination finally in reach. "Yes, Nate."

His nostrils flared again, but he drew a measured breath, watching her through narrowed slits. Then, he rolled her to her back and straddled her. Hands braced on the mattress by her head, he hovered over her until she was completely, blessedly surrounded by him.

Direct gaze searing with temptation and promise.

Full, lush lips parted with shallow oxygen exchange.

Straining muscles covered in ink that rippled with tension.

Bulging biceps and coiled forearms.

Wide chest and pecs and six-pack abs that were more like a case.

Veins and tendons and dark skin.

Firm, solid thighs and, between them, his beautiful erection. Thick and long. Velvet over steel.

As if liking her attention, he rolled his hips, grazing her belly with the hard length. So badly, she wanted to touch him, but she sensed that might trip him over some kind of edge. Keeping her arms at her sides, she looked him over again, enjoying the view, growing wetter with the perusal.

He pressed his hand between her breasts, splaying his fingers, and eased it lower. Rough calluses deliciously grazed her flesh. Watching her, he made a path past her abdomen to her mound and cupped her heat. She bucked into his touch, but he merely tilted his head as if coming to a conclusion.

Rising, he sat on his haunches and reached for the condom. Gaze locked on hers, he bit through the foil and sheathed himself. "There's a difference between want and need. Earlier, you asked me what I wanted and I said you." He flipped her over onto her stomach and covered her with his body, settled his hips between her legs. While she was still reeling, he brought his lips to her ear and shifted behind her. His thick crown parted her folds. "Thing is, baby. I don't just want you. I need you."

He traced the shell of her ear with his tongue and brought one arm up beside her face. Ink and skin blurred together to create a hazy kaleidoscope. Soughing for air, for relief from the painful ache of desire, she rolled her hips.

He groaned and chuckled against her cheek, the sound low and strained. "Tell me what you want, what you need, and I'll give it to you."

She was going to die in a puddle of unspent yearning if he didn't stop torturing her. "You..."

No sooner had she whispered the word and he thrust inside. Stretched her. Filled her. Stole her breath and sanity.

He stilled as if to give her a moment to adjust, then slid his arm between her and the mattress. His fingers scissored around where they were joined, palm pressing her clit, and tingles shot through her. She moaned, rolling her hips, but not getting much relief because of his weight. His other arm worked under her chest until he cupped the side of her face and cradled her head in his hand.

She blinked, completely leveled by the conflicting emotions his move instilled. The sweetness of holding her while he sinfully worked her body. Covered it. Surrounded her. And like before, she had no idea what do. She was entirely at his mercy, willingly so, and overwhelmed by desperation to ease her need. There was something utterly freeing and frustrating about it. Like hanging by her fingernails from a ledge and simultaneously letting go to plummet.

His breath caressed her cheek. "Tell me you want me." The grated, whispered demand made her heart pound harder.

"I want you."

He pulled out and thrust inside, his palm adding pressure to her clit. She cried out at the violent pleasure.

His nose brushed her ear as he tilted his head. "Tell me you need me."

"I need you." So, so, so much.

Again, he repeated his motion, and she pinched her eyes shut at the jarring satisfaction. "Then, I'm yours, baby. For as long as you'll have me." Another thrust. "You're mine."

Oh God. "Nate..."

He groaned. "I know, baby."

This time, he didn't thrust, he drove home. Swift. Brutal. With short, firm plunges, he pounded into her. Repeatedly. With each filling, his fingers slid along her folds and his palm added more and more pressure where she needed it most. She could do little more than lie there, taking him, completely submissive under his weight.

And she loved it.

He enclosed her body with his, stretched her to the point there was no room for doubt. Her breasts, crushed against the mattress, became more tender as her nipples peaked. Tension knotted her shoulders as she sought her release. His grunts fueled her on and a warning of an impending explosion clutched her midsection.

Fisting the sheets, she splintered. Light and kinetic energy blasted through her, rendered her motionless as she came on a silent scream. She trembled under him, felt the white-hot burn through her whole system. Again and again. Gasping, she opened her eyes.

He never let up. "You're not done." Harder, he pumped, and they drifted higher up the bed. His palm smacked the headboard as if to gain leverage. "Come again."

The graceful motion of his body and shift of muscle against her contradicted the carnal, fraught way he took her. Savage. Dominating.

He dipped his head and latched onto her neck, swirling his tongue over the spot that made her eyes roll back in her skull. His

174

fingers moved from her folds and flicked her clit, then he pinched the nub and...

She buried her face in the sheets, trying to chase yet another white light. With every retreat, he rubbed her sensitive flesh, and with each plunge, he filled her anew. Rhythmic. Beautifully jarring. A mating and a promise and a declaration.

He grew rigid behind her and pulsed deep inside her. Opening his mouth wide on her shoulder, he groaned. Loud. Long. "Now, baby. Christ, please."

Knowing he was on the brink, holding out for her, and that she was the very thing standing between him and bliss, was enough to send her to the cliff with him. She whimpered and...

Something seismic ruptured inside her. She bowed and came a second time, the orgasm ripping through her. Muscle locked around bone and her cells liquefied. Unable to take it, she wailed into the mattress as quake after quake assaulted her.

He cursed a wicked streak and dropped his forehead to her nape. Froze. Shuddered. Rolled his hips. Pumped several more times. And...collapsed onto her with a grunt. He pulled out, rolling to his back beside her, chest heaving. They lay next to one another for long moments, obscenely panting.

Finally, an eternity later, he removed the condom and stared at it.

She could barely blink. "There's a trash can on the floor beside the bed."

He glanced over with a groan and discarded the condom. "Thank Christ. I don't think I can move." His brow furrowed and he gingerly bent his knee. Rubbing his thigh, he turned his head and looked at her. "Doesn't look like you can, either."

"Maybe next week. With proper motivation, that is." Lord, she felt good. Sated and exhausted and properly sore in all the right areas. "What's wrong with your leg?" He kept massaging it.

"The injury. Stiffens up sometimes. I'm fine."

He probably needed fluids. Gearing herself, she shifted to the edge of the mattress. If memory served, he had a couple sports drinks up here from her fever.

"Where are you going?"

She paused on his side of the bed. "To get you a Gatorade. Be right back."

"If you can walk, I did something wrong." He patted the sheets. "I'm fine. Come here."

Leaning over him, she smiled. "You did everything right. Now be quiet." She gave him a brief kiss and made her way to the kitchen on shaky, spent legs. Funny, she'd never moseyed around her suite naked before. She snatched a bottle from the fridge and returned to find him sitting up, leaning against the headboard. "Drink. Rejuvenate."

He smiled and took the bottle. "Thanks."

She climbed back in and covered them with blankets. He downed half the drink before recapping it and setting it on the nightstand, then laid on his side to face her.

His gaze swept over her as he propped his head in his hand. "You're goddamn beautiful after you come. All the time, actually, but especially after sex."

The air seeped from her lungs. "That's much better than I'm sorry."

His brows pinched as his throat worked a swallow. "Would it be redundant to apologize for saying sorry? My intention wasn't to hurt you. The opposite." He tucked a strand of hair behind her ear, gaze following the movement. "I don't know what the hell I'm doing, Olivia. Literally and metaphorically."

The point being, he was trying. That's all that mattered. He wanted to evolve and move on. "In the past, what did you do when faced with something uncertain?"

"Fight blind." He twisted his lips in thought. "Or run. Depends."

"Well, you're not alone, so fight with another set of eyes. And I'll catch you if you run." She grinned. "I'm very fast."

Amusement shone in his eyes. "Olivia Cattenach, are you telling me you'd chase me?"

She suspected she would, to the ends of the earth and back. He'd lit a spark inside her, and not just lust. His dark side called to hers as if reaching out for a mutual healing. Somehow, he was filling a need she didn't know she had. Companionship. Strength. Safety.

"Are you thinking about leaving?" It hadn't occurred to her, but there wasn't anything tying him here.

Gradually, he sobered. After the longest pause, he cleared his throat. "If there was the slightest chance I was capable of leaving you, there's a greater one I never will." He closed his eyes as if frustrated. "I don't understand how you get my thoughts out of captivity and sprung from my mouth." He looked at her with a frown. "What I mean is, I plan on sticking around until you ask me to leave."

"Because you promised Justin?"

"Yes." But he absently shook his head in denial like he wasn't aware he was doing it. "He said something once. We were talking about old girlfriends and I asked why he didn't have a current one. He gave me that cheesy grin of his and replied, *if you're with someone who makes you a better person, hold onto them. I haven't met her yet.*" He huffed a laugh and rubbed his eyes. "Totally forgot about that."

And he chose now, right this second, to remember. Because he thought she made him a better man. The compliment wove around her jugular and squeezed. "You're a good person, Nate."

He slapped his hand between them on the bed with a weary sigh. "I think you're the first person to ever think such a thing. Definitely the only one to say it." His brows rose as if solidifying his argument.

"Justin knew. He wouldn't have sent you here, otherwise. Aunt Mae wants to adopt you, plus you have the respect of my ranch hands. You even managed to win over Amy and Nakos. No small feat with those two." She rubbed her thumb across his lower lip. "I do believe you're outnumbered."

His hesitant gaze trailed a path over her face like he was trying to memorize her features. "I should get back to my room." He leaned in and kissed her forehead.

"Why?"

He paused, blinking as if he genuinely had no clue how to respond. "Isn't that what you want? Besides, the others will know something's going on tomorrow morning if I'm up here."

One step forward, two steps back. "First, you've been crashing on my couch for more than a week. Second, if they haven't figured out what we're up to, they're blind. Third, I'm not ashamed to be with you. And lastly, no, I don't want you to go." She took his hand in hers. "How am I supposed to wake you up doing naughty things if you're downstairs?"

His mouth opened and closed on a frown. "Are you sure?"

"Turn off the light. Yes, I'm sure."

After a pause, he whistled for Bones, then reached over and switched off the lamp, flooding the room in moonlight. Once Bones jumped onto the bed and settled, Nate eased closer to her and reclaimed her hand, threading his fingers through hers.

She snuggled up to him, tangling their legs and burying her face in his chest. Hard and impenetrable as he was, he made a good pillow.

He sighed and kissed her hand. "Perhaps you could explain these naughty things you mentioned. To prepare myself."

She smiled against his hot, scented skin. "Where's the fun in that?"

Chapter Eighteen

Nate's first cohesive thought? He'd piled on too many blankets last night. He was hotter than hell. The second thought being, Bones had grown awfully affectionate if he was licking Nate's neck to wake him.

Wait...

A female hum vibrated his skin, followed by the scent of rain.

On a sharp inhale, his eyes flew open. Olivia's room. Sunlight. Auburn hair in his face. Breasts crushed to his chest. Her hand roaming from his hip to his ass as they lay on their sides, facing each other. Her tongue...driving him insane.

He groaned. "What time is it?"

"Almost eight." She kissed his chin and smiled at him, her cornflower eyes alight. "Good news. At breakfast, Nakos said he gave the guys the rest of the weekend off to gear up for spring harvest. We can stay in bed all weekend, if you want."

Want? She was grabbing his ass and sending the nerves behind his ear—make that his neck again—into hyperactive by using that damn talented mouth, and she wondered what he wanted?

He tried to think through her assault. His heart thundered. If it was almost eight, he'd slept nine solid hours, nightmare free. Plus, she'd already had breakfast, which meant she'd snuck in and out of bed without him knowing. Christ, she was some kind of sedative if...

"Ah, the rest of you is fully awake now, too." She lifted her head. "Good morning." Her husky voice and wild morning hair were a one-two punch of sexy and cute.

Since he needed to kiss her more than he needed air, he did. He slanted his mouth over hers and she welcomed him inside with lazy, seductive strokes of her tongue. She tasted like melon and smelled like heaven.

Though the blood heated in his veins, the kiss was unrushed, and he didn't mind. Any of it. The fact that one of his first instincts of the morning was to kiss her, an act he rarely participated in, and that it was more about sentiment than seduction, should have his triggers kicking in. Instead, he sank into her, oddly turned-on and confused.

179

Hell, her lips were soft. She was soft everywhere, but her mouth fascinated him. She always seemed to use the right amount of demand, depending on his mood, and kept pace like she could read his mind. She had this quirk of going after his lower lip before parting hers, caressing and testing, then exploring. She was a hot, wet cavern he could spend hours navigating. No two experiences were alike with her and with each instance he found himself falling deeper into her web.

Another thing he didn't mind and should.

She eased away with a contented hum, nuzzling his jaw, and the rasp from his stubble scratched the air. "Think you can let me run the show?"

He paused.

Honestly, he didn't know. He'd never ceded control in the bedroom and rarely did out of it. Twice now, he'd taken her rough and hard. According to her and her reaction, she'd enjoyed herself. Hell, he'd more than enjoyed it. She was dragging him out of his world and into hers bit by bit each second of the day. Damn if she wasn't making him feel less like an asshole and more like a part of the human race, too.

Would it kill him to try her way? She hadn't steered him wrong yet.

Panic didn't pound his temples, so he nodded.

Urging him to his back, she straddled him. His pulse shot up twenty beats, but he was more curious than uncomfortable. She leaned over him, hands planted on the mattress above his shoulders, her hair a red curtain. The position had her pert nipples grazing his pecs in a groan-inducing tease.

"Let me know if it's too much." Her gaze warm, her smile warmer, she gave him a brief kiss and dipped her head to swirl her tongue over his collarbone. "Still breathing?"

No. Seemed he'd forgotten how. At the reminder, he sucked oxygen and closed his eyes.

Between her sexy little mouth and the feather-light brush of her hair, his skin was on fire. Just when he thought he was getting used to her touch, she proved him wrong. As she moved lower, he got caught up in her slender frame shifting over him. The fair skin, the scattering of freckles, her auburn strands...the fact he was letting her be on top.

He was so enthralled that when she sucked his nipple into her mouth, he barked a shout of surprise. He bucked into her ministrations and grew frustrated not knowing what to do with his hands. Twice he reached for her and wound up fisting them instead. By the time she got to his other nipple, he was losing circulation in his fingers.

She knelt between his legs, kissing his navel, and her intentions became clear. Air burned in his lungs at the effort of breathing. She grabbed his hips, kneading, and he slammed his eyes shut.

It had been eons since he'd had a woman go down on him. He considered it foreplay and too much of a hindrance to his in-out motto. Truthfully, he could count on one hand the number of times he'd allowed it and he'd still have fingers remaining.

Closer, closer, she inched.

Once her breath fanned his shaft, he was throbbing and climbing out of his skin. Anticipation clawed his gut. His heartbeat cracked ribs. His muscles threatened to solidify with tension. Loving and hating every second, he pressed his palms to his eyes.

And then she took him in her mouth, and it was lights out. Scorching heat and wet suction. Firm fingers around his base, pumping the life right out of him. He bowed off the bed in an effort not to thrust, grinding his hips. His crown hit the back of her throat and he roared.

He slapped his palms to the headboard. Said her name a thousand times.

Christ save him, she started using her tongue. He sprang from her mouth with a pop, and she licked the underside of his shaft. Swirled around his crown. Cupped his balls.

Sweat broke out on his forehead as he fought the urge to shove himself deeper, to let his baser side take over. Utter torment. Sheer pleasure. The combination felled him. Worse was he had no clue how to handle it. Though there was something tragically exhilarating about handing her the reins, it went against every rule he'd put in place. For a reason. The level of trust he'd given her alone had his windpipe collapsing.

Again, she took him deep in her mouth, and he dug his fingertips into her headboard. He bent his knees, pressed his heels into the mattress, and carefully rolled his hips, making sure not to raise his pelvis off the bed and hurt her.

She hummed around his shaft as if encouraging him. Vibrations. Fire. His balls tightened and his lower back pinched in warning.

"Baby, I'm..."

Faster, her hand pumped. Harder, her mouth sucked. Firmly, she massaged his sack.

Uhn. "Shit...baby." A growl raked his already raw throat. *"Now."*

He threw his head back and came on a blinding stream of misery wrapped in bliss. Jerking, he let out a carnal groan that emptied his lungs. She swallowed his jets, mercilessly never easing up, and his release dragged out an eternity.

When his shuddering finally subsided and he collapsed, arm over his face, she kissed his hip, his outer thigh, then the inner. Her fingers traced patterns on his skin and wove through the light hair on his legs.

Chest heaving, he lifted his head to look down at her. And mercy. If he were the type of man to weep, he might've right then.

Cornflower gaze on her task, she outlined the series of red scars from where shrapnel had embedded itself during the explosion. There were seven in total, all ranging from a one-inch circle to a three-inch linear line. Some were raised, others barely noticeable. He'd been lucky that none had completely severed muscle or tendon and had been easily removed surgically.

But the tender way she touched them, ran her lips over the marks, was like getting hit all over again. This time square in the gut. Like he was five-years-old and had scraped his knee, she acted as if she could kiss it better.

His chest tightened and he rubbed his eyes, unable to watch. Jaw clenched, he shook his head. Some memories couldn't be erased or rewritten, no matter how endearing the attempt. But she just kept right on trying, going at him with enough compassion to level even his glacially reserved heart.

And it was working. Sometimes, she even had him believing her efforts were worth it.

It had been so long since he'd allowed hope to take root. He didn't trust the emotion. As a kid, he'd prayed to someday not be transferred from one foster parent to another. None had been home, nor the people inside his family, and he'd desired only that. The displaced faith of a young, stupid boy. As a teen, he would've settled for a friend. Just one person who didn't seek him out for an end game or because they needed him for dirty work. By the time he'd grown into a man, all humanity had been stripped from him. His life had become about existing, nothing more.

One foot in front of the other. Rinse and repeat.

Then Justin Cattenach had landed in his unit. He'd shared stories of his family as if incorporating Nate into the fold, welcoming him in. Had made the effort to ask about his life, not only hearing the answers, but truly listening like he gave a damn. He'd been the only genuine friend Nate had ever known. With one lopsided grin, he'd turned Nate into a somebody. Proved he wasn't a ghost among the fray.

And Nate had repaid the favor by getting the poor, sweet bastard killed.

On Justin's dying breath, he'd sent Nate to Olivia. To look after her. Protect her. But she'd picked up where her brother had left off, infiltrating Nate's mind and body until he didn't know whether to believe a lifetime of experiences or the whispered words and actions of an abandoned angel.

Hope? Love? All weaknesses he thought he'd scraped from his mind, had purged from his soul.

Damn it to hell. He had to tell her the truth. Somehow, he had to find a way to explain he was the guy who'd screwed up, that he was the reason her brother was gone. Until then, he was only compounding more lies and hurting her. If Nate—a frigid, useless asshole—was falling as hard for her as he suspected he was, then she was probably already there.

How was he supposed to rip her world apart a second time?

"Where did you go?" She pressed a kiss to his hip, then climbed up his body to lay beside him. Curling against his side, she cupped his face to force him to look at her. "You seemed like you were miles away."

Sighing, he wrapped an arm around her to tug her closer and kissed her forehead. "Just recuperating. Your mouth is a weapon of mass destruction."

She laughed in that whimsical, sleepy way that caused his heart to leap.

He turned on his side, sharing her pillow. He stared into her eyes, the bluest damn things he'd ever seen, and wondered if he could be patient enough to return the favor.

Since the second she'd stood in front of him in all her beautiful glory, he hadn't been able to get certain fantasies out of his head. Like tasting every inch of her soft, fair skin and playing a twisted version of connect the dots with her freckles and his tongue. But he wasn't exactly a romantic guy and he knew even less about...seduction.

Her eyes narrowed playfully. "What are you thinking about? Tell me."

"I'd rather show you." He rolled her to her back and rose over her. "Where to start?"

She grinned. "Wherever you like."

He grunted and brushed his lips across hers. "Here?"

Her lids drifted closed. "Seems as good a spot as any."

Tilting his head, he teased her lips apart with his own and dipped his tongue inside. At the first brush of hers, he retreated and did it again. He'd devoured her before and it had made his blood boil, but this measured enticement had everything inside him rousing to take notice. Chills of awareness skated over his skin and his heart thumped as if the organ wanted to reach through his chest to get to her.

Groaning, he went for a longer swim and, with their mouths wide, he swirled his tongue around the tip of hers. Her uneven exhale caressed his lips and he groaned again. Instinct told him to claim, but he dialed it back and kissed his way across her jaw to her throat. She tilted her head back, her fingers stroking his scalp.

Funny, he'd never entertained the notion of his head being an erogenous point, yet her touch seemed to send his pulse out of whack. She'd done it before when they'd kissed, but he paid closer attention this time to the nuances, the details he'd overlooked.

He moved lower to the light dusting of freckles on the swells of her breasts. "I goddamn adore your freckles, baby."

"Really?" She gasped when he took a nipple into his mouth, tracing the areola with his tongue. "I didn't think they were all that attractive."

Lifting his head, he met her gaze. "They are." Then he shut her up by giving the other pebbled peak equal attention. While they were both damp, he teased them into stiff buds with his thumbs. "You're beautiful."

She gripped his head and arched, silently seeking more. A flush worked up her chest to infuse her cheeks while she looked at him through heavy lids. She sunk her teeth into her lower lip, reddening it to a darker hue.

How could he have gone his whole adult life without this? Watching her pleasure, her need slowly build, was hotter than the surface of the sun.

He licked a path to her navel, and the scent of rain on her skin mixed with her arousal. Heady. Addictive. She rocked her hips as he spread her legs, settling between them. Instead of giving her what she wanted, he tortured them both by kissing her inner thigh, then grazing it with the stubble on his jaw.

Whimpering, she threw her hands over her head, closing her eyes once again.

Christ, he was going mad and she wasn't even touching him. He kissed her other thigh, dragging his lips north. With every centimeter of progress, she panted wilder.

Grinding his shaft into the mattress for relief, he set his hands under her hips and lifted her pelvis clean off the bed. Because it was fantasy number seven-hundred and twelve, he bit the perfect round globe of her ass. She cried out and trembled, nearly flailing out of his grasp. Encouraged, he bit the other one.

Her head whipped to the side, fingers white-knuckling the pillow, her cheeks crimson with desire. "Nate..."

And suddenly, her pleasure, her pain, was his, too. Her every quake and moan and inhale became his own. He couldn't tell which one of them was doing what, couldn't see they were two separate people anymore. Where she led, he'd follow. He'd do anything, give up everything, to keep her.

"Be my oxygen, baby, and I'll take your breath away." He had no idea where the sentiment had spouted from, but it was the first thing that had come into his head. No truer words had passed his lips.

"Oh God, Nate. You already have." Her lashes fluttered and she looked at him. Begging and pleading. Destroying him.

Again, a surge of adrenaline hit him and demanded he take. Gnashing his teeth, he fought it and dipped his gaze to her small triangle of red curls. Heart pumping, he parted her folds with his thumbs. It had been some time since he'd done this, but he remembered a few tricks. And she was ten times the woman than his previous partners.

Watching her closely, he ran his fingers through her slickness and coated her swollen nub. She thrust her head back and mewled. He sank two digits inside her and curled them. Her walls greedily gripped him. Then, he flicked her clit with the tip of his tongue, and she started to unravel.

While he pumped his fingers and flattened his tongue over her hot little button, she undulated against him, rolling her hips and issuing the sexiest noises known to mankind. He kept at her, and it killed him to keep the pace steady when she smelled irresistible and tasted even better. Faster, her hips rocked and, a few thrusts later, she contracted around him.

She wrinkled her brows in a pain/pleasure mix that froze on her face for several elongated moments. She trembled, her whole body, and he eased her down slowly while he hit the end of his rope.

When she soughed air again, he rose, went into her nightstand, and rolled a condom down his throbbing length. Kneeling between her legs, he grabbed her thighs and brought her knees up to her chest, spreading her wide.

He leaned forward and kissed her, hard, then waited for her eyes to open. "Come on, baby."

There. *Right there*. All that blue.

She held his face and smiled at him. "Can't talk right now."

"You only need to feel." He buried himself inside her and stilled when she gasped. "Feel me." He pulled out and pushed back in. Heaven. Goddamn heaven. And she was right there with him, succumbing. It was evident in her eyes, in her parted lips, in the way she held him. All he could do was surround himself with her, with them. "Christ, baby. Feel me."

With a hand behind his head, she brought his mouth down to hers and kissed him.

His hips pistoned as he took her with punishing thrusts that matched his errant need, the kiss a direct link to the conflicting sentiment of emotion. His body said claim. His heart said keep. And he couldn't get his mind to engage any thought tied to reason.

Her hands shook against his cheeks, and he worried it was too much for her. But when he broke away from her mouth and glanced at her, he realized she was close to coming again. He worked his arm between them and circled her clit with his thumb. On a cry, she raised from the pillow to rest her forehead to his.

The intimate, charming gesture knocked the wind out of him. Fighting, clawing, he said her name. An oath. A prayer. And she whispered his as an orgasm claimed her.

Wild. Untamed.

He followed, helpless to do otherwise.

Chapter Nineteen

Behind the barns and near the open pasture, Olivia took a sip of lager and grinned at the story Amy's brother Kyle was telling Nate about Justin's first black eye, right after he'd broken his leg falling from a cottonwood.

A bonfire crackled in the center of their small circle of chairs, a radio off to the side playing flashback songs from the nineties. Temperatures had finally begun to warm, yet the nights still held a nip in the air. The scent of firewood mingled with fresh grass and blooms.

It had taken two weeks, but the winter wheat had been harvested. They were relaxing this weekend before planting the spring crop. Most of the ranch hands had gone into town, aside from her few close friends, to let off some steam.

She glanced at the blackened sky, twinkling with stars, and a pang of longing hit her. Between Kyle's story and working the fields, she missed Justin something fierce. Spring had always been his favorite season.

"So then, he waddles right up to me and says, *I'm not gonna tell you again. I can ride faster than you with a gimp leg and blindfolded.*" Kyle laughed. "Eight years old, and he was stubborn as hell, even then. He's got this giant cast covering him from thigh to ankle, and the dumbass tried mounting the horse. Fell right off and took a faceplant."

Nate chuckled and glanced up from the block of wood he was whittling in the chair next to hers. "Sounds like him, all right. I'd like to tell you he grew out of his obstinate behavior in the military, but that would be a lie."

Nakos cleared his throat. "Must run in the family."

Olivia sent him a baleful glance. "Said the pot to the kettle."

With a grin, Nakos looked around her to Nate. "What are you making over there?"

"No clue." Nate continued to work the tool, wood shavings piling at his boots. "Don't really think about it."

"He made me several carvings of Nessie." She stared at her dog between their chairs. "And Bones. Right, boy?"

The dog barked twice, earning a grin from Nate.

"That's it. She's sunk." Amy pointed her beer bottle at Olivia. "Feed into her Loch Ness obsession and she'll do whatever you want."

"I resemble that remark." Olivia glanced at Nate.

He winked at her, then examined what he'd done. "Huh. Looks like this one's for Amy." In his palm was a carving of a camera, no larger than his fist. He tossed it to her two seats down and leaned over to grab his beer from where he'd set it on the ground.

Amy's brows went up. "This is really cool. Thank you."

"Speaking of cameras..." Nate tipped his head. "I saw your photos in Olivia's living room. They're good. When are you going to start using your new equipment?"

She twisted her lips in a pout. "I haven't taken anything out of the boxes. I'm just not comfortable with not knowing who they're from."

Olivia pinned Nate with a glare, silently telling him to spill the beans.

He scratched his brow with his thumb and shared a look she couldn't decipher with Nakos.

After a few beats, Nakos nodded in gradual understanding. "Uh, they're from me."

Olivia looked between the men, wondering why Nate seemingly wanted Nakos to take credit.

"What?" Amy's eyes flew wide. "But, why? And to not tell me?"

Rubbing the back of his neck and disrupting his ponytail, Nakos shot a flickering glance at Nate and back again, obviously uncomfortable. "Yours was busted and I had plenty in savings. Consider it a gift."

She blinked at him as if she'd never seen him before and they hadn't grown up together. "Thank you. I'll pay you back."

"You absolutely will not." Nakos waved his hand in dismissal. "Take photos. That's reward enough."

"But..." She frowned, looking at the carving from Nate. She brushed a strand of long cocoa hair from her face. "Okay. If that's what you want."

Closing his eyes, Nate sighed, one corner of his lip curling in satisfaction. He sent Nakos a nod Olivia interpreted as *thank you*, then took a long pull from his bottle.

Olivia shook her head, not understanding, but kept mum. Honestly, she was just glad he and Nakos were getting along. In fact, the two were developing an interesting bromance. Every time she caught them, they were together working on something or talking.

It made her heart happy Nate was settling in, making friends. He didn't seem to have anyone of substance in his life and deserved to be around people who cared about him. Nakos wasn't the only one, either. Amy adored Nate to death and the other guys always made it a point to acknowledge him.

Ever since he and Olivia had sex that first night, he'd gotten better about other things, too. He smiled more and brooded less. At dinner and breakfast, he sat at the table instead of standing or taking his meal to the porch. Aunt Mae had even coerced him into dessert a time or two. He didn't hesitate when leaning in for a kiss or to hold Olivia's hand when they watched TV. And he never fell asleep without pulling her to his side so they were wrapped up in one another. He hadn't gone back to his bedroom, either, except to change, and he'd get no complaints from her.

Their lovemaking was still intense but, afterward, he was forever gentle. She hoped he would start wanting to be more intimate in that regard. Not that she didn't love wild sex. However, he kept falling back into his comfort zone whenever things got heated. She couldn't pinpoint why, but she suspected there was a part of him holding onto something dark. At times, he looked at her like he had something to say, to admit. Yet he'd clam up and shake his head.

"Oh, I love this song." Amy pointed to the radio. "This was from our senior prom, remember? I haven't heard this in ages."

Olivia recognized Peter Gabriel's, *In Your Eyes*, but forgot it had been their prom theme. "It was, wasn't it?"

"You were a terrible date." Amy looked at Nakos. "This was the only song we danced to."

"Hey, I agreed to attend, not dance."

"Wait." Nate leaned forward. "You two used to go out?"

"No." Amy snorted a dismissal. "Nakos went to school on the reservation. For functions, he'd go with one of us to be included."

"Against my will."

Olivia laughed. "Hardly. And you wanna talk about bad dates? At least yours didn't try to get under your dress at the after party."

"God, he was a loser." Amy sighed and blew a strand of hair off her face. "I can't believe you dated him. For *three months*. And he thought sneaking you into a hotel room was a clear path for sex. Forcefully, I might add. Wow."

"I think he was more clueless than malicious." Olivia figured he'd assumed sex was a part of the whole prom experience. She might've considered it had he not acted like a petulant child.

Nate bared his teeth. Seethed. "Where can I find this person?"

Everyone stared wide-eyed at him, but it was Nakos who eventually broke the silence. "Tom Henderson. Quarterback of the football team and had his eye on Olivia since freshman year. He converted to a Mormon after graduation and lives in Utah now with five wives. Or something. And don't you worry, he walked out of that hotel limping and bleeding."

"My hero." Olivia rolled her eyes. "I did knee him in the balls. I had it handled."

Kyle took a bow in his chair. "And I escorted the fair maiden home."

"That you did." She smiled at him and set her hand on Nate's rigid arm to calm him down. His mouth was still in a tight line, but his shoulders sagged. "Riding on the back of your ten-speed was awkward in an ankle-length gown."

"Shut up." Kyle laughed. "I had Dad's car, thank you very much. And we had fun the rest of the night, if I recall."

Nate tensed again under her palm. She squeezed his arm.

"Sweet Baby Jesus." Amy gagged. "Tell me you two didn't hook up. I might vomit."

"I second that." Nakos rubbed his stomach.

Olivia tilted her head. "Want to tell them our naughty tale?"

Kyle grinned. "If memory serves, we were in your bedroom, it was dark, and we..." He paused. "Watched *The Breakfast Club*. Twice. Popcorn might've been involved." He glanced at his sister. "Get your mind out of the gutter. Sleeping with Olivia would be akin to incest."

Nate let out a quiet, long exhale.

"Be sure to remember that." Amy looked at Nate. "So, any sordid high school tales from Chicago?"

"No." He rubbed his jaw. "I didn't attend dances. They weren't my thing."

And he'd been in juvie by the time his senior year had rolled around. What a shame, too. Prom was like a rite of passage and he'd missed out.

"Well." Olivia rose. "I'm going to bed. You guys okay putting out the bonfire?"

The others nodded and said goodnight as Nate stood to follow her. With the dog at their heels, they headed inside and to her suite, where she stopped in the living room and eyed her stereo. An idea bloomed, and she sorted through her CDs.

Nate came out of the bedroom, minus his shirt. "You coming?"

"In a sec." She loaded Hoobastank's *The Reason* and told Nate to wait there. She went into her bedroom and fished through her closet, grinning when she found what she was looking for. She changed and stepped back into the living room, arms spread. "Ta da."

He turned and froze. His gaze skimmed down the length of her navy blue slip dress and back again, heating with desire on the second pass. "What's that?"

"My prom gown. Can't believe it still fits. Barely." She wiggled. "You like?"

"I just swallowed my tongue, but why are you wearing it?"

"Because you didn't get a prom." She walked to the stereo and hit Play. "Now, dance with me."

His mouth opened and closed, but he didn't move.

She tilted her head, studying him. It didn't matter how many times she looked her fill, seeing him was always a bolt of electricity.

His feet were bare and his jeans hung low on his narrow hips, worn in all the right areas. His hat was off and she had the strongest urge to rub his bald scalp. Contours of muscle and tats came to life when he shifted the slightest bit. Veins and tendons protruded from his dark skin. His clenched jaw ticked in what she'd learned was nervousness.

But his dark, puppy dog eyes searched hers. In question. With understanding. And a flicker of hope.

193

He cleared his throat. "I don't know how to dance. I've never done it before in my life."

"I'll teach you."

Closing his eyes a beat, he sighed and looked at her again. First at the dress, then he met her gaze. "I don't need a...prom. Or whatever this is you're doing."

"Sure you do. Everyone should have a night to dress up and act like a frivolous teen." He'd had so many opportunities stolen from him. She could do this one thing for him, even if it was just the two of them in her living room.

"I'm not dressed up." He glanced at himself. "I'm barely clothed, in fact."

"And thank you for that."

He smiled as if unable to help himself and ran a hand down his face. Shook his head. Looked at her gown again. A furrow grew between his brows. "So, that's the dress your date tried to...?" He growled.

Lord. She held up her hands. "Do remember I kneed him in the balls and Nakos broke his nose." She waved at herself. "Note I'm standing before you in one piece, unharmed."

His eyes narrowed.

"Dance with me. At the very least, you can give me a better memory than when I last wore this."

A glance heavenward, and he walked over to stand in front of her. "You don't play fair, baby. Fine. What now?"

Taking his hands, she placed them around her waist. "High school dances are elementary. We really just have to sway back and forth." She wove her arms around his neck and brought them flush together. Grinning, she looked up at him. "See?"

He grunted. "I see you have no shoes on and I'll probably break your toes."

"Your optimism is staggering." He was adorable all pouty-like. She took a small step to the right, and when he followed suit, she did the same to her left. After a few beats, he relaxed. "Not so bad?"

"If you were my date back then, I might not have minded doing this. The monkey suit, though? No thanks." His hands skimmed up her back and he drew her closer as the song ended. It started again since she'd put it on repeat. He glanced down his nose at her. "Any particular reason you chose this song?"

194

"Caught on to that, did you?" The lyrics were about starting over after finding a special person who gave proper motivation to want to be better. "I dub this our song."

"Our song?" Up went his brows. He glanced away as if listening, then huffed a laugh. "Okay, baby." His throat worked a swallow. "Does this make you my girlfriend or something?"

She rose on her toes and whispered, "I think I have been for a while." At his blank stare, she grew confused. "What term would you use for what we are together?"

He shook his head. "This is your world, Olivia. Your home, your family, your friends. I don't have the foggiest idea what the hell is going on. I just follow you. You're the only person in my world."

Shocked, she paused. If that wasn't the sweetest, most misguided thing she'd ever heard, she'd climb the Laramie naked. "First, just because this started as my world, doesn't mean you're not a part of it. These people? They like you. A lot. Family doesn't always mean blood and they are your friends, too, not just mine."

She took his face in her hands, his stubble rough on her palms. "And that thing they say about one special person in your life? It's a myth. Family, friends, romantic love...it's all precious. Humans, as a species, weren't meant to have just one person. And if they're lucky, if the gods are smiling, they don't."

Studying him, her heart grew heavy. Lord, she wished he'd met Justin sooner. "Luck may not have been on your side, but it is now. You're here, in a new world. Shed the old one and let go. There are people everywhere around you who care."

His fingers twitched on her back. The longer he stared, the more shallow his breathing became until she swore he quit altogether. For a moment, she got a picture of the scared little boy he used to be, hidden beneath the man who still held onto those fears as if they were all he deserved. Clear as day, he was trying, wanting to grab hold of what she offered with both hands. Yet the censure in his soulful eyes said he couldn't quite bring himself to believe.

And she fell in love with him right there in her living room in her bare feet and an old prom dress. She'd laugh if she didn't feel like crying.

Love. She'd been surrounded by it in one form or another her whole life. But not like this. Not in a tragically consuming, she-couldn't-catch-her-breath kind of way. Yet, she loved him. The desperate, lonely boy. The rogue turned soldier. The man whose heart still beat despite life's attempts to crush it. A hero. His defiance, his charm, his utter selflessness in the face of tragedy...

He wasn't just it for her. He was everything she dared not wish for herself.

Truthfully, she'd been no wiser than him. In the wake of her parents' deaths, she'd clung to those she had left and built her world around them. He'd been right before when he'd claimed she didn't seek anything for herself. And perhaps that had been a good thing, else she might not have recognized the real deal when he rode in on a Harley with a cargo of baggage and a *If You're Reading This* letter.

This wrecked, beautifully built man had awoken her, and she hadn't even known she'd been asleep.

Carefully, he gripped her wrists and moved her hands from his face to the back of his neck once more. Then, with a swallow working his throat, he brushed a strand of hair behind her ear. His quiet sigh went right through her, but his tender gaze wrapped her inside him.

One corner of his mouth curled like he wanted to smile, but couldn't commit. "So, was that a yes to the girlfriend question?"

Damn him. She dropped her forehead to his chest and breathed a laugh. Just...damn him. "Yes, Nate." She lifted her face and smiled. "That was a yes."

He grunted and shoved his hand in her hair, holding the back of her head and encouraging her to rest her cheek on his pec. The other arm banded around her back as he started to sway again. She reveled in his warm embrace and the safety there, breathing in his scent.

After a moment, he dropped his chin on top of her head. "Aren't couples supposed to go out? Not that I have a shred of experience in this area, but shouldn't I be taking you on a date or something?"

Pressing her lips together, she smiled against his skin. Lord, he was adorable. "If you want. Why don't we do something you're comfortable with?"

His hand skimmed up and down her spine. "How about a ride on the Hog tomorrow if the weather holds?"

She grinned up at him. "Heck yeah. I've never been on a motorcycle."

"Well, what do you know?" He dipped her and held her suspended over his arm. Pinning her with an amused glare, he smirked. "Something I can teach you for a change."

She grabbed his shoulders and laughed. "I thought you couldn't dance."

"I'm faking it." A grin split his face and, had he not been holding her, she would've melted into a puddle. "Tell no one."

"Your secret is safe with me."

He brought her upright again and she wrapped her arms around his waist to grab his shoulders from behind. She buried her face in his neck and contentedly hummed when he held her close.

"Question." He smoothed her hair. "Why do you do that? Press your face against me?"

"Because you're warm and you smell good and I like being close to you." She blinked, concerned. "Does it bother you?"

"No. I like it." He dipped his head and brushed his nose against her cheek. "Just curious. You do it a lot."

"It also gets me in target range to do this." She licked his pulse, teasing him with the tip of her tongue, knowing it drove him mad every time.

He inhaled, fingers clenching her strands. "Pretty sure you're not supposed to get this feisty at prom."

"Good thing no one else is here." Nuzzling his neck, she lightly scratched her way down his sculpted chest, past the rivets of rock-hard abs, and cupped his length through his jeans. He made a choking sound and she grinned. "Since I'm never going to wear this dress again, how about you tear it off me and take me to bed?"

Without hesitation, he did exactly that.

Chapter Twenty

"Oh my God. This is awesome!"

Nate laughed and revved the Harley's engine to speed down the almost deserted two-lane highway. Wind whipped his face as Olivia's squeal filled his ear. He grinned again, eyeing the flat prairie and long grass swaying across the horizon. The Laramie Mountains shadowed the distance and fencing kept cattle from wandering. The cobalt sky went on for miles.

He didn't dare go much faster, not with Olivia onboard and only one helmet, which he made her wear. But they'd been riding over two hours and she hadn't shown any signs she wanted to head back.

He leaned into a curve, and she wrapped her arms tighter around his waist. Damn, but it felt good having her behind him, her thighs cradling him and her scent of rain melding with late afternoon spring. When he got the chance, he rode often, loving the solitariness of the open road and vibrations under him. It gave him a chance to clear his head, to breathe.

But her? With him? A turn-on to the nth degree.

He checked the mirrors and yelled over his shoulder. "Ready to go home?" He wanted a shower and then to sink inside her. Maybe not necessarily in that order. "Before you answer with no, understand that I'm hard as a rock and your breasts crushed against my back isn't helping." Nor were her hands that kept wandering.

Her laugh wrapped around his balls and cut off circulation. "Okay, bad boy. Take me home."

Christ, finally. If someone had told him six months ago he'd choose a woman over his Hog, he would've had them committed. Instead, he anticipated the second he could get her alone and naked as he turned them around, gunning for the ranch.

Once in the driveway, he removed her helmet and threw her over his shoulder. Her husky laugh overrode the sound of his boots as he climbed the porch, stepped inside, and kicked the door shut. He headed right for the staircase before they could get interrupted by one of the many people who frequented her house, stopping only when he got to the third floor.

He deposited her on her feet in her bedroom. "I need a shower and then I'm yours."

"How about a bath instead?"

One eyebrow quirked, he looked at her.

"With me?" She kicked off her shoes and pulled her tee over her head, revealing a blue bra shades darker than her eyes. Her auburn strands resettled into chaos. She gave him a teasing smile and backed toward the bathroom, crooking her finger. "Hot water. Bubbles. Slippery skin and soap...everywhere. I can make it worth your while."

No doubt about that. He groaned and grabbed her waist. Her toes dragged on the floorboards as he carried her into the adjoining bath.

Giving her a quick kiss, he released her. "On with it."

She filled her square tub with water and suds while he stripped, then she put her hair up in a knot as steam enclosed the generous space.

He climbed in with her back to his front and nearly groaned at the hot water lapping his body. Maybe there was something to this bath thing, especially if she made a habit of joining him. He made quick work of washing the road sludge off him, then took his time with her, and the whole room smelled like rain. Since he'd used her soap, he did, as well.

Nestled between his thighs, she reclined against him, seemingly interested with tracing the inked designs on his forearms. She often did it after sex, too, gaze lost in thought and like she needed the constant connection.

"I think you should take Rip up on the job offer."

He'd almost forgotten. "Why? Trying to get rid of me?"

She laughed. "No, and I love having you around, but I figure police work is better suited for you than ranching. You've been doing great and the guys think so, too. Yet...I don't know. You might be more content, more comfortable to have a badge pinned on your shirt. Some purpose. You can still help out around here and live in the house."

Her suggestion and observation wasn't that far off. He'd had a gun in his hand since he'd enlisted at age eighteen. "I'll think about it."

She grew quiet and contemplative again. Up and down and around went her fingers over his tat sleeves. "Have you visited Justin's grave? Talked to him like I recommended?"

Damn. What had made her travel that path? Between spending time with her, his early morning exercise run, and working with Nakos, Nate hadn't had much time. Besides, what the hell good would it do?

"It makes me feel better. I get the impression you've had something on your mind. Maybe hashing it out with an old friend will help." She squeezed his arm. "Up to you."

The way he saw it, standing graveside for a soldier whose memory haunted him hourly wasn't going to make a dent in his absolution. He had enough ghosts. Chatting with one of them was only bound to make him more batshit.

"Okay," he said to appease her and tried to find something to change the subject. "I haven't taken a bath since I was a kid." He kissed her temple and laced their fingers together, enclosing her to him by crisscrossing their arms. "One of the families I was placed with didn't have a shower. That may have been the last time."

She made a noise as if distracted. "I loved bathtime as a girl. Got my imagination going. I'd splash around for hours. My parents would have to haul me out."

Like food, bathing for him had always been about need, not pleasure.

Their many differences juggled inside his mind and his gut tensed. For weeks, they'd been playing this game of house, of being a couple, and he didn't know how much longer he could do it. The heavy burden of Justin's death kept dragging him back under, reminding him none of this was real. As soon as she learned the truth, everything good he'd ever known would be gone. From day one, she was destined to be his mirage—a tease for what he'd secretly desired, but could never have. The longer he kept at the lie, the worse it would hurt her in the end.

And there would be an end.

"You want children, don't you?" His voice was as rough as the rawness in his throat. But he'd done this to himself. He'd allowed her in, just like he'd done with her brother. Selfish to the core. "You said that once before, right?"

"If for no other reason than to carry on the Cattenach legacy. But, yes. I want kids for personal reasons, too. A big family and a noisy house." She turned her head and looked at him. "I assume you don't, based on your childhood?"

Intuitive little devil. "What the hell do I know about family or raising a child?"

"Most people don't when they first start out. They muddle through."

Yeah, but they had some kind of memories or examples to fall back on. Nate had a cluster of strangers who barely tolerated him on a great day, rendered him invisible on a good one, and used him as a verbal or physical punching bag on a bad stretch. What he knew about right or wrong could fit in an envelope. Kids should be loved and nurtured and made to feel safe.

None of which he'd been given. It made him physically, violently ill to think about what kinds of traits he'd pass down, how pure innocence could be tainted with his DNA.

When he just stared at her, at a loss, she slipped out of his arms and rotated to face him, wrapping her legs around his waist.

Her patient gaze searched his. "If I were to tell you I was pregnant, what would your reaction be?"

Even though he knew her question was hypothetical, his heart stopped dead in his chest. Just...stopped. Panic clutched his windpipe, blocked his airway, and collapsed his lungs.

His reaction? No. Christ Almighty, no.

As if he hadn't screwed up enough for two lifetimes, ruined lives, that would be the worst imaginable thing possible. He'd destroy hers. She was everything beautiful and kind and good this miserable existence called life had to offer. And a...mistake such as that one, just like what he'd done to Justin, couldn't be taken back. Real or not.

But then he lowered his gaze to her abdomen, or where it would be were she not chest-deep in water and suds, and his pulse gained momentum. He knew her body, every precious inch of skin and subtle curve, and a picture shoved to mind. Of her belly swollen with his child. Her delicate fingers resting over the bump. A grin on her glowing face as she reached for his hand to place it under hers.

Something warm filled his chest and expanded, muting the pain he forever carried inside and illuminating corners. His lungs filled. His heart puttered anew.

And shit...his eyes burned.

"Right now." Her lilting voice soothingly cooed to him, the tone as soft as she was making his resolve. "What are you thinking right this second? Once the *oh no* sensation passed, what was the first thing you felt?"

More images came. A little girl with auburn strands and cornflower eyes running through wheat fields, sunlight kissing her fair skin and freckles. A boy with shaggy chestnut hair like Nate's used to be before he'd shaved it, laughing beside her on horseback, his dark eyes smiling in a way Nate's never had. That sense of protection and utter adoration he attributed to Olivia filled him, watching the two small forms disappear over a ridge.

"Happiness," he whispered, choking on the admission. But he shook his head in denial. It couldn't be, could it? Olivia's face grew hazy through a sheen of...tears as he looked to her for guidance. "Happiness?"

Was that what this was? Maybe. He wouldn't know.

Fuck it all. Gutted, he met her gaze again and made a God-awful noise like a dying animal. Because, yes. This was what he imagined happy felt like.

Calm as you please, she set her wet hands on top of his head. "And there's your answer. It doesn't matter where you came from." She placed her palm over his heart. "What matters is what's in here. And you, Nathan, are a good man. You will make a great father someday because you know how awful it is to go without, to be hurt, and you'd never instill what was done to you on another. You're also street smart with honed instincts. But, most of all, despite not having been shown any, you are capable of love."

Christ. If she'd stabbed his carotid with a rusty utensil, it would hurt less.

Nostrils flared, throat on fire, eyes wet, he struggled through the uprising insurgence of mutiny inside his skull, his chest. Every-damn-where. "Baby..."

"Shh." She pressed her lips to his and spoke against them. "You're okay. You're safe."

Hell. For the first time, he just might be. "What are you doing to me?" Gritting his teeth, he hissed and cupped her jaw. Gave her a little shake. "Olivia, baby. What are you doing to me?"

"Nothing. Just giving what you should have had long before we met."

That wasn't nothing and they both knew it. Family, friendship, loyalty, respect, a sense of worth, of belonging, and...a home. Were there no lengths she wouldn't go to?

Her sad, sweet smile was the last straw. She'd broken him. For good.

Rising, he climbed from the tub and held out his hand for her. Once she'd stepped onto the mat, he dried her off, then himself, and carried her into the bedroom. He laid her down on the bed and rose over her. Braced on his forearms, he studied her pretty face, took in each aspect to be sure his suspicions were right. In awe, he gave up fighting and shook his head.

Love. That's what looked back at him.

Though she didn't offer the words, three little syllables he'd never heard, she told him with one glance. He'd seen it often on others, had longed for it himself once upon a time. He relished the flame it kindled in his chest, let it burn and smolder, knowing he'd never feel it again. She should give this gift to someone deserving, and he wouldn't dare tell her in return, but he could show her what she meant to him.

He reached for the nightstand, but she grabbed his hand. "You had frequent check-ups in the Army? You're safe?" At his nod, she swallowed. "So am I, and I'm on birth control."

No protection? She drove him to the brink of sanity, made his heart bleed, and he should genuflect merely being in her presence...but she wanted to drop the last barrier he had at his disposal?

Before he could wrap his head around that, she rolled him to his back and straddled him. Holding his face as if he were the precious one, she leaned in and kissed him. Soft. Tender. A brush of her lips and a sweep of her tongue. She said everything and nothing, and filled the infinite space in between.

Unhurried, he attempted to relay his sentiments in return. How unworthy he was of her. How she was the very thing he never knew he always wanted. How, heaven help him, she showed a monster like him what it meant to be significant.

And with her hair a curtain to shield them from outside world, he gave her his complete trust, put himself in her hands. Let himself slip into the delusion one last time.

She shifted and took him inside her, never breaking from the kiss. Unimaginable heat and soft flesh cradled him, inch by excruciating inch, until he was buried so deep, there would be no resurfacing. No recovery.

His sinuses prickled. His eyes burned. His throat constricted.

She paused, keeping them suspended on the edge of oblivion, and he couldn't move. Couldn't breathe.

He'd not, in his wildest fantasies, imagined just how glorious she'd feel with nothing between them. Heightened. Overpowering. Intense. The sensation took sensitive and gave it a steroid chaser.

Worse was what followed. The blatant, unrefined emotion, the sensual slowness in the way she handled him. She caressed his shoulders, his arms, and laced their fingers. Still, her hips didn't shift, nor did she attempt to seek pleasure.

No. Instead, she made love to his mouth.

He sensed what was coming, but was helpless to stop her. Always before, desire and need had taken hold, had made being with her fierce and passionate. Though those elements hovered in the distance, this moment would be permanently hung on his memory's wall.

Because she made love to him. And he let her.

With a tremor and a shaky exhale, she rocked her hips, her cornflower eyes locked to his. She kept him trapped in her gaze, in the torrent of emotion he found there. Over and over, so damn slowly that he broke out in a sweat, she rode him. Days, years, millenniums passed until her body told him she'd had enough, that she needed him.

Untangling their fingers, he sat up and wrapped his arms around her, never veering from her eyes. The punch of intensity at the connection slammed into him. Her breasts were crushed between them, she held his jaw, and they shared oxygen a suspended beat. Kingdoms could have been erected and destroyed, he'd never be the wiser.

Eyes open, he kissed her—the pressure light, wide-mouthed, and with the barest hint of tongue. And then he thrust. He used his arms as momentum to have her grind as his hips rose. She trembled, whimpered, and her lashes fluttered.

"Don't close your eyes," he pleaded. "Look at me."

When she complied, he thrust again. Heat exploded and planets collided. She rode him, matching his tempo, holding her face close to his so that there was nothing and no one but her. Pace painstakingly deliberate, he repeated the dance, bringing her down around him as he rolled his pelvis.

He flattened his hands on the smooth expanse of her back, then detoured south to grab her ass. Damn, the motion was amazing. Jarring. She wrapped her arms around his neck, caged the back of his head by crossing her wrists. Still, they watched each other, lips mating, bodies knotted, and her heart pounding against his chest.

The result was an epiphany, his version of an apocalypse. Because there would be no life without her. Truthfully, his existence started just a couple short months ago.

And it would end tomorrow when he told her everything.

For now, tonight, he had her. He gave her everything he had left so she'd hopefully find it in her heart, in some distant day, to forgive him. To understand.

She breathed his name, and it took immeasurable restraint not to kick up the rhythm as she grew close to unraveling. Quaking, she looked at him. Pleading. Searching.

"That's it, baby. I'll catch you." Somehow. But who'd break his fall?

Her walls fisted him. "Nate, I—"

He crushed his mouth to hers to stop what she was about to say. It couldn't be taken back and she'd only regret it later. While she came, splintering in his arms, he grieved for the words he'd never get to hear. But that was his punishment. He deserved far worse.

With a shout into her mouth, he followed her and clung to her shaking body as he emptied inside her. Leveled, gasping, he rested his forehead to hers.

Taking in her flushed cheeks, her lips reddened by his kiss, and the sleepy wantonness lingering in her gaze, he died all over again. Christ, he'd never get over this. Over her. He'd almost rather be clueless than know there could be good memories to override an eternity of horrible ones.

Fisting his hand in her strands, he pressed her face into his neck and slammed his eyes shut when the hot threat of tears rose anew. Goddamn agony.

Somehow, he breathed through it, shoved emotion aside, and eased backward onto the mattress. With her on top of him, he kicked the blankets until he could reach the edge and covered them.

Her cheek on his chest, he smoothed her hair from her face and skimmed his hand up and down her spine. Kissed her strands. Let his lips linger. Breathed in her scent. Basked in her warm, soft skin against the hard planes of his body. And stored all of this for later.

"Nate?"

Christ, please. Save him.

"Not tonight, baby. Go to sleep." Arms around her, he held her in a cocoon and prayed she'd listen.

After a few minutes, her breathing evened and he sighed in relief. Once he knew she was out cold, he carefully rolled and resettled her on her side of the bed. He tucked her in and slipped from under the covers to get dressed.

From there, he headed downstairs, packed his meager amount of things, and secured the canvas bag on the back of his motorcycle. Then, he gathered the carved figurines he had lying around and set them on the dresser in the bedroom he'd been using. Hopefully, they'd make her smile and not cause more grief.

Finally, he climbed the stairs to the third floor and sat in the chair in her bedroom.

Watching her sleep, with a heart so heavy it may as well be lead, he dreaded the moment she opened her eyes. The irony wasn't lost on him and only made a mockery of the situation. A month ago, he'd been poised in the same spot, trained to her every nuance and twitch after her injury, scared out of his ever-loving mind she wouldn't wake up.

Elbow on the chair arm, he rubbed his lips. Her long, pale lashes shadowed her cheeks and her auburn strands fanned the pillow. That lush little mouth of hers was partially open as she slumbered away. Her habit of setting her hand under her head and her bare shoulder peeking out from under the blankets only added to the adorableness, fed into the naughty sprite image he'd first envisioned.

He watched her through the night, and when morning broke, he rose to wait for her in the other room.

She'd been right about one thing. Turned out, monsters were capable of love after all. But it didn't mean they should.

Chapter Twenty-One

Stretching, Olivia rubbed her bare legs against the sheets and reached for Nate, but his side of the bed was cool. She blinked against the morning light filtering through the blinds as disappointment hit her.

Figuring he was out running, she smiled and recalled last night while burying her face in the pillow. He'd finally let go. The emotion pouring through him in the way he'd made love to her had been amazing. Earth-shattering. Soul-crushing. After all the horrible things he'd seen and done, that were put upon him, he seemed to be shedding the past and looking toward a future.

About time.

Another stretch, and she slipped out of bed with the sheet around her middle. She padded into the living room, only to abruptly halt.

Nate sat on the sofa, elbows on his knees and head in his hands. He was fully dressed in jeans, boots, and a tee, and the tension radiating off him stalled her heart. Muscles rippled and ink came alive as his fingers fisted.

"I need to tell you something." Slowly, he lifted his head. Shadows darkened, creating caverns under his eyes, and leaving misery etched in the depths. Concern and guilt twisted his mouth.

Oh God. "Is Aunt Mae all right?"

He gave a tight nod. "Everyone's okay. Come sit down."

Nervous, she made her way over on shaky legs and perched on the edge of the cushion. Stomach somersaulting, she looked at his profile.

He flew off the couch like the hounds of hell were chasing him and stalked the room. Eventually, he landed on the other side of the coffee table and ran a hand down his face. "I've had all night to play this conversation out in my head and…" He dropped his arm, hand slapping his thigh.

"You're scaring me."

On a sigh, he pulled his phone from his pocket. "When we were overseas, Justin used to play this song over and over again if he missed home. You, in particular. *When You Come Back to Me Again* by Garth Brooks. Do you know it?"

She shook her head, heart pounding. Justin wasn't much of a country music fan, so she was a little surprised. More over, what did this have to do with whatever had Nate agitated?

His thumbs flew over the keypad. "I think it was intended to be a romantic love song, but he interpreted it differently." He set the phone on the table as a melody played. "Listen to it."

"Okay," she breathed and stared at the cell. She gripped the sheet tighter to her chest with trembling fingers as her pulse tripped, wondering what was going on.

A haunting voice sang a metaphor of ships lost at sea and safe harbors, about sinking without the ties of love to keep them going. She imagined Justin in camo gear, in the desert, earbuds in and listening to this song. How scared and helpless he must've been, how alone. How the world he'd enlisted in was very different than where he'd been raised. No safety net, no people who loved him.

By the time the second verse started, unstoppable tears trekked her cheeks and a hot ball of emotion wedged in her throat. And when it was over, her chest cracked wide open. Burying her face in her hands, she sobbed.

"I'm sorry, baby. I'm so sorry. I did this to you."

Letting out a quivering exhale, she wiped her cheeks and looked at Nate.

Hands at his sides, expression fraught, he shook his head repeatedly. "I took him from you and I'm so goddamn sorry."

Dread settled in her belly. "What?"

"I was the commanding officer who sent him inside that building to die." He slapped his chest and fisted his hand over his heart. "Me." His mouth trembled and his eyes reddened, but he sucked a breath and clenched his jaw. "I made a mistake, a stupid error in judgment."

A block of ice formed in her stomach and spread to every organ. "What are you talking about, Nate?" From the moment she'd found out Justin had been killed, she'd been bitter, angry with the soldier responsible. And Nate was claiming he was that person? "You lied to me?"

Nostrils flared, eyes wide, he gave her a look of such helplessness that the glacier in her belly began to defrost. "I should have told you that first day. I don't know why I didn't. But then things with us evolved and…got out of control."

"Out of control?" Anger ramming her temples, she stood. "Out of control is an icy patch of road like the one my parents hit. I let you into my house, my home, my life. Oh God. I let you into my bed, my…" She clutched the sheet over her heart. Because he was in there, too, embedded deep. Betrayal tore through her, ripped her apart. "I trusted you. I thought you were a good person who just had a crappy start in life…"

Her own words shot back to her and ricocheted inside her skull. She straightened, glancing away. The things he'd told her, had admitted reluctantly, trickled to the surface.

Shoving aside memories and conversations, she honed in on the major ones. Him, a scared little boy in foster care, wanting to be accepted as family. Him, a teenager, making misguided decisions for the sake of forming friendships. His initial inability to be touched or sleep through the night or even eat without remorse. And at the root of it all—blame.

The wind rushed out of her lungs like a gale force. Stock still, she blinked as the fury and deceit dissolved into curiosity and compassion. The one defining factor in Nate's life, in the way he thought and behaved, boiled down to guilt.

And none of it had been his fault. Yes, he was a grown man now who made his own decisions, and yes, his choices weren't always the right ones. But they were formed with good intentions. Most of all, his blame had, nine times out of ten, been displaced.

Reasoning this out, it was entirely possible he was wrong about Justin, too. In fact, odds were in that favor.

"That's what I've been trying to tell you, baby. I'm not that guy, not a good person. I'm no one's hero."

Eyes wet, she lifted her gaze to his. What stared back at her leveled her to the ground and stole the beat from her heart.

The man before her, who'd not been shown an ounce of compassion in all his thirty years, held her gaze with abject empathy in his. Distressed, frantic, and bordering on vicious, his eyes pleaded with her to absolve and condemn him in the same beat.

Because he loved her. It was as obvious as her grief.

Panting, he pressed both hands to his chest. "I promised him I'd take care of you. And I will, from a short, safe distance. I'll leave

211

you alone to live your life. But should you ever need anything at all, I'll come running. Always. You have my word."

His throat worked a swallow and he bent to retrieve his phone. Gaze down, he turned away. "I'm sorry, Olivia. If you trust nothing else, believe that." He strode toward the door, and panic gripped her.

"Wait."

He paused, his back to her.

"Explain." When he didn't move, she bit her lip. "Tell me what happened the day he died. All of it."

He hung his head. "I did, months ago when I arrived. Everything I've told you from that point forward has been true, aside from my lie of omission."

Then she was missing something. "I want the details, Nate."

A sigh, and he faced her. He rubbed his jaw, his expression pained. "I don't see what good it'll do to—"

"I need to know."

He studied her a long, tense moment, then glanced heavenward before shoving his hands in his pockets. "Like I told you, we were sent to this small abandoned village. Troops had gone through before, but our sergeant got a tip there might be refugees hidden there. Six of us went to do a sweep with me in charge. We were supposed to be in and out."

Looking away, his gaze seemed lost in thought. "We split into three teams of two. At every structure check, the guys radioed me updates. At the last one, Justin swore he saw a kid in the doorway. The building was no larger than a gas station and half of it was in rubble. I thought he was crazy or it was shadows playing tricks on him since we'd seen not one soul up 'til then."

Shifting balance to his other foot, he cleared his throat. "As we were about to go inside, one of the other teams reported in and had a question. I…" He frowned suddenly as if remembering something, confusion furrowing his brow.

"You what?"

His gaze flicked to hers and away. "I told Justin to wait a second and was on the mic for a minute at most." He rubbed his chest as if it hurt. "When I turned back, Justin was gone." He shook his head. "I forgot about that. He must not have heard me." He blinked, skimmed a hand over his bald head. "Anyway, I ran in and rounded a corridor. Justin was halfway down the hall, rushing toward me, waving his hands." He stopped abruptly and looked at her. "Are you sure you want to hear this, baby? It's—"

"Yes." She wiped tears from her cheeks and sniffed. "Tell me."

He lifted his hand and dropped it as if to say *fine*. "The bomb went off and we both went down. When I got my bearings, I dragged Justin out and, with the rest of the guys, waited for the evac team."

Except that didn't seem like all of it. Judging by his gutted expression, what followed the explosion had been hell for him. And no wonder. He'd watched her brother die right in front of him. His friend, a fellow soldier.

"Justin was killed in the blast?"

Nate's gaze shot to the left and he paused. "Yes," he finally said, his voice low and rough. "It was...a suicide bomb and he was closest to it."

Silence hung as she tried to absorb what he'd told her. The longer time passed, the more she realized how fate and destiny were a frightening thing.

"That's the truth? All of it? Everything?" Because her heart was breaking for the umpteenth time. Not only did Nate not appear responsible, he'd had to stand by while the only person to date who'd cared about him was killed. Violently. Brutally. In front of his face.

"Yes." Shoulders slumped, he avoided her gaze and kept his down.

"Justin went into that building against your orders. Had you been with him, you both would've died. Am I understanding that correctly?"

His gaze jerked to hers, fury darkening his irises. "Don't." He took a step forward and pulled himself short. "This is not one of those circumstances you can excuse like before. I was no good then and I'm no good now. This is an uncrossable red line. Whether Justin ignored me, figuring there was no threat, or whether he didn't hear me, I'm still accountable." He pointed to his chest, ramming his finger into his breastbone. "I was his superior and should've paid better attention. I was responsible for him. *Me*, Olivia. I took away something you loved more than anything."

She choked on a sob. "You built the bomb? You set it off? You sent Justin inside knowing he'd die?" Lord, she couldn't breathe.

213

How many more victims did this incident need to claim? How many more hurts could be laid at Nate's feet before he finally broke? "If the roles were reversed, would you want my brother blaming himself for your death?"

He snapped to attention, his body rigid. "Don't you dare, baby." His chest rapidly rose and fell. "Don't pretend a part of you didn't get buried with him. I would do anything to give him back to you. What happened that day is a knot in my gut that never unfurls. There's no forgiveness here. I don't deserve it. Any of this. Not him back then or you now."

A sound passed his lips, part revelation and wholly disheartened. He ran a shaking hand down his face, and when he looked at her once more, there was nothing left in his gaze but a hollow, empty void.

Agonizing seconds went by, then he strode to the door and paused with his hand on the knob. He pinched his eyes closed. But it was his low, tortured admission that clawed her from the inside out.

"I wish it had been me."

The door shut quietly behind him.

Time collapsed and the room vacuumed of oxygen. The longer she stood in the middle of the room, alone and gutted, the more she bled out until she was a numb, vacant shell.

Had she been too quick to forgive him? Was she letting her feelings for him pollute rational thought?

She didn't think so. Aside from failing to tell her about his role in Justin's death, Nate had never lied to her. In fact, getting him to talk about his past, about anything, had been like pulling teeth from a rabid wolf. No one would make up stories like that. Besides, his behavior backed up everything.

What was she supposed to do now? Could she fix it, make him understand? Did he just need space?

Justin. Dear, sweet Justin. That's what she needed. To talk to her brother and gain some clarity, some insight. Then maybe she would know how to approach Nate and figure out what to do.

Heading into the bedroom, she dressed and went downstairs. Bypassing the kitchen where the sounds of Aunt Mae were clinking and clanging, Olivia opened the front door and stepped onto the porch.

Humidity and the scent of hay, of untamed land, bathed her face as she made the hike to the cemetery. Sunlight shone and heated her chilled bones while her shoes crunched on gravel. Eventually reaching her destination, she shut the squeaky gate and knelt at Justin's grave.

"You tricked him into coming to Meadowlark, didn't you?" She sniffed and pulled a couple dandelions from the base of his stone. "I figured it out, little brother. You knew Nate had no one and nothing to go back to once he was discharged, so you put a failsafe in place in case you weren't able to bring him here yourself." She nodded. "Well done."

She sat in the damp grass and crossed her legs. "Except he thinks he's responsible for your death." Her chest hitched and she rolled her lips over her teeth to stave off tears. "You jerk. Why'd you have to go into that building? Huh? You up and left me." Angrily, she wiped her wet cheeks. "All this time, I've been furious at the wrong person. I blamed your superior because it was easier than blaming a dead man." She shook her head. "So much blame to go around. But no one's really at fault, are they? Not even you."

Leaning back, she rested on her hands. "I went down to the creek the day you died. At the time, I didn't know you'd passed yet, but I had this strange urge to go. Nakos threw a fit, of course." She laughed. "I really went to see you, I think. Habit, perhaps. We always met there to play, remember? I crouched by the bank and thought about all the things we'd done and seen, all our memories. Everything we were and could be. And I was angry even then because you'd gone off halfway across the world." She sobered. "So, I went down to the creek to see you, but you weren't there. I suspect a part of me knew you were dead the moment it happened."

She tilted her head. "You broke my heart and I was mad. Have been since we buried you. Survivor's guilt, I suppose." And the situation rammed home. "That's Nate's problem. He was given no sense of self-worth. You befriended him, made him start to view things differently, and then you died on his watch. Now he doesn't know how to deal with the fact that you broke his heart, too. He didn't know he had one."

And there was no doubt. Nathan Roldan had heart. Too much of it. If he didn't, he wouldn't carry such immense remorse around like it was his due. He wouldn't have followed through on a promise to watch over a woman he'd never met. He certainly wouldn't have been willing to evolve from a lifetime of loneliness in order to seek a connection.

Blowing out a sigh, she stood. The visit had done exactly what she'd been hoping it would. "I know sending him here was to help him, but you gave me the bigger gift." She brushed off her pants. "Love you. Say hi to Mom and Dad."

As she strode out of the cemetery, she whispered, "Thank you. I've got it from here."

Chapter Twenty-Two

Every instinct told him to run, to get as far away from the pain as fast as possible. But he'd given his word, had made a promise, and he'd keep it. Though it wouldn't be right under her nose on the ranch, Nate would protect Olivia just the same. Pain be damned.

On his Hog, he tore down the road, heading for town with two goals to accomplish by day's end—to find a way to stay in Meadowlark and to make sure he'd never be in a position to hurt Olivia again.

He'd barely made it out of the Cattenach Ranch gate and his chest pinched from missing her. And he'd better get used to it. Not that he ever would. Christ, he never should've touched her, never should've let her try to...heal him. His own misery was something he'd grown familiar with eons ago, but this particular level went beyond that to an amplified version of hell.

The look on her face, the hurt in her voice, the way she'd tried to justify...

No. *No, no, no.*

Pulling off the main road a few minutes later, he parked in front of the white brick police station and dismounted. Mission one.

He opened the exterior door to the stench of burnt coffee and Lysol. The semi-spacious room had brown and white checkered linoleum, yellow walls stained with what he hoped was time, and four empty desks in a square facing each other. Off to the right was a hallway. Next to it, a counter with a coffeemaker circa turn-of-the-century. To the left was an office.

He went that way and stopped in the doorway. Pictures of family and—bears?—hung on the walls. Behind an enormous desk teetering with manila folders was a window facing east, the blinds closed.

Rip glanced up from behind a pile of folders, his Fu Manchu twitching. "Look what the cat dragged in. What can I do you for, son?"

Nate crossed his arms and leaned on the jamb. "Did you check my references?"

"Yep."

"Is the job still open?"

"Yep."

He nodded. "I'll take it."

Rip paused. "Good. You can start on Monday."

Nate didn't think there was anything more frightening than finding Olivia face-down in a creek, but Rip's grin might do it. His slightly crooked yellow teeth flashed for a fraction of a second longer than was comfortable, then disappeared behind a frown.

The sheriff stood. "Come on. I'll show you around."

He took Nate down the hall, showing him two cells and a closet, then pointed to a door, claiming that it led to a basement for storage. Next to it was a flight of stairs to a second floor. Rip jerked his chin at the bathroom on the way back to main reception.

"That'll be it." He adjusted his brown hat that matched his uniform. "The board up there's got the schedule rotation and anything Casper County sends us. We can hold arrests overnight for booking, but no longer. Shifts are twelve hours, four days a week. Three men on at night, three during the day, including me. Be here at seven a.m. Monday morning. We'll get you registered with a badge and weapon." He gave Nate a once-over. "And uniform. Anything else?"

Easy enough. "Know of a place where I can crash for a while?" Mission two.

Rip frowned. "Thought you were staying with Olivia." When Nate said nothing, Rip's brows rose. "Gotcha. Whelp, no motels in town. However," he jerked a thumb at the ceiling, "there's an apartment upstairs. Can't even walk up there it's so cluttered. Years of files. If you're willing to haul it all to the basement, it's yours."

Done and done. "Mind if I get started?"

"Have at it. Coffee's over there." Rip lumbered back into his office.

Grateful to have something to do to keep his mind off a certain redhead, Nate went outside, pulled his Harley around the back, and brought his bag inside. He climbed the stairs next to the basement door to the second floor and...stepped into a clusterfuck. A flick of the wall switch had florescent lights humming and confirming said clusterfuck.

What looked like a twelve-by-twelve studio apartment was covered floor to rafters with boxes. Hundreds of them. Hoarders weren't even this talented.

Easing around one stack, he wormed his way to the center of the room. Kitchenette to the left, bed and dresser to the right, and a bathroom straight ahead. Blocking it was a red plaid couch.

Heaving a sigh, he dropped his bag and grabbed the box closest to the doorway, then carried it to an area of the basement that appeared unused. And repeated the mind-numbing task until dark descended and his back complained. At least he'd made a path to the bed.

Deciding to call it, he mounted the stairs for the last time and came face-to-face with Nakos. Perfect. Just...perfect.

He eyed the foreman's flannel, jeans, and cowboy hat. "Hi."

"Nice digs. You might have more room in one of the holding cells." Nakos held up a six pack. "Want one?"

"Hell yes." Nate issued the foreman inside and removed the crates covering the couch. "I can't promise this is clean."

Nakos shrugged and plopped down, anyway. A plume of dust rose around him.

Nate accepted a beer and sat with a cushion between them, laying his head back. The material smelled like moth balls. "If you're going to kick my ass, you don't need to get me drunk. I'll let you win without putting up a fight."

In response, Nakos studied him out of the corner of his eye and took a sip from his bottle. "Haven't heard your side yet."

"Olivia's is the only side that matters."

Up went Nakos's brows. "What kind of friend would that make me if I didn't hear you out?"

Nate did a double-take.

"What? We're not friends? You wound my delicate sensibilities." Another sip of beer. "Do you need a hug to prove it? You won't get one."

Unsure what to think, Nate glanced away. Sighed. "I repeat, Olivia's is the only side that matters."

"Interesting you should say that. Wouldn't that make her right?"

Nate bit his tongue, but curiosity got the better of him. "Right about what, exactly?" He was worried sick about her—wondering if she was handling the truth okay or not, if she was still crying in the way that ripped his very soul from his body...

"She refused to get specific, but she insists you think you did something unforgivable." Nakos picked at the label on his bottle. "Did you?"

"Yes." No. Hell, he didn't know anymore.

Retelling what went down in Iraq had triggered some facts he'd forgotten. Like how Nate had instructed Justin not to go inside the structure alone. And part of Justin's sputtered, pain-filled last declaration that forever played in a loop in Nate's mind.

"Shit, it hurts, Nate. I'm so...cold. Take care of my sister. Promise me you'll...take care of...Olivia."

He heard it in his sleep. While awake. Randomly and all the time.

Except, when he'd hashed out the specifics to Olivia, he'd remembered something else.

"Not...your fault. Go, Nate. She'll...take care of...you, too."

It was the last thing the sweet bastard had said. His dying thoughts had been to absolve Nate. To send him straight into the arms of the person Justin loved most.

Whether Nate had chosen to ignore the statement until now or whether the pain from his injuries had rendered his ears mute at the time, he didn't know. But watching the life drain out of his friend had been ten times more agonizing than the shrapnel embedded in his leg. It rippled through him, even almost a year later.

"She's crawling out of her skin." Nakos looked from the bottle to Nate. "She scoured the town, the ranch, everywhere looking for you. She assumed you went back to Chicago and was ready to hop a plane until Rip finally told her you were okay. Wouldn't say where you were, though." He sighed, gaze roaming over Nate. "I thought she was two feet in the madhouse, but you're not faring any better, are you?"

Shit. She wasn't supposed to be trying to find him. Thinking about him at all, in fact. She should be pissed off and glad to be rid of him. He'd lied to her. Had hurt her in unimaginable ways. Right?

Doubt reared in his head. Whatever. Regardless of fault, Nate still should've had Justin's back. Paid better attention. And Olivia should hate him for failing.

Thing was, Justin and Olivia were too close to him. At every pass, they had Nate second-guessing his share of blame. Nakos, however, had always played it straight and told Nate exactly what was on his mind. What Nate really needed was guidance from an unbiased outside party.

"Let me tell you a story." He took a long pull of beer for courage, and then laid it on the foreman. All of it, leaving out no details or sugarcoating the particulars.

Born to a junkie four weeks premature. The abandonment. How no one had wanted to adopt a crack baby. Foster care. The sometimes neglect and random beatings. The gang. Juvie. The Army and meeting Justin. And…Nate's role in his friend's death.

For almost an hour, they sat on the foul-smelling couch. Nakos listened, not once interrupting. Nate's throat and chest were raw as he relived it all. And when he was done, he slumped on the cushion and closed his eyes.

Exhaustion and confusion gripped him, but he felt suddenly...lighter.

"No wonder." Nakos, eyes sober and mouth downcast in sympathetic understanding, looked at Nate. "It's no wonder your walls have walls and you're reluctant to accept anything resembling kindness. Honestly, before I knew you better, I just figured it was PTSD or that you were a bonafide asshole."

He turned on the sofa to face Nate. "I can't pretend to comprehend what you've been through. I have two loving parents and Mae, not to mention Olivia and Amy. I never had to question whether they gave a damn."

"I don't want your pity."

"Good. You won't get it. Pity is for those who are too dumb to rise above the past." The foreman's eyes narrowed. "You do have my sympathy. What you had to deal with was wrong. Flat out, wrong. But if what you said about Iraq is true, I'm not getting how you were at fault. You want to blame someone, blame the people who made the bomb in the first place, the very ones who used a little kid to get their fanatical point across."

Nakos rubbed his neck, his olive skin growing ashen as if disgusted. "Having said that, I did know Justin very well, and if he were here right now to see how you were beating yourself up, it would kill him a second time."

Shit. Closing his eyes, Nate skimmed his hand over his clenched gut.

"And I also know Olivia better than anyone." Nakos's determined gaze nailed Nate to the couch when he refocused on the foreman. "She's a pain in the ass, stubborn as hell, and has a heart bigger than a church full of saints, but she's not stupid. If the goal is to not hurt her, you're going about it back-asswards. You told her the truth. All your secrets are out. And what was the first thing she did?" He tipped his bottle at Nate. "She went after you."

Well, Nate had wanted the foreman's insight. He'd gotten it. Hell, he didn't have a clue what he'd been expecting to hear, but shock blew him away nonetheless. This place, these people, were like being dropped in another dimension with no compass or instructions. Another world he never fathomed could exist.

Nakos stood and glanced around. "Kind of downsizing your life, if you ask me. Smells like someone's great-grandmother's attic, too."

Despite the chaos in his head and turmoil in his chest, Nate huffed a laugh.

A wry smile, and Nakos set his empty bottle back in the cardboard case on the floor. "Here's my take. If you love her, denying her happiness and the man she wants is no way to prove it." He crossed his arms. "And if you still question the worth of that man, consider the motives. Nothing you've done, said, or thought up until now has been about your needs or desires. Yet you feel bad for circumstances beyond your control. Which means you have a conscience. Sounds like you're not the bad guy you thought you were."

Oddly...touched, Nate watched Nakos stride toward the door. "Hey." He waited for Nakos to face him. "She would've been better off with you."

A slow shake of his head, and Nakos offered a regretful smile. "We had all our lives to go that route. She was waiting for you." He turned, paused, and slapped his hand to the jamb. "Oh, and I want a picture of you in that ugly Meadowlark Police uniform. I'll put it on my holiday cards for a good chuckle."

Laughing, Nate scrubbed his hands over his face and sat in silence awhile.

His head had too much crap shoving around and vying for attention to make decisions tonight. The last thing he needed was to act impulsively. Best to sleep on it. Tomorrow was another day.

But, damn. Olivia was upset. Looking for him. Worried.

Christ, he missed her. Not even a day, and he was experiencing something akin to withdrawal. Where her warmth had filled him, now there was cold blackness. He'd spent his whole life wanting what she offered, and now that it was right in front of him, it seemed too good to be true. A taunt from fate. A joke at his expense.

That was the root of his hesitation. Yes, guilt was a living thing inside him. Yes, he'd probably spend an eternity trying to prove he was worth her. Yes, he'd made terrible mistakes. But no, he wasn't God. She'd been right all along. Her little experiments had done a number on his mind and pulled him out of himself to see her view.

He'd done everything she ever asked of him, but one. Talk to Justin. Nate suspected the reason for his adamant refusal was because, somewhere deep inside, he knew once he did, it would mean letting go. Shedding the past. The pain. The skewed image he'd carried around.

Saying goodbye to the first friend he ever made.

Damn it. Needing something to do, he rose and rummaged in his bag for sweats. A run should exhaust him enough to allow him to collapse into sleep.

After he changed, he went downstairs and introduced himself to the three night shift officers, then stepped outside. Humidity and the threat of rain lingered in the cool air, but it was perfect for a run. Without any direction in mind, he took off under the disguise of a full moon.

And wound up in front of the Cattenach Ranch.

Huffing, he set his hands on his hips. It figured. All roads led to her, didn't they? Even the one Justin had laid.

To wind down, Nate walked up the driveway and stopped at the base of the porch. The house was dark, quiet, while crickets chirped and an owl hooted. It was too late to be here and he didn't have a clue what to say to Olivia even if she were awake.

He went to turn away when something reflected out of the corner of his eye. He eased closer and found his whittling supplies in the metal bucket on the steps. In his haste, he'd forgotten to grab them. Glancing around at the sinister shadows the trees created and the utter stillness, he shook his head and said screw it.

Snatching the bucket, he strode around the house and headed for the cemetery. If he was going to do this, to say goodbye to Justin, then it was best Nate be alone with his demons. The pitch blackness worked for him, too.

His shoes crunched on loose gravel and slipped on a couple patches of wet grass as he climbed a hill, rounded a bend, and came to an abrupt stop at the fence. The place was even creepier and ethereal at night. He'd never been comfortable in cemeteries, yet he opened the gate and made his way to Justin's grave.

Adoring son. Loving brother. Faithful friend. Devoted soldier. Fallen but never forgotten.

Damn if that didn't sum up the guy in too few words.

Nate stared at the stone, rubbing his chest and trying to figure out what he was supposed to do. A vision of Olivia from the first time she'd brought him here filtered to mind. She'd sat right down and started chattering. He'd been too shocked and enamored to pay attention to what she'd said, though.

Regardless, he plopped on his ass and put the bucket in front of him. He pulled out supplies and a chunk of wood, letting his hands do what they wanted while he cleared his head with the task.

"Your sister says I should talk to you, that it makes her feel better." He frowned. "Between you and me, it's making me feel like an idiot."

His strokes of the knife grew sharper, forceful. "Actually, that's not true. I'm pissed off. I gave you every go-away vibe I had in reserve, ignored you hard as I could, and you befriended me, anyway. Flapping your gums and making me laugh." His arms ached with the tool's ministrations. Short, blunt strokes increased in violence. "Screw you, bastard. You made me like you. Did you ever listen to me when it counted? No. You got yourself killed."

He froze, realizing what he'd said. "You died and left me here for the fallout. Your sister was a wreck. She still weeps at the littlest reminder of you." He sighed, his anger deflating. "Hell, I miss you, too." He refocused on carving. "Tell anyone and I'll deny it."

After a few beats of silence, he stared at what he'd done—a figurine of the sun with triangular beams and a heart at the center.

He shook his head. "That sums you up, doesn't it?" he mumbled. "Bright as the effing sun and loveable as shit."

With a swipe of his thumb over the front, he placed the carving at the base of the grave and set his supplies in the bucket once more. Then, he flopped onto his back and rested his head on his bent arm.

Stars winked overhead in the inky sky and it reminded him of a couple instances where he and Justin had done this very thing overseas. To unwind or clear their heads or to let crap wash off them. Nate had never done anything like it until Justin had made him, nor had he since being discharged. He'd forgotten how relaxing it was to lay and do nothing. Just...be.

"I'm in love with your sister." He pressed his thumb and forefinger into his eye sockets. "As I did with you, I tried to fight the connection. But you two are like kryptonite to a loser such as me."

Letting the cool breeze float over him, he exhaled, releasing all the tension and pain and trials he'd endured. They were too damn heavy to carry any longer.

"You might've warned me she was so damn beautiful." He turned his head and eyed the grave. "Seriously. One minute she's sexy as hell, the next she's too cute for words. And Christ, she's always got something to say. Funny and clever, like you."

His gaze drifted away, blurred. "She makes it hard to catch my breath and, yet, I can't seem to breathe without her. I'm beginning to want things, stuff I never thought I could have. Happiness, for one." He closed his eyes. "Happiness, Justin. Imagine that."

Groaning, he threw his arm over his face. "And it's annoying how, ninety-nine percent of the time, she's not wrong. Is that a female thing or target specific to her?"

Because she'd been right about this. About everything, thus far.

Talking to Justin did help.

Chapter Twenty-Three

Olivia pulled her truck in the driveway and cut the engine, then pounded her fist on the steering wheel a trillion times. Not that it helped her frustration level, but it beat screaming through town like Wee Willie Winkie after a meltdown.

All day yesterday, she'd torn Meadowlark apart trying to find Nate. After little sleep, she'd headed out to do the same thing this morning. Nothing. Nada. All Rip would tell her was Nate started work on Monday and that, last he'd heard, Nate was fine. The good ole boys club, protecting each other. Rip must've assumed Nate needed time.

She wasn't fine. And she didn't believe for one second Nate was, either.

Helpless tears of concern and fear threatened again, so she climbed out of the truck and stalked toward the barn. Perhaps Nakos had heard from Nate.

Sunlight beat down and the grass was damp with dew. Spring clung to the tepid air and birds chirped. A breeze whirred the leaves budding on the trees. Flowers poked through the defrosted ground, ready to bloom. She wanted to napalm all of it, obliterate anything joyful and cheerful until she saw with her own two eyes that Nate was all right.

Nakos stood outside the first barn, clipboard in hand. "*Hebe*, Olivia."

"Have you seen him?"

He focused a little too hard on the clipboard, flipping papers. "Who would that be?"

"You know who." She crossed her arms. "Nate. Where is he?"

Giving up the pretense, he lowered the clipboard and stared at her, gaze understanding. "I may or may not have hung out with him last night."

"Where?"

"It doesn't matter and I'm not telling you." He held up his palm when she bared her teeth. "He's figuring stuff out, little red. Give him time. He'll come around."

Shoulders deflating, she pouted. Nakos wasn't going to cave.

"Did he..." Crap. Her throat clogged with tears. "Is he really okay?" She sniffed. "And if you lie to me, I'll fire you."

A smile teased his lips. "You won't fire me and I've never lied to you. He'll come around. I promise."

She looked at him another moment, then spun on her heels. "I'll kill you both as soon as I find him."

Nakos's laugh faded as she stomped up to the house.

Kicking off her shoes in the tack room, she shoved through the kitchen door. Aunt Mae was at the table, papers scattered everywhere in her version of organization. Eyeglasses perched on the end of her nose, she glared at a page in her hand, then one at her elbow as if comparing.

Olivia knew better than to bother her aunt when she was doing monthly statements, but this couldn't wait. "Did he call? Has he come back?"

"No, baby girl. I'm sorry." Aunt Mae removed her glasses and set them aside, then smoothed her white strands. "Let me make you something to eat."

"No, thanks. I can't even comprehend food right now." She blew a hefty sigh and glanced around. Pancakes and sausage in mass on the counter. A pot of soup going on the stove. Normal, as always. Except Nate *wasn't here*. She rubbed her forehead, achy from crying. "What are you working on? Looked like you were upset."

"Oh, well. You should take a look." Aunt Mae shoved her glasses back on and passed Olivia a paper. "That's the bank statement for last month. The numbers are off. There are too many funds."

"Okay," she said slowly. "Perhaps one of the suppliers haven't withdrawn yet."

"I thought the same thing, but I looked into that already." Aunt Mae handed over another paper. "That's the employee payroll. I compared check numbers to what was on the statement." She removed her glasses yet again and stared at Olivia. "Nate's are the only ones that haven't gone through."

Olivia froze. "What do you mean?"

"I mean, he hasn't cashed or deposited one check since he arrived."

"What?" She glanced at the page, then her aunt. They paid the ranch hands every two weeks. Off the top of her head, that was roughly five to six checks Nate hadn't cashed. And she'd handed them to him herself. "Why would..."

Oh no. Oh God.

He'd refused to take payment from her. That's what this was about. He wouldn't accept money for what he wrongfully assumed was atonement for his sins. Because he wasn't on Cattenach Ranch to work. He was here to fulfill a promise. In his mind, anyway.

Hands shaking, she set the papers down. The room blurred in a haze through hot tears. Her stomach plummeted to her knees.

"I have to find him," she whispered.

No one had ever shown him they cared. Aside from her brother, nobody had ever bothered to try. Nate had stumbled through life on a wing and a prayer. It was shocking he'd turned out as charismatic as he had, considering.

And after the way he'd left yesterday, the things he'd said, she could only imagine his state of mind right now. Though hesitant, he had started to reach for happiness, to believe the things she'd told him.

But to have that ripped away, like Justin had been taken from him, even if by Nate's own hand, would probably send him spiraling. To Nate, he wasn't worthy of her or the life she'd offered, and a lifetime of being alone and in pain was his punishment.

Lord, she had to find him before his conscience undid all her progress.

"I'll be back in a little while."

In a daze, she climbed the stairs, rummaged in the box Nate had made for her, and pulled out Justin's letter. She put it in her back pocket and went back downstairs to the kitchen.

"If he calls or stops by, text me right away."

Aunt Mae nodded, her smile sad. "Sure thing, baby girl."

Olivia made her way outside and stopped near the herb garden, trying to think.

Nate's motorcycle had been at the police station when she'd stopped in, but parked in back out of view. Which she'd stumbled onto by accident trying to turn the truck around in the small lot. He couldn't be far if he was on foot. She'd already checked the diner and storefronts nearby. The ranch hands had searched the property yesterday with no luck.

So, where the heck was he?

229

Two sharp barks rent the air and she turned. Bones loped down the hill on the other side of the wildflower patch, his black and white fur flowing due to his speed. He barked twice more.

The poor dog had spent the night whining, pacing from her third floor suite to Nate's bedroom and back again. This morning, he'd taken off for the barn when Olivia had gotten in her truck.

Bones stopped feet from her, barked twice, and turned as if wanting her to follow him.

"Did you find him, boy?" Lord have mercy, please. "Where's Nate?"

The dog took off in the direction he'd started, and Olivia jogged to catch up. She followed him up the hill and around the bend, Bones stopping periodically to wait. Once he made a hard left at a cottonwood, she realized where he was leading her and picked up speed.

Out of breath, she halted by the cemetery gate and nearly collapsed to her knees.

Nate, his back to her and facing Justin's grave, stood with his hands on his hips and his bald head down. He wore a black tee and sweats, smeared by grass stains. Judging by that and the wet patches darkening his pants, he'd been sitting at one point. Had he been here all night?

Relief crippled everything else, and she slapped a hand over her mouth to hold in a sob. She breathed through the assault, remembering her frantic searching and frenetic worry, and closed her eyes.

When she opened them and he stepped back like he was going to turn around, rage took over and shoved gratitude into the backseat.

***

"You!" The cemetery gate squeaked open and slammed shut.

Nate spun at the feminine shriek and found one purely pissed off and furious Olivia Cattenach stomping toward him.

Homicidal eyes red-rimmed, lips firm, auburn hair flying around her head, and a fierce wrinkle between her brows, she launched at him. He barely had time to set his feet and her fists were pounding his chest.

230

"You...jerk!" Punch. "How could you take off like that?" Punch. "I looked everywhere for you." Punch, punch. "All day, half the night, and this morning."

Christ. He lifted his hands, not to fend her off because, well, she wasn't actually hurting him in the slightest, but he was worried she'd hurt herself. "Olivia—"

"No. You don't get to speak. You said enough yesterday. It's my turn." And...she was back to wailing on him. "I was worried sick." Punch. "I thought you were dead in a ditch..." Inhaling suddenly, she straightened, her pretty eyes bugging into something downright scary. "You're laughing at me?"

He rolled his lips over his teeth, but it was no use. A laugh emerged. "I've just never heard anyone actually say that before. The dead in a ditch thing. I thought it was some cliché manufactured by parents to frighten kids into obedience."

"Well, it's not. I literally searched ditches on the side of the road." Her voice rose two octaves above banshee. "Ditches, Nathan! And you didn't cash your paychecks. After what you said, how you wished it had been you..." Punch, punch. Then, she choked on a sob, her arms falling limply at her sides. "The suicide rate is high for returning vets and you looked dejected when you left and I couldn't find you and..."

Fear melded with gripping loss, twisting her face.

Ah, shit. "Come here, baby."

He pulled her to him, but she climbed up his body and clung to him. Arms around his head and legs banding his waist and face buried in his neck, she trembled as hot tears splashed his skin.

"I'm sorry." Closing his eyes, he cinched her higher and threaded his fingers in her hair. Christ, the thought had never occurred to him, that she'd jump to that kind of conclusion. "I'm so sorry, baby." He kissed her strands, lids pinched tight, his insides spilling all over the grass. "I'd never do that. I swear. No matter what, I'd never do that."

Panting, she seemed to be winding down from her jag. "For Justin. The promise?"

Yes. He owed it to her brother to live his life to the fullest. Justin's time had been cut short. He'd never have the opportunity to fall in love or hold his child or tell another ridiculous joke. But due to him, Nate *would* have that chance. He was here, happiness at his feet, because a redheaded kid from Wyoming had persistently chipped away at Nate's resolve in the middle of a godforsaken desert.

"And for you." Nate skimmed his hand over her strands, eternally thankful to have her in his arms. She triggered the calm in him, easing the tension and taming his beast. He breathed in her rain scent, absorbed her warmth, and shook with gratitude. "You know I keep my promises. I swear to you on my pathetic, empty heart that I will never leave you again."

Finally, she lifted her head, looking at him with those holy-shit blue eyes framed by wet lashes. She cupped his jaw, his stubble a scratching sound against her palm. "I like to think of your heart as uncharted." She offered a weak smile.

Damn, but she felled him. He brushed his nose against hers, at a loss.

"Go in my back pocket." She sniffed. "Please."

Adjusting her in his hold, he reached into her jeans and pulled out...Justin's letter. Nate had carried it around everywhere with him. He'd recognize that yellowed envelope and Olivia's name in chicken scrawl anywhere. He jerked his gaze to hers in question.

"Read it." When he started to object, she ran her hand over his head, her gaze following the movement. "I want you to read it."

Since it seemed important to her, he ignored the cold sense of dread and his pounding heart. Sitting with her in his lap, he took out the folded sheet of paper and opened it behind her back. As he clenched his jaw to read, she rested her head on his shoulder.

Olivia,

If you're reading this, I'm with Mom and Dad. I'm not much for writing, but since this is the last you'll hear from me for a while, I'll try to be epic. No pressure.

This also means Nathan Roldan is probably with you, delivering my letter. I know he's huge-nor-mongus (I declare that an actual word. Notify Webster immediately), but he's harmless. He's a gentle giant, honest to God. Without him, I might not have gotten through this adventure. You're safe with him. I have no idea what circumstances caused my death, but don't dwell on them, and instruct Nate not to, as well. They don't matter.

I could fill a notebook with memories of us but, instead, I'll pick one. It stands out to me the most and is something I'll carry with me to the other side. Us, standing graveside, as they lowered our parents into the ground. For most, that would be a horrible day. It was cold and wet, everyone was wearing black, and people were crying. I was too young to understand the significance at the time, only that I was scared and confused. But you took my hand, squeezed it, and told me everything was going to be okay.

And you made sure of that. You were the best big sister a guy could ask for. Never did I want for anything. You put me first and took care of me, so it's time I did the same.

Which brings me back to Nate. I suspect he has no one in his life and no home of his own. I choose him for you. Whether he's a friend you nurture or a soul mate that develops into love, don't let him walk away after reading this. Don't let him become a passing stranger delivering a note or an acquaintance you see once in a blue moon. Take care of him and let him take care of you. Grant me that one thing.

Tell Aunt Mae I love her so much. Thank her for rescuing us and for giving up her life to come back to the ranch. She treated us like her own and I want her to know that hasn't gone unnoticed. Tell Nakos to stop gawking at you and find his real love. Also that the buckle on saddle eight is loose. It's not, but mess with him one last time for me. I'll miss him. And tell Amy to smile more like she used to. She has my permission to call you Liv any time she wants because you hate it and it gives her pleasure to annoy you. I'll miss her tons, too.

Now, this letter will self-destruct in ten seconds, so I'll be brief in my last order. Do not think of me and cry. I know you and that's what you're doing. In fact, only think of me twice a year—Spring and Winter harvest. That was my favorite and I'll watch over you while you plant.

I'll miss you most of all, Scarecrow. I love you. Be happy.
Justin

Through a sheen of tears he attempted to will away, Nate refolded the letter and put it back in Olivia's pocket. Then, he set his chin on her shoulder and held her silently until the gutting sensation passed. Talk about cracking his chest cavity wide open.

Christ, he missed the little bastard. He'd thought highly enough of Nate to manipulate fate in order to intertwine his life with Olivia's. To make sure they wound up in the same place. And leave it to Justin to try to make his sister laugh while saying goodbye. Just like him—funny, sweet. Truthfully, and he'd said this all along, Nate was the lucky one to have known Justin, not the other way around.

He stared at Justin's grave, at the headstones of Olivia's parents, and sighed as melancholy swallowed him whole.

Some time later, when he thought he could speak, he pulled away and pushed her hair from her face, holding her head in his hands. And again, he was struck stupid by her beauty. Yes, she had a pretty face and gorgeous hair and adorable freckles and huge eyes and a pouty mouth. But it was the whole package that was beautiful—the components that made up her personality, rendering her unique. She was witty and smart and hard-working and unselfish and stubborn to a fault.

And mercy, did he love her.

"I'm probably going to screw this up, but hear me out." He rested his forehead to hers. "You know my background, but I don't think you can fully understand the...loneliness involved. Or how it messed up my head. It started with Justin and continued with you, but somehow you cracked through years of ingrained lies to show me the truth. I'll never be rid of the guilt. I don't think that'll ever go away. Stupid mistakes were made, yet I know now not everything was my fault. You showed me that, baby."

He kissed her wet eyes, wiped her damp cheeks with his thumbs. "Something else I realized, that took me too long to comprehend, was my life didn't start in a Chicago hospital. It began in the desert with your brother. And if you'll let me, I'd like to spend the rest of it with you."

Her chest hitched and more tears spilled. "Nate—"

"Let me finish. This isn't easy for me and..." He shook his head. "Actually, it is. Being with you is easy. That's what I'm trying to say. Nothing in my life has been simple. Love was never supposed to be a part of my plan. I have no clue what I'm doing, I have nothing to offer you in return, but I do know how to love. Because you showed me. And I do love you, more than I thought was possible. Forgive me and let me keep loving you. Please, baby."

She looked at him, tender gaze sweeping over his face, and drew a slow inhale. "There's nothing to forgive. That's what I've been trying to tell you all along." She blew out a ragged breath. "Forgive yourself for thinking you were ever less than what you are—a good man."

Gaze determined, she held his jaw. "I love you."

A strangled sound died in his throat and he glanced heavenward. Breaths soughing, he struggled not to split apart, atom by atom. Unimaginable heat blasted behind his ribs, filled the fissures of darkness, and all he could do to hold it together was close his eyes.

She stroked his head with aching gentleness, wrapped her fingers around the back of his neck. "Get used to hearing it because I'm going to say it a lot."

"Never," he rasped and looked at her. "I'll never get used to hearing it." It was one thing to spot the emotion on others, to find it in her eyes when she gazed at him, but something else entirely to have her say the words aloud. "No one's ever..." He sucked air. Cleared his throat. "Please say it again."

She grinned, and the last remnants of his old life cindered to dust. "I. Love. You."

Nope. Never get used to it. Fisting his hand in her hair, he pulled her to him.

As he sank inside her kiss, in the sanctuary and refuge she forever offered, he was jarred by the freedom, as well. To let go and just...be with her was liberation at its very core. No secrets or lies or shadows threatening to consume. Nothing stood in their way and no one could steal his chance at happiness. Not even him.

Bones barked and pawed at Nate's pant leg.

He chuckled under his breath. "I love you, too, boy."

With a contented hum, she smiled against his lips. "I hope you realize that leaving and scaring me makes us even for the creek incident."

He eased away and glanced at the thin, red scar by her hairline, traced it with his fingertip. "Not even close, baby."

She laughed. "Is that a challenge?"

"Don't make me sic Nakos on you. I'll do it."

Another laugh, and she rolled her eyes. Adorable. "I can handle him."

"Yeah, but can you handle me?" He gave her a hard, quick smack on the lips and stood. If it put her in a coma, he didn't care. He was going to make love to her all damn day and through the night. Bending, he wrapped an arm around her waist and tossed her onto his shoulder. "I think not."

She giggled as he strode through the gate, Bones at his heels. "Where are you taking me?"

"Home, baby. We're going home."

*Read more about Nate & Olivia's ever-after in
Nakos & Amy's story, BENEDICTION,
coming in Fall 2017.*

Want to help an author? Please consider leaving a review
and tell others about the great romance you just read!

www.AuthorKellyMoran.com
Enchanting ever-afters...

Sign up for Kelly Moran's newsletter and get a FREE eBook!

ABOUT THE AUTHOR:

Kelly Moran is a best-selling & award-winning romance author of enchanting ever-afters. She is a Catherine Award-Winner, Readers' Choice Finalist, Holt Medallion Finalist, and a 2014 Award of Excellence Finalist through RWA. She's also landed on the 10 Best Reads and Must Read lists from USA TODAY's HEA.

Kelly's been known to say she gets her ideas from everyone and everything around her and there's always a book playing out in her head. No one who knows her bats an eyelash when she talks to herself. Her interests include: sappy movies, MLB, NFL, driving others insane, and sleeping when she can. She is a closet caffeine junkie and chocoholic, but don't tell anyone. She resides in Wisconsin with her husband, three sons, and her two dogs. Most of her family lives in the Carolinas, so she spends a lot of time there as well.

She loves connecting with her readers.

Made in the USA
Columbia, SC
20 July 2021